# The Stone Folk
# & Other Stories

By Meredith Anne DeVoe

The Stone Folk & Other Stories
by Meredith Anne DeVoe

The Stone Folk & Other Stories is a work of fiction. Any resemblance to any events or characters, living or dead, is purely coincidental.

## Contents:

*Dedicated to B.*
*You are everything we ever wanted.*

## The Soul Shepherds

The center of the lush meadow was serene, with daisies and yarrow barely waving in the soft morning light, unaware of the roiled and bloody muck they would soon become. Atal sighed, gathering with the others at the sideline. He could see among the war-clad men and women milling at the rise to his left, a number of his kind mingling invisibly with the warm-blooded. There was a stir and a shift in attention as boats hove to shore at the river that edged the bottom of the meadow. Shadow figures like Atal's were also among them on the boats, and waiting on the stony shore.

A female voice spoke from behind him. "There are too many of us here, Atal. That means you haven't told us everything." Atal turned slightly toward Jahl, a slight crooked grin completing the crooked angle of his long nose. Jahl's green eyes were fixed on him probingly through wisps of her black hair.

"You'll see."

The warriors at the top of the rise began dinning their spears on their shields and chanting as the raiders at the river disembarked and formed tight knots. They crouched and began their own low invocation, staring up the hill from eyes painted to look dark and fierce.

Some of Atal's tribe were already unhurriedly placing themselves around the meadow. In a few hands, the curved blades glittered in the early sun. Atal's friend, Hurk, spun and caught his dagger idly in his pink-palmed, black hands. Atal heard a snicker from Jahl. "Show off," she said, grinning.

The battle lines were coalescing, the black-clad army at the river's edge into vanguards and the green army at the hilltop to Atal's left into one long wall of death. Drumming began and the army at the left poured down the hill, screaming. Birds exploded from the grass and flew toward the trees. The armies met with a clang, and the chanting ceased, replaced by grunts and shouted names and shrieks of pain. Already those of Atal's kind were at their work, cutting here, gathering there. Even now, some of them were working their way to the edge of the meadow, daggers bright with ichor in their right hands, their left hands leading the dead; who invariably looked surprised and confused. A woman was led by Hurk, who carried the soul of the woman's unborn child gently in the crook of his arm. As they passed Atal, the baby looked at him with knowing eyes, the umbilicus trailing off into light against Hurk's dark robe. In moments, it would grow to stature and Hurk would set it down to walk the spirit road with its mother, Atal knew.

The battle was slowing down, both defenders and invaders tiring. Atal turned to Jahl. "Follow me, and bring your people." She nodded and turned to the dark figures behind her. Atal nodded to Hurk, who remained behind on the field of battle while the bulk of Atal's people moved over the rise toward the village several furlongs beyond.

Atal could see the small town first by a smoke rising from between green hills. As they approached, the thatched roofs came into view, and individual vegetable patches. Beyond the village were the pastures, but the livestock had been gathered into the common enclosure and the open fallows were empty... except for a dark-painted crowd of raiders, just emerging from the cover of trees, on the opposite side of the village. There was plenty of time, no reason to hurry. Atal and his following rambled easily over the fields, arriving just as the painted warriors descended upon the hamlet with fire and blade upon those too old or young or ill to fight.

Atal entered the home of the chieftain's family. This one was not fired; the invaders knew there was treasure within. The doors were barred, but that meant nothing to Atal. Even before he entered, he counted the souls inside. Numerous children, two very old people, two pregnant females. One stood tall over the others, and was clearly the chief. She bore a sword, ready to defend all within—but there was a mark already on her. As Atal waited while the screams and shouts outside grew closer, and a banging began on the strong oak door, this woman's eyes swerved to meet his. Atal felt chilled to the bone.

It happened occasionally. It was usually someone very old or very young, or gravely wounded, who hovered on the edge of life. This woman, though, was strong and vital, standing bravely over her house. As Atal's eyes met hers, he saw in her everything he was sworn to protect—life, humanity, a strong spirit free from the terror of death and the dead. For a long moment, he took in her green eyes, her dark-blonde braids, the red gown crisscrossed by gold and beads, the shield she clutched in front, the sword she held pointed to the ground at her left—she was left-handed, he noted—the unusual folds in her ears, the curve of her shoulder and the deep and seething breaths she took.

Atal turned to view the men hammering at the door. Their leader, a vast and tall man, stood just behind, ready to charge into the door once it fell. Atal knew men, saw in his eyes the violence and mercilessness he savored in his mind. The prurient cruelty. The contempt for life.

The door hinges shattered and the oak fell inward, thudding on the floor. Atal did the unthinkable.

With the swing of the chieftainess's sword, Atal reached with his curved blade and severed the silver cord at the heart of the man with a deft flick; the man's limbs splayed helplessly in mid-strike. The woman's sword swung upward, catching the artery beneath the jaw line. But as his blood sprayed out, his soul already stood weaponless and bewildered in the dark of the room as his insensate corpse fell forward onto the shattered door.

The woman didn't waste a moment but jumped up on the back of the huge man whose corpse filled the doorway and shrieked fiercely at his shocked followers. It was only then that more of Atal's people appeared within the house, their faces just as confused as those of the men outside, who were now backing away from the door.

But the moment did not last, for the remnant from the battle in the meadow were now returning to the village, screaming revenge. The painted men turned to face this new onslaught while the woman stood berserk at the door, swinging her sword about her. Atal moved away, but not without a backward glance. The mark was still upon her.

Hours later, Atal walked from the village to a nearby hilltop. From there, he could see the spirit road stretching away into the evening sky. A few still walked it, but not in numbers like earlier. He himself had helped many to find the road, and helped with those who stubbornly refused—out of jealousy or unforgiveness—to leave the living and go their way. Atal knew where the road led, to Brightness ineffable, out of sight; and that none returned who walked it. He knew that their journey was appointed. He knew that a house in the village was filled with living souls who were marked for the road, but there they were.

A figure was approaching—Hurk. He came and stood by Atal and gazed down at the houses.

"Did he at least have the mark upon him?" Hurk murmured.

"You know the answer." It had not been the big warrior's time.

"Then he will bring his rightful anger to the Throne. He will be heard. I am sorry, my old friend."

"I know how far outside the bounds I stepped. I..." Atal sighed deeply. "I am not even sure I can say that I am sorry. I know..." His words fell apart with mixed commitment and regret. Hurk reached over and squeezed his shoulder for a moment before turning away.

For some days, a few of Atal's people lingered around the village, reaping the souls of those whose injuries were mortal. Some followed the invading tribe retreating on their boats, for the same reason. Atal went to find the one who had been there longer than any of them; Kirkal, the local soul shepherd. Kirkal had arrived more than a century before with the settlers of the area. For generations, he had needed little help overseeing the departures from the tiny farming community as it grew into a town. Kirkal was expecting Atal's visit and showed no surprise at his approach. The two bowed respectfully. Kirkal faced Atal squarely.

"Surely you saw that the mark was upon her." It was a statement, not a question. But then he surprised Atal. "What about the unborn child? Did he bear it?"

Atal was stunned. In the moment, he had not taken notice. The mark was no more than a shadow upon the heart, a smudge of ashes, a shadow of an unseen hand. Atal closed his eyes and brought the memory back to mind of that moment in the front room of the chieftainess's house. Try as he could to see it, there was no shadow beneath the woman's heart. Instead, two bright lights. Atal's eyes flew open. How had he not seen it? "Twins, Kirkal! The woman bears twins. And no mark upon them."

Kirkal nodded knowingly. "Erigal, the woman—her father was a twin, as was his grandfather, and that one's grandfather—he it was who led the people here from farther south. It may be that she is destined to die, and very soon. But perhaps it was not to be by your hand. No healer here has the skill to be sure of delivering a child from a dead mother's stomach."

Atal nodded gratefully. He took a deep breath, perhaps his first in days. "Still, there is the warrior. There was no mark on him. And I cut his silver cord. And others in the house bore the mark. A price will be exacted." He looked at the ground, his face pinched with pain. "How I wish it were mine to pay."

It was deep in that night that he knew. A celebration had gone long into the night, and one young couple had met in the barn. A lamp had been kicked over and a fire spread in the straw. Meanwhile, Erigal was in labor.

Atal led his people into the flames where children and old people were overcome by smoke. Most of them were led out before the tongues of flame could reach their bodies. Erigal was being led out from the house by the chief, her husband; both of them were badly burned. Every few steps, Erigal stopped and clenched, involuntarily pushing. The mark was very dark upon her now—and another, below her heart. A life for the warrior's life.

Atal followed her closely. Jahl stepped up beside him. They shared a brief gaze, and Jahl nodded. Erigal stopped and clenched one more time; she crouched down, pulling her robe to her waist. Souls were passing by, escorted by Atal's dark people. Their faces turned towards Erigal, but they did not pause on their way. The woman pulled a shawl from her shoulders and lay it between her feet and with a final scream, her newborn slid onto it.

Her husband supported her by the shoulders while a younger woman wrapped the child in the shawl. The cord still connected the baby to Erigal, whose blood pooled around her feet. She was collapsing, and the second child was not delivered. Kirkal stood at a short distance, watching.

In a few minutes, Atal himself cut the cord connecting Erigal's life to her magnificent frame, while Jahl waited a few moments for the unborn twin. Erigal stood gazing down upon her former self. Jahl stood up, holding a tiny slip of soul to her chest. Erigal watched her husband trying to revive her, while fruitlessly the village healer attempted to retrieve the dead twin from her belly, pushing down on her flaccid stomach. The living newborn, its cord now cut, mewed in her cousin's arms.

Erigal then nodded to Atal, and they turned to go. Dawn was breaking over the river, and the spirit road led above the smoke and the terror and the mournful cries, while the black moon silently witnessed, and the white moon hid its face beyond the horizon.

After some time, Atal was aware that the dead twin was walking beside his mother. Atal looked at the twin, and saw the cost of his impulsive choice. This boy was to have been a delight to those who knew him. He would have shot arrows with piercing accuracy; sang with such a heavenly joy. The girl he would have loved would have been blessed, and their children beautiful. But even now, all that was changing; erased from the future. The bride and children were his brother's. And his brother would always carry the loss of his twin, a sadness no one could fulfill. His choices would be confused. Within generations, his line, the line of Erigal, would fail. Future paths shifted, this one trailing off to nothing.

Atal grieved. It suffocated him. Erigal and her people continued on the spirit road, but Atal staggered to a halt. The curved dagger weighed heavy in his hand. He stumbled down to the river's edge and stared into the water as the sun rose higher. Smoke from the village soured the loveliness of the morning. Atal held the dagger over the shining water, and let it drop.

But it would not. It returned to his hand, where it belonged.

Hurk, Jahl, and the others stood by him. Their faces did not judge him. It was time to go for now, but they would be returning in numbers to this place, he knew. Before they moved away toward their next appointment, Atal looked back up the meadow. From the crushed grasses and mired places where warriors had struggled and spilled blood, from a rut where a body had been dragged away for burial, a daisy had raised its head to the morning sun.

## The Beautiful Child

Div was a Dweller in a House of The Brightness.

She had had her marriage, her family, outlived her husband, seen her children grown and with families of their own. Now she was old, but not yet finished. Going to dwell in the House, where she was not in the way, Div felt at peace with her life.

She rose with dawn and reached for the Brightness, with her body and her soul, moving through the slow dance with a few others, reciting the prayers, coming to stillness and gazing with closed lids at the unseen the Brightness, praying that it would light the dark places in herself, in others near and far, in all the world of water and stone. They prepared and ate a morning porridge and drank tea while planning their day. They worked in their fields, carried water, wove cloth, chopped firewood. They visited the poor, healed the sick, and bore the burden of carrying out the justice meted out by the community upon the guilty — mostly, overseeing their work of reparation; occasionally, punishing; and rarely, putting to death.

On worship days, she dressed in white with all the others and led the songs and prayers in the House of The Brightness with other faithful in the community. There was no special garb or mark that set the Dwellers apart from the others except for their close-shorn hair.

Meditating continually on the Brightness, many found that the plants they tended lovingly grew with supernatural speed and size and beauty; or the cloth they wove from common linen was fine and pearly and filled the weft seemingly on its own; or that the cider they pressed became a heavenly mead that brought a shine to the faces of the congregation on the Longest Night and filled them with hope and joy. They could spin threads of gold from the shine of sun on oats as it waved in the wind, pluck crystals from the drops of rain that fell in the forest, create fabric dyes of deepest hues by pouring water while gazing on rare woodland flowers. Many were able to do these things, but not all found their "gold-skill". Some, like Div, were blessed instead with a rare level of peace, love, or truth that lifted others up. Div's own "soul-skill" was her ability to sit and know that the Brother of the Brightness sat close as a lover, so that others who sat with her also knew his touch and breath.

Div walked often to the top of the nearby mount, to keep her body lean and her heart strong and to breathe the freshest air. From there, she could gaze westward over the shining sea. She would then descend to the nearby village of Gladwaters and walk along the river road, watching the people at their work, praying for them.

On such a walk, she passed a house where the mourning was loud and long. She stood by the door and called her blessing to the house. No one answered, so she waited. Finally a child emerged, stared at her for a moment, and said, "My Mama died."

"I am so sorry, child. Brother of Brightness give her soul rest."

The girl took her hand and led her across the threshold into the dim interior. Numerous children and adults crowded the room around a shrouded corpse that lay on the table. A youngish man sat at her head, a newborn squalling in his arms. She moved toward him, taking the child to comfort it. Eventually, it cried itself to sleep as she walked up and down the hall. She went back to the room where the body of the young mother was laid out and led the family in prayers. She went to hand the newborn off, but the father stood and told her, "Take the babe away, Mother. We have nothing to feed him."

"Is there no one to nurse him? No goat or sheep in the place?"

"See all these children. The goats we have are not sufficient for them. The girls will have to mother the young ones, and they themselves too young. Please, take him and raise him in the House of the Brightness."

"What is his name?"

"Eradis."

Div stayed for the burial and carried the child back to the House of the Brightness. There was always a girl or two there who had given birth in the shelter of the House, and one became wetnurse to the newborn. The boy Eradis grew up in the House of the Brightness, as Div grew older.

From a young age Eradis had an unusual talent for gold-skills. Not just one, but it seemed that any that he witnessed for any length of time became his own. He could produce gold and silver, silk and perfume, dyes and gems in such abundance that the House itself began to be decorated with windows of sheets of clear crystal in jewel colors, the walls with murals of living colors, with gold leaf and carpets like mountain meadows.

Div herself went on a pilgrimage that took her away for almost ten years from the House in Gladwaters to visit other Houses of the Brightness to teach and encourage the faithful. She walked on her own feet the whole way, hundreds of miles, with only a staff to acknowledge her advancing age.

By the time she returned, she walked into a place she hardly recognized. New buildings had sprung around the place. The original House was but an entryway to a lofty arena, splendid with colored windows, gilded and plush, redolent with incense, brightly lit—not with candles, but with lamps that burned pale, cool light, night and day, within crystal globes that sat upon golden stands. She stood in the midst of all this opulence, stunned at the transformation, and dismayed.

Worshippers entered, for it was the time. They gathered under the massive dome in their jewel-toned tunics.

The Dwellers came into their midst in a procession, singing the same hymns as of old, but their robes were no longer white and simple. The colored and gold embroidery and gems covered them from neck to ankle. Their shorn heads bore headdresses of the same. The necks, wrists and ears of many were piled with gems and gold that clanked and clattered as they raised their heads and arms. They carried crystal globes before them. And the brightest of them was in the hands of Eradis, who was now a man of arresting beauty.

The varicolored congregation subsumed her. But she had always been tall, and if anything her white tunic and white hair against her sun-browned skin made her stand out among the vibrant colors. The eye of Eradis caught hers. He smiled widely, lighting up his olive-skinned face, his green eyes brilliant with pride. Div merely returned his look, holding herself still.

The ritual of the Brightness went on very much as it always had. The hymns were led by a choir whose voices had been finely trained. The timing and diction and cadence of the prayers were perfect. Div looked about and took account of who were the Dwellers, leading the ritual. Some she recognized, most were new since she had gone away. She closed her eyes to all the splendor, and found the Presence near her. There was little sense of sharing that spirit with anyone else around her. She stood still in her place until the last of the worshipers had filed out and were standing about outside in social groups, talking and laughing.

Still, Div stood, until the sound diminished and all she heard was the chirping of sparrows and the wind in the trees. Then she turned to go out the way she had come in.

Just outside, some of the Dwellers awaited. She greeted those she knew by name and was warmly embraced. Finally she came to Eradis.

"Peace to you, Mother Div," he said warmly, smiling broadly. He took her hand and bent over it, bringing it to his forehead. Then he stood straight. "Be welcome from your long journey. Come and take of the noon meal with us."

She bowed her head slightly in accession. He held out a hand to show the way, but she fell in behind him with Morda, an old, brown woman with a round face that seemed to fold in half across the bridge of her nose when she smiled, which she did now as she took Div's arm and held her close. It was as if ten years had not passed, between them. Div's eyes met hers and although Morda smiled, the sadness in her dark eyes was unmistakable.

The meal was sumptuous. There were attendants filling their goblets—crystal, not stoneware—with water, milk, or wine, such as they wished. Div took a small piece of the duck, some sliced fruit, and some cress salad. Eradis kept looking her way, his eyes shining, yet a question hung at the back as well, dimming the shine more and more as the meal progressed. Div silently ate what was on her plate and drank water.

While Eradis's attention was taken by another, she asked Morda to show her to her old room. Morda took her to the cottage down near the stream where all the Dwellers had once lived. Now it seemed nearly empty.

"The new cottage up the hill, the one we passed with the roses growing by the doorway—that's where most of the newer Dwellers live now. Only me, your old room, and a couple of other souls stay here now. During the meal, I made sure Loli, a new Dweller you'll meet—oh, you'll love her, Div—anyway, she shook out your bed and dusted everything and opened the windows up. It's just as you left it."

It was small and spare. Rustic. She herself could see the contrast between it and the affluence on display in the new House, in the dining hall. It gave her eyes a rest to see something she remembered so well. The whitewashed plank walls, the grey stone floor, the sheepskin rug, the undyed wool blanket on the bed. The small stoneware vase where she used to keep a single flower once in a while.

"Bless you, Morda. Bright One, bless you. I'm going to wash and rest now, if you don't mind."

"Of course. Here comes Loli with some warm water now. There's a fresh tunic and skirt cloth in the cupboard. Rest well."

\*\*\*

She awoke from a dream of pale desert under buttermilk sky, the promise of dawn painting the horizon, the stars fading overhead.

Through such a place she had journeyed and fallen in love with the silent stillness. She had fasted for many days by a spring of clear water. It was there that she sensed the Bright One so strongly, she might have starved and not regretted the empty husk of herself left sitting by the spring. But he had made it known to her soul that she had more to do, and needed to eat and become strong again. A shadow had passed over her closed lids, she opened them to see a child standing there. The child pulled a loaf of bread from her bag and handed it to Div before filling her waterskin and running up the bank, disappearing into the sun that peered over it. She had returned to the world on the strength of that bread, walking many miles back to the nearest village.

But in her dream, the sky began to turn fantastic colors. The sun leapt above the horizon in a riot of gold, fuschia, carnelian, chartreuse. The small clouds grew, with golden edges. They became cabochons, each holding within it a blinding glare from the sun. The sun smiled brilliantly at her, and then inhaled. As it inhaled, the light was drained from the sky-jewels. She was a pearl on the white sands. Dimly the jewels fell behind the horizon and the sun, now filling the sky, burned her until she cracked open—

It was a rap on the door of her room. She sat up, rubbing her face. "Just a moment," she croaked.

Loli had left a bottle of water on the stand, and Div took a long drink. She wet a cloth and ran it over her forehead, eyes, and mouth. She stood straight and recited a prayer, calming herself, and drawing vitality and strength from the Brightness. Then she opened the door.

Eradis stood there. Garbed simply, he looked like the young man she had left behind, who had been like a son to her and the other Dwellers. He smiled happily. She embraced him; he stood several inches taller than her now, and a rim of dark beard ringed his face.

They walked in the garden, and she told him briefly of her travels. He told her how he had been given a new position created for him, that of Head of House. His gold-skills had enriched the House so much that Dwellers from other houses now came to be trained in them.

"I see all around me the fruits of these, your gold-skills. There truly never was a Dweller that I have seen nor heard of in all my travels as accomplished and adept such as you are in these things." Her words hung in the air.

"Mother… I am sensing a 'but' in your words." They stopped in the shade of the roof of the House.

"Eradis, anyone would find your accomplishments admirable. And yet, I wonder. What of the soul-skills?"

His smile faltered for a moment, and then brightened.

"Mother Div, isn't that a matter best left between one and the Brother? How can we measure a soul-skill, or know if it is genuine? Gold and gems can be assayed, and their value set. Even silks and spices that find their way to the tables of the King, he rewards us for, richly. Their value is objective. Soul-skills are strictly subjective. What price is peace, or love, or faith?"

"And yet it is those things that give value to the other. What is the value of gold or gems? Can the hungry eat them, can the sick take them and be well? Can the lonely embrace them, can the broken heart be wrapped in your silks and made whole? Can they sing to the motherless, or bring life to the dead?"

"There is great joy to be found in gazing upon beautiful things. Even healing for the soul. In their sparkle and shine, the Brother's light is reflected."

"They dazzle the eye because of the light of the sun and the moons that reflect off of them. Can they shine in the dark? And yet that is where the Bright One shines the brightest."

"Mother, have you seen my lamps? For it is I who invented them, and they dim not! There is always light to gleam on the beautiful things, to chase away darkness, to light the way."

"Eradis, are you blinded by that light to the true Brightness, the Bright One? What need have you of his presence, his love, his truth, if you fill your life with artificial light, man-made light?"

Eradis laughed. "The same can be said of candles. Even of the sun and the moons. What about them?"

"The old songs and prayers clearly tell us that those point us to the true Brightness. They come and go, and in their rising and setting, in their waxing and waning, in the limited life of a candle, they show us our need for an unfailing Brightness—"

"Which I've created! Don't you see? We don't need faith to see light, it can always be in our hands. Right here, right now." From a pocket, he brought forth one of the crystal globes.

It was a pretty thing. The shell seemed to be glass, or perhaps quartz. It was somewhat cloudy, obscuring the source inside; a point of steady bluish brilliance. Eradis spoke low words to it and the light swelled so that Div had to avert her eyes. Seeing this, Eradis's face fell.

Div stood still, again seeking the nearness of the Bright Brother. Behind her closed lids, she felt the Presence lighting her. But Eradis was only a shadow before her.

She opened her eyes and looked upon his beautiful face. It was dark and brooding, hurt and resentful. "Eradis, my beautiful boy. You have done so many beautiful things. I am quite overcome. I need time to get used to all you have done here. Please, give me time."

His face softened. "Of course, Mother Div." He hesitated. "Welcome back." He once again put her hand to his forehead, then walked away, it seemed to Div, stiffly.

Div fell back into the rhythms of community life. As much as she had enjoyed her travels and the fulfillment that came from serving far and wide, it was wonderful to be back in her place, as much as it had changed. She visited with her children's families. The House had been such a huge crowd, they had missed each other in the mass of people. She saw a great-grandchild held aloft in the House of the Brightness and its name chanted by the congregation. Where there was depression, or grief, or strife within a house, she brought the Presence with her.

The girl Loli was eager to find a soul-skill, and spent many hours walking and talking with Div. Loli's cropped hair was bright red, her skin crowded with freckles, her physique robust and she was always laughing as she hefted loads, carried water, played with children by the hour and along the way taught them their letters and numbers. Everyone was saying that her soul-skill was joy, for she had an overflow that lifted others up as well.

One evening Div met Loli coming along the path. She looked a ghost of herself. She almost brushed by Div without acknowledging her. Div stopped her, taking both her arms, which were like ice.

"Loli, are you well?" Loli shrugged. Her mouth drooped in a way uncharacteristic. Div took her back to her room in the cottage and brought her some tea. She was recovering from whatever funk she was in, but said she was tired and wanted to sleep. Div prayed with her, imbuing the very air of the room with the nearness of the Brother; and closed the door to her room. Within a few days Loli was back to her jovial self, the incident seemingly forgotten.

It was some weeks later before she found Loli outside again, this time sitting on the stoop of the cottage in the middle of the night. She hardly seemed to know her own name. She was unsteady on her feet as Div guided her in and led her to her bed again. The next day Loli was listless and silent, and claimed to feel ill and unable to help with the children. Over a few days, again she recovered. Div said nothing.

The third time, there was snow on the ground. Morda found Loli this time, collapsed by the pathway, near death from exposure. They got help to carry her inside, and keep her by the fire until she was warm, but her eyes were still dull. After getting some broth in her, they led her to her bed, the room warmed with a brazier. She lifted her dull eyes to Div's. "Will it never be summer again?" she asked in a hollow voice. "Eradis has the summer in his eyes."

Div spent much of that night pacing the common room. She had a long conversation with the Presence. Loli recovered more slowly after that, it was days before she was back to her merry self.

A few days before the Longest Night, Div, Morda, and Loli sat at the common room table, knitting. The door opened on the winter morning, and Eradis stepped in and closed the door. Loli became very still, her knitting forgotten in her hands, her face pale. Eradis saw Loli looking at him, and his beaming smile faded.

"It was you…" murmured Loli.

"It was me,…what?" said Eradis, innocently.

Loli shook her head. "I don't know" she said under her breath, rising and disappearing into her room.

Eradis had stepped in to talk to Morda about a new Dweller whom he thought would like to stay in the old cottage with them. They went into a spare room and Div heard them chatting. "Head of House," she muttered. She had got used to many new things in the past weeks and months, but this simply wouldn't stop irking her sensibilities. Eradis wasn't despotic, but many decisions that the whole House would have made together were simply made by him. He decided, for instance, who would come to dwell and who was turned away. And it seemed to Div that all the newer Dwellers were young and lively. Was there no place for the introverted, the aged, who still wished to serve and had something to give? She enjoyed the energy and vibrance of the younger Dwellers, but missed the motherly and fatherly grey heads, the blind and the lame whose griefs and pain and struggles brought something valuable to the soul of the community — wisdom, compassion, hunger for the Presence.

Eradis and Morda left and Morda returned in a short while with the new Dweller. As Div might have predicted, she was young and fit, brown and pretty and full of laughter. Her brown hair formed glossy curls, even cropped short.

Div began keeping an eye on the sweet young girls. Loli and Suri, the new Dweller, became inseparable and worked side-by-side in the children's house, almost as children themselves. Perhaps Suri would also find joy was her soul-skill, Div thought.

Next, it was Suri who stumbled into the cottage of a spring evening, tears streaming down her face. Div was in her room and heard Morda asking Suri what was the matter. Div came out to find Morda seated by the fire with a shivering Suri. Her eyes were blank and hollow. Suddenly, she shook herself and cried out, "I was meant to get help! Loli needs help!!" She got up and dove for the door but couldn't make it halfway there before collapsing.

"Where is Loli? What's wrong?" Morda shouted. Suri pointed weakly toward the door and said, "the children's house…" Div ran out the door into the spring night toward the small house where children were taught and cared for during the day while their parents worked. She found Loli lying by the pathway. She was dry and empty as the shed skin of a cicada.

Loli was dead.

Div cried out and then closed her eyes, looking for the Presence. She tried to fill up so much with the Brother that he would overflow from her into Loli. For such had she done more than once, and seen the dead return, especially if they were young and their stories yet untold. But not this time. Loli's eyes had closed forever, and she had returned to the Brightness.

Several people had heard Div's cries and those of Morda, and came running. Everyone was asking questions, or crying. Some were saying they were going to get Eradis, and in a few minutes she heard his voice.

He was laughing as though drunk.

All fell silent as he approached, shouting. "Loli has returned to the Brightness, Bright One be praised!" A few voices tentatively echoed the blessing, but Eradis exploded in a fit of giggles, which shocked everyone.

Morda sat on the ground, cradling Loli's body. "Brother of Brightness, have mercy! Are you moonstruck, Eradis? Our sister is gone."

"And she was always so full of joy, should we not be celebrating?" Eradis grabbed a young woman nearby and swung her around him. "Loli was always giving and giving and giving joy, she lived to give, she must be dancing with joy in the Brightness, should we not do the same to sing her home?" The young woman pulled away from him and vanished among the others standing there.

Div stood up from where she also sat near Loli. An answer was beginning to form in her mind. "Yet you yourself never give of your soul, only your gold. We are called to be givers. But you, you are a taker, Eradis. Your soul-skill is taking. You took everything from Loli until she couldn't give any more. Then you also took from Suri."

Eradis couldn't help it, he threw his head back and laughed, and then howled wolf-like at the red moon that hovered overhead.

"Bright Brother," murmured many around him. People drew away, but Div came closer. She sought the Presence and felt him, before her, behind her, above and below, at her right and her left hand, and within her.

"Take from me, Eradis. Take it all. Take everything." Eradis's smile fell away.

"You don't have what I need, old Mother." He actually looked sad, and even more beautiful sad than he had ever looked. "I love you, Mother Div, but you offer me water, and I need wine."

"I love you, Eradis, like my own children and grandchildren and great-grandchildren. But you saw others giving of their souls, and you turned it around so you could take. This is a blasphemy, a perversion of all that is sacred to the Brightness. Turn away from this evil and come back to the Brightness."

Eradis laughed, but it was edged now with cynicism and mockery. "Mother Div, your time is over. It is time for you to depart." Someone gasped.

Morda stood and approached. In Div's soul, she saw her as incandescent with the Presence, warm and sure as a mountain in the sun. "No, Eradis. You are the one who must depart. Soon, the Warranters will come and look for you for taking the life of one of our family. He is already being notified. And I have little doubt but that the consequence meted out will be a life for a life. Go now, and see if you can escape that justice."

Eradis looked frightened and sad. "Mother Div..." But she looked at him with hard, grey eyes.

Then he turned towards the others who stood about. "You people made me the Head of this House, but I will not stay where all I have done for you — the wealth and beauty I, *I* have brought to this community, the prosperity and the prominence, are valued as nothing. I go. Those who will follow me, come now. Take such treasures as you can carry. We depart this very moment!"

Such was the power of Eradis's charisma that about a fifth of those standing about — all younger members of our House — turned and left with him, a few immediately, and a few more who lingered indecisively before joining the group that marched with Eradis up to the House of the Brightness, where his globes lit the colored windowpanes from within night and day. They carried away most all of the globes that night, the beautiful vestments, much in the way of food, gold and silver coins and bolts of silken weavings. No one stopped them. Soon they had mounted the few good horses the House owned and ridden into the night.

By the time the constabulary arrived, they were long gone. The Warranters followed them through the night and the next day but returned empty-handed. Meanwhile, the Dwellers buried Loli and cleaned up the mess left behind in the House of the Brightness.

It was said that Eradis and his followers went first to Bend-in-the-River, but moved on from the kind of scrutiny one found in a small and wealthy city to a place high in the hills, farther to the west, north of the port city Dastenn. His many followers came and went.

As for Div, she lived long also in the House of the Brightness, drawing her own vitality from the Presence. One day she crept into the House of the Brightness, shrunken and leaning hard on her staff, and was later found sitting in the center of the House, her soul having gone wholly into the Presence forever, smiling, and tracks of joyful tears still drying on her wrinkled face.

# Io

The cobbled streets of Dastenn were filled with a roar of people of all colors, dressed in jewel tones and masks of animals and fantastic creatures, dancing up streets and down to a furious music of drums and trumpets, bagpipes and flutes. At every corner, the band and the beat changed, and the movement of people collided and eddied like a river's confluence under the bright sun. There were long, broad ribbons passed from hand to hand, tying the people to one another, pulled and waved; but forbid it that any of their length should touch the ground. It was a game, and a ritual, and a festival all in one.

For those who tired or were thirsty, there were many stands selling refreshments, and the wayside trees' spreading roots were populated with people resting, watching, laughing at the antics.

While they drank their chilled beverages from cleverly folded banana leaves and ate their meat or vegetable filled pastries from dishes of the same, they ignored eyes that watched hopefully from deep folds in the tree roots.

Finally, a bonanza! A young woman discreetly wrapped her meat pie in the leaf, having sampled only a bite, and shoved it behind her before rising with her companions. Before they were three steps away, Io had secreted it in the pocket of her tunic and retreated to the folds of the tree roots.

Her stomach growled, but she waited until she had collected more half-eaten meals and even an undrunk cup of fruit squeeze — it had a fly in it, which she ignored — and made her way up the tree, one hand carefully holding the juice cup, to a hidden crotch stuffed with leaves and rags to make a bit of cushion. Her little brother was awake, eyes glazed with hunger, and he wordlessly fell on the almost-whole meat pie and drank most of the juice. Io ate the other bits of pastry while she combed his brown curls with her free hand. It was almost enough, and the day had just begun.

Refreshed by the meat pie, her brother, Leep, began to chatter. He was curious about the dancing and the ribbon game, which he wanted to join.

"No, Leep. The game is too dangerous for children. See, they are watching from balconies, and throwing bougainvillea petals down. It's raining colors on the dancers."

She pointed to a house across the way, where she herself had brought a bushel of collected petals to sell to the house matron the day before. Beautifully-dressed children clung to the iron railing of a balcony, the full-length windows wide open.

"Later, there will be games for the children when things calm down a bit. See, part of the game is to keep the ribbon tight, so that if someone falls, they can be pulled up by those around them. It reminds us that we catch one another when we fall. The Bright Brother teaches so." Despite her smile, Io's sadness returned to her. No one had caught Leep and her when they lost their father and mother.

Leep cried out his happiness when a group of tumblers came leaping and diving over and under the bright ribbons, which rose and fell to accommodate them. The crowd roared their pleasure. Even Io was caught up in the spectacle, and mirrored Leep's smile. The drums and trumpets played louder.

"I have to wee." Leep said suddenly. His face looked anxious, and Io nimbly descended the massive tree between ridges on the trunk, with Leep following behind. She helped him down and took his hand firmly in hers as they navigated into a nearby alley with a privy stall. They stayed to avail themselves of a public water point, which Io had visited before dawn to clean herself and comb out her long, dark hair with her fingers before braiding it over her shoulder. She washed Leep's face and ran wet fingers through his dusty hair. She instructed him to wet his hands and clean beneath his clothes as well as he could, then finally wash his hands and arms well.

They spent the remainder of the morning finding food. There was so much to be had that once they were full, they saved things that would keep—candied nut clusters, whole fruits, dried spiced meat, hard cheese cubes—in the bag Io kept slung over her shoulder with all their worldly worth inside; normally, the bag hung quite slack on her hip. The bounty could feed them for days.

As the day wore on, the ribbon dance came to an end, the ribbons themselves worn to a raveling and left, bunched, by waysides all over the city. If there was one in good condition and not too dirty, it swelled the bulk of Io's bag yet more.

Passing an alley, she saw someone's laundry hanging low, and a sweet little blue tunic, just Leep's size. It made him presentable to participate in the children's dancing. She promised herself that she would return it to the alley later; they were only borrowing. She watched from the sidelines as he bounced through the circle game, his brown locks bobbing and flopping.

The game over, the crowd mixed chaotically as parents sought their little ones. She saw Leep threading his way toward her, a great smile on his bright face.

Someone jostled her from behind, hard, crying out their apologies. She looked away only for a moment.

Leep was gone, like the black moon, vanished in the sea of people.

She sought his curly head everywhere. She cried out his name. Family groups were moving away from the center of the wide street, new visitors surging in. Io ran to the middle of where the game had been. She accosted the game's organizers, but they shrugged as they looked about. After an evaluating glance at Io, her faded and worn tunic and ratty footwear, they didn't seem very concerned and soon were moving away themselves.

It was getting toward evening by then and food vendors were multiplying. Io ran from cart to table, looking among the gathering customers clustered around each, the smoke from grills stinging her eyes, the smells of roasting vegetables and meat lost on her.

No Leep.

Io's head was spinning, her throat a painful knot of anxiety. She looked around for where, if she were Leep, she might have gone. She hurried down an alleyway that had a public privy. She called his name, but he was not there. IShe kept down that alley and emerged on the next street, looking around for a few moments before continuing on one more intersection to the place where stood the tree they lived in. Hastily she climbed up but found the space between trunks empty.

She ran up a large limb that thrust out over the street, looking through clusters of green and gold leaves, up the street and down.

For hours, Io toured the streets and alleys until she herself was lost. She called Leep's name until she was hoarse. It was long past sunset when she heard him crying. Her heart stopped and she stood, finding the direction from which it came.

There was an iron fence enclosing a strip of flower garden between the street and a tall house with great windows, lit golden from within. She listened carefully, and decided his crying was coming from the window nearest the corner. It was partially hidden by a rampant vine that covered much of the corner of the house and was lush and thick enough to hide inside. She climbed the stone corner post of the fence, and then the vine on the front of the house until she could look right into the window.

The glowing opulence of the interior stunned her. The walls were pale yellow, the curtains sky blue. The furnishings gleamed with rubbing, and there was a case of books and small statuary on either side of the tall fireplace.

She heard Leep whimpering, together with the voice of another child. "Don't worry, Leepy. Mum and Dad will find your sister. You can sleep in this bed, next to mine. Didn't the bath feel so nice? And wearing clean clothes? They'll wash out the juice from your tunic. Do you want more cake?"

Io strangled the cry that wanted to issue from her throat. Relief wrestled with anger, and even a kind of hysterical laughter that "Leepy" was taking baths and eating cake while she worried herself sick. Her head bowed on the windowsill, thankful that he was well.

A woman entered the room. Io crouched lower behind the sill. She watched what must be the other, unseen child's mother, taking in her brocaded evening robe, elaborately dressed hair, and the kohl on her eyelids. She was several years older than Io. The woman smiled warmly.

"I miss my sister!" she heard Leep sob, and it was all Io could do to not leap through the window and scoop her brother up. But she held back.

The woman bent over Leep. "Of course you miss your sister. She's all you have, isn't she? But for now, you need to rest. That arm was badly broken. You were such a brave boy. Wasn't he, Manas?"

Io lifted up higher on the sill, trying to see inside to where the children were, against the outer wall, apparently, and difficult to see from the window without putting her head past the gathered curtains. The woman was moving around the room, loosing the blue hangings so they fell together, covering the windows, and closing the louvered shutters. Io just had time to hang down flat against the wall before the blue curtains fell over the window where she was. She had to climb lower so that the closing shutter wouldn't pinch her clinging hands.

She heard voices, and the light through the louvers dimmed as the woman was evidently putting out lamps. Io climbed down all the way, and hid herself in a trumpet flower bush against the foundation of the house. She slumped in relief, and cried tears of outrage.

Who were these people and what right had they to scoop up her only family, all that was left to her after their desperate flight from the mountain that rained fire? But seeing Leep, just for a moment, clean and fed and laying in an actual bed, with linens, oh, how she wanted him to stay there, warm, safe, fed. Her inner conflict dizzied her as she gazed through the bush at the tall house on the other side of the quiet street.

At least an hour passed while she thought, and cried, and even ate some of what was in her bag to quell the growling in her stomach. Then she climbed back up to the window. The shutters were only a moment's difficulty, and then she was in the beautiful room, now darkened.

She crept to the bed where she had glimpsed her brother. He lay atop snowy linens, and his right forearm was splinted and wrapped thickly. She approached him and whispered in his ear, "Leep, it's me, Io." He woke groggily, and his arms slipped around her neck. She felt the splint against her ear, and then he was pulling that arm back to himself, apparently dismayed for a moment, having forgotten about the splint and wrappings.

"Io!" –she shushed him. "Io," he whispered. "Are we going back to the tree?"

"No, Leep. These people want to take care of you. You can stay here for a time. I will come back and see you."

"I want to go with you!"

"How will you climb the tree with a broken arm? And what happened? Whisper, now."

"I was crossing the street after the game. Someone ran into me. Then the boy, Manas, tripped over me and spilled blackberry squeeze all over me. His mother took me into the alley to wash me off but then she saw my arm. It hurt so bad, Io. They asked where my parents were and I said I only had you, Io. They asked me where we live and I said we lived in the tree on Stonemason Street. They brought me home and a bonesetter came. They gave me a bath, and dinner. It's so comfortable here, Io. Everything is so smooth, and soft. I'm not used to it. I want to go with you."

"Listen to me, Leep. You are going to stay here, and eat lots of good food, and sleep in a soft bed, and let your arm heal. I am going to come every night to visit you and make sure you're okay. When you get better, then we can... well, we'll decide what to do."

Leep's dark blue-green eyes were wide, and even in the dim light Io could see the pupils dilated slightly from whatever the doctor had given him to dull the pain. Tears collected on the lower rims and spilled over into the hair above his ears. He nodded solemnly, his head and eyelids beginning to droop.

"Does it hurt, badly?"

"Not too much now. I'm really tired, though. We had a big day, didn't we?"

"We did, Leep. Kiss me goodnight, little brother." His cherry-like lips brushed her cheek and he laid back on the linen. She laid down beside him until his breathing became regular.

She awoke suddenly, hours later, as the rising white moon peered through a slat of the louvers. She arose quickly and exited the window.

In the early morning, the night fishermen's returning-song wafted faintly from the direction of the river. A bell rang softly from a House of the Brightness. The streets were empty, not even a rat, for the sweepers had done their work in the night, removing every trace of yesterday's festivities.

Io found her way slowly back to the tree. It was lonely without Leep to wrap herself around protectively. She knew she had done the best she could by him. She fell asleep and awoke in the full morning.

Without her brother to look after, Io was able to find work tending the ovens in a bakery. She also had to split and stack the wood, shovel the embers and ashes from the ovens when it was glowing hot and close the door after the bakers shoved loaves in with a long peel, carry sacks of grain from the market in a heavy barrow, and many other tasks while the bakers kneaded balls of dough as large as a man before letting them rise and splitting them into balls, to be baked as loaves.

Besides a large loaf a day, she was promised a copper each week and a silver at the end of the month, and a place on the floor to sleep as her work began well before dawn when the third watch bell rang. Although in truth, she was up an hour before, slipping into a window to see how her brother was keeping. Most nights, she didn't wake him, but left a leaf or a pebble to show him she had been there.

Returning to the bakery, she laid and built the fire until the bricks of the oven glowed with heat. The bakers were already mixing the dough in mountains of buckwheat flour. They loaves rose in the gathering heat, and finally after Io had shoveled the embers out of the oven, they loaves were put in to bake. Io closed the door with an iron hook.

The embers were placed in bowl-like pans and carried away for other uses. Vendors used them to grill fish and vegetables to sell to people walking to work. Hawkers ran with them to neighborhoods where they cried their wares and harried servants rushed from kitchens where the fires had gone out in the night to buy a scoopful of them. Io was familiar with these early morning activities.

She hung her bag always where she could see it, high up in a corner of the bakery. The owner was a red-faced woman named Caro, who came to oversee the doings of her employees and check that the loaves were of a size, shape, and color that never varied. She squinted at Io, but her look was not unfriendly, and while she shouted unneeded instructions at her occasionally, it was more old habit than anything else, and she did the same to the two men who mixed the dough. They appeared to ignore her, but it was remarkable how consistent the loaves were. The men lived elsewhere, but Caro had an apartment above the bakery.

It was high summer, and all of them streamed sweat while they worked. Io, wrinkling her nose, wondered if the loaves tasted saltier in the summer months, as the men shucked their shirts as they worked the huge mounds of dough.

After the loaves were in the oven, everything was washed and swept well, and the sponge mixed for the next morning. Only then did they receive their daily loaf, and their liberty for the evening and night. The only days off were the Longest Day, the Longest Night, and the Equinoxes; and a few religious days, for Caro was observant.

One afternoon Io left the bakery to visit the bathhouse where she would dip in the natural hot spring and wash off the sweat, flour, and ashes, and change her clothes—for she now owned two sets, Caro having given her an old, overly-large tunic, and Io had bought trousers from a fripper's cart. She returned to the bakery to wash her dirty clothes and hang them over the cooling ovens. It was too hot to stay in, though.

Before they had had to flee Bend-in-the-River, Io had gone to school. There was a House of the Brightness in the town, and a young man would walk out to her village and teach all who wanted to learn their letters and sums. Io did not wish to lose her reading, so she sought things to read as she wandered the city of Dastenn. Signboards, handbills, broadsides, terse menus chalked on pub fronts.

Seeking cooler air, Io wandered uphill to a part of the city she had not visited recently. There was a House of the Brightness there with an arched doorway inscribed with words graven into the dark wood. The stepped moldings were lined with them, arching overhead. The sayings were teachings of the Brother of Brightness. Each week she tried to memorize one to carry with her. They reminded her of her mother and father, who quoted such things often, and Io hoped they would be pleased that she was still guided by the doctrines.

For a number of nights, Io had climbed through the window only to find Leep so deeply asleep that she was unable to rouse him enough to talk. Then there were four nights in a row when she wasn't able. The vines about the windows had been trimmed after blooming with fragrant white flowers. And a guard was posted to walk the narrow garden.

Finally, she was able to slip by him, only to find that the window was shut and locked against the night. She realized the whole house was dark and silent. Her heart dropped into the earth. Where had they taken her brother?

Walking home, she berated herself. She should have introduced herself to the family—they said they would look for her. She would have taken him out of the house when he was well. But to what? To live again in the tree? She would have to leave the bakery in order to look after him for he was too young to be on his own. She couldn't go back to that, and take Leep with her back to desperation.

After her work hours, she took her daily loaf with her after bathing and went to the rear gate of the house where Leep had been staying. Leep had told her their name was Marteague. She had bought a large sheet of paper and wrapped the loaf, tying it with string. At the gate, she spoke to the old man posted there. "Peace to you, brother."

"Peace to you," he said in return.

"My mistress craves that the family in this house sample her bread. I can deliver loaves each day by sunrise. They are the best quality, and I believe Mistress Marteague will be pleased." She smiled broadly as she held out the wrapped loaf.

"They've traveled."

She allowed her face to fall in mild disappointment. "I see." She brought the loaf back to her chest, but glanced down at it. "It's a shame to let this go to waste. Will they travel by land, or by sea?"

She smiled again, noticing the guard's eyes were on the loaf. She held it out just a couple of inches.

"They sail at the turn of the tide."

"How wonderful? Where are they going to?"

He shrugged. "Do I know?"

She toyed with the paper wrapping of the loaf. "And what is the name of the ship they sail on?"

His eyes met hers, narrow. Then he shrugged. "The *Delphine*."

She smiled, and passed the loaf through the bars of the gate. Then she turned and ran for the bakery to collect her still-damp change of clothes and her bag, and then to the docks of Dastenn, her heart in her throat.

At the docks, she threaded her way through the crowds, asking for the *Delphine*, getting no more than a terse gesture farther down the line. It was late afternoon. She asked a smiling man selling passage on a schooner when the turn of the tide would come. He told her that it would be just after midnight, but full boats would cast off and position themselves favorably in the bay to be ready. Some were already moving off, she realized. She thanked the man and continued down the row of boats. The quiet chaos of loading cargo and passengers and supplies was layered by the scream of gulls and the clang of bells. Another ship was casting off far down the pier.

Suddenly she saw it—the *Delphine*. A caravel painted white and blue. She froze, and did what she thought of as "fading". She stood still and forced herself to breathe slowly. She made her body language say that she was nothing, not worth notice. She prayed to the Brother to calm herself. And watched, and noticed.

There was plenty of loading still going on, although the passenger gangway was roped off at the bottom. She drifted over toward the cart loaded with grain sacks. A young man came down the cargo gangplank and threw a sack over his shoulder and turned with fluid motion back up the corrugated plank. She stepped up and perfectly mirrored his motion, picking up a grain sack and following him up the plank and down the hatch. He strode into the dark bowels of the ship and to the bay where the grain sacks were stored. She watched as he tossed it down, but ducked behind a bulkhead as he marched back. When he was gone she placed her grain sack down and tucked and patted it to match the ones he had stacked so perfectly, then jumped back behind the bulkhead as he returned with another sack. She saw him hesitate for perhaps a half-second as he met the extra, unexpected sack but then he threw on the next one and turned back.

Her eyes were adjusting to the absence of light, and she prayed in the dark. Finally, as the young man returned yet again down the hatch, she stood plainly in the aisle. She jumped aside as if surprised as he came. He frowned at her slightly. "Sorry, where is the kitchen? I'm new."

He took a moment to evaluate her. "Galley's forward." He pointed past the hatch to the front of the ship, and then skipped lightly up the ladder, gone.

Io made her way around barrels and boxes in the direction he pointed to and found the galley compartment. A woman with blond hair, mixed with grey and tied with a scarf, was already busy at an iron stove over a boiling pot. Io knocked at the propped-open door and the woman turned suddenly toward her. "Evenin' meal's not for an hour yet, young puss."

"I was told to help you, mother."

Her face brightened. "The Steward hired you to help me? How many summers have you seen? Maybe twelve?"

"Fourteen, mother."

The woman turned and looked her up and down. Io averted her eyes deferentially. "Where may I put my bag out of the way, mother?"

"You call me Cook. And there's a peg behind the door. There you go. Now, roll up your sleeves and look alive, and wash those greens." Io picked up a tub of green vegetables and hesitated. "Well, I can see you're as green as those greens, anyway. Some help Guck sent me."

"I'm very good with ovens, Cook, and with bread."

"Is that right. Well, then. The loaves are rising, get the oven going. The wood's on the other side of the companionway. That'll be the ladder, to you, land-mouse."

A while later Io had the fire in the tiny oven as hot as it was going to get. She asked about the scuttle for the embers and Cook had to hunt for it. By the time she found it the oven was ready. The embers from this went back into the cook stove, and the loaves—after the first which Cook had shaped while Io watched carefully to see how she wanted them—into the bread oven. Io closed the door. She had danced carefully around Cook as the plump woman moved about the tiny space. Overhead a bell clanged. The floor suddenly shifted underfoot, causing Io to grab a support post.

"Wouldn't you know. I hope the bread don't fall. Sun's gone, light the big lantern, -what did you say your name is?"

Io saw no reason not to use her own name, and she told her.

"We'll make a messman out of you yet, Io."

Io allowed herself a small smile, and took a deep breath.

"Well don't just stand there looking pretty, we've got cleaning up to do!"

After they had the kitchen area spotless, they were able to eat a hurried meal themselves before the bell rang for mess. Cook snatched down trays and tureens from a cupboard and servants began appearing at the kitchen door. Each bore chits for meals which were passed to them by Cook and Io. Finally the paying passengers were fed, and a couple of boys showed up for food for the crew. Some would eat now, and some after the changing of shifts, in just under an hour. They washed their own serving bowls and trays, but it wasn't long before the trays and tureens sent out earlier to passengers began to arrive and needed washing. By then the water was boiling and all, even the huge stew pots, were scrubbed and hung up overhead or secured in the ventilated cupboards. A few stragglers came to the kitchen who had missed the meal, and it was clear that Cook had their respect and that she doled out the food accordingly.

It was the tenth hour before Cook pulled the kitchen door to and locked it with a key that hung from her belt. She hustled toward a tiny enclosure. Io called out, "Cook, please, where will I rest the night?"

"Well, didn't the Steward give you a place? No mind, we'll hang up a hammock for you in my cupboard. Best you're safe away from the men."

Only when Io was hanging in her hammock in the dark, stifling closet of a room, swinging gently beside the snoring form of Cook, did Io give thought to whether Leep was even on board. It was too late, now, if he wasn't. She heard the cries of the sailors and felt the surge of the sails as they caught the wind and the tide and headed out of Dastenn Bay. She didn't even know where the ship was going.

When she was smaller, when they lived on the farm, her mother would take her out on the river to catch fish when the silver eels made their mad mating dance at the water's surface. Heedless, they writhed their watery dance, flashing in the dawn light, practically leaping into the nets. They filled their boat with the sleek creatures, as did a few dozen others who had the legal right to fish on those magical few days of spring. They would eat fresh eel for days, smoked eel for months.

So Io was not altogether a stranger to the ceaseless motion of a boat, but had never been on anything so enormous. Swaying in the dark, she was full of anxiety.

"Cook, please. Might I go out and look at the stars?"

A snore was her reply. Carefully Io climbed down from the hammock, gently slid the lock open on the narrow door, and made her way up the companionway to the deck.

In the dark, shapes of men and women moved about the deck, and low voices murmured. Gazing toward the stern, she could see the elevated rearward deck, with soft light in tiny windows. She moved as close as she dared, but did not want to encounter anyone.

Someone was moving toward her. She jumped back down the companionway and hid behind a bulkhead, her heart thumping. When no one came after her, she went back to the cupboard where her hammock hung. Somehow, she fell asleep.

It was just before dawn when Cook's voice sang out, "Rise and shine, young puss. Time to get the grub on." Breakfast was bread remaining from the night before, for the crew, with hot coffee. For the passengers, there were trays of cheese, butter, boiled eggs, and fruit to be laid out for them or their servants to retrieve. Breakfast had been cleaned up and the noon meal started when Cook told her to take the opportunity to use the head and maybe go up for one or two sniffs of fresh air. "No more than three, mind you, the stove won't stoke itself!"

After using the head, Io no more than peeped her head out the hatch, looking toward the stern. She didn't know who might notice her among the bustle on deck, so she took her three breaths and ducked back down into the shadows.

Someone else was in the tiny kitchen with Cook.

Io tucked herself in under the companionway. She heard Cook's voice gabbling on about the list of fresh food to be purchased at the next port, and then she segued into "Thank the Brightness I've got a helper, and she's a handy one, too, Guck, although she'll need a bit of training up. I suppose I've also got you to thank for finally getting me a mate?"

"What are you going on about, Cook? There's no second cook on this journey."

"Well, who's the girl running the stove and kneading the bread, then?"

The man scoffed. "Looks like you've a stowaway on your hands, Cook."

"So you didn't get me any help. How many months have I told you I needed a hand down here? Well, can't we keep her?"

"Not if she's come aboard without pay or permission. Where is this girl, anyway?"

"She's just gone to use the head. Can't we keep her on? She's been awfully helpful. You want to go back to half-baked bread, and overcooked stew?"

The voices got louder, and she was sure she smelled the aroma of bread that was ready to come out of the oven. She might as well face whatever was going to happen, and make herself as indispensable as she could. She appeared in the doorway, saying in a loud voice, "Your pardon, Cook, but the bread's got to come out of the oven quick, or it'll burn!" She dashed between the Steward and the oven, opening it with a fair bit of drama as it bloomed with a bit of smoke. She shoved the peel in, and laid each loaf on the huge wooden tray on the counter quickly. It was dark, but not burned.

The Steward had backed halfway out of the door. He signaled with his head to Cook, who followed him out into the hold. Io heard the Steward attempt to take control of the conversation, but Cook wasn't having it, referencing Io rescuing the bread as an example of how needed she was. Io continued to tend to the fire and watch the stew, meanwhile wiping and cleaning and tidying everything in sight. Finally she heard Cook come in the galley. She turned slowly, to see the older woman sitting on a stool, leaning in the corner, arms crossed, muttering curses.

Io faced her with a meek aspect. She had a good idea what was coming. Cook gave her a powerful speech about her "insinuating herself into my kitchen and bringing no end of trouble down on my head" but gradually the speech changed tone to how badly she needed a helper and how unjust it was of Steward Guck to have expected her to do for over a hundred crew and passengers all on her own.

Finally her words were spent. Io knelt at her knee.

"I am sorry I troubled you, Cook. I was desperate to get on board and I was sure I couldn't buy passage on such a fine rig. I'm not running from anyone. I'll tell you everything, Cook, but we've got to get the stew into the tureens." She got up and began again to work furiously before the servants and passengers arrived. Cook didn't speak to her for the rest of the day, but she didn't get rid of her, either.

Until that night, when they rolled into their hammocks.

"All right, Io. Let's have the story."

Io told her about Leep, how they were orphaned, and how he came to be on the ship—she hoped.

"What, you're not even sure? Some ship's stewards, they'll toss you over the side for stowing away."

Io lay silent. Their bodies swung gently back and forth. Cook never blew out the oil lantern but turned it down to a tiny blue pearl of flame. It cast faint, odd shadows on the plank walls. Like the river cows moving under the surface of the river, when she was a child on the boat with her mother. A tear found its way from the corner of her eye to the hair at her temple. "He's all I have, Cook."

Cook harumphed in the dark. When the snoring began, Io wept into her sleeve until she too fell asleep.

Days passed like this. They worked from dawn to deep night. Life went on above them on the deck, and below them in the hold, and the sea passed by far below that, but they lived between the kitchen and storerooms. Cook advised Io not to be seen above, lest the Steward change his mind about her. So Io had no opportunity to see about Leep.

One evening she couldn't stand the twilight of the hold anymore, and before going to sleep she crept up the companionway. The fresh breeze was a balm, and the stars a glory. The red moon was sinking under the sea in the west. There seemed to be a stir of interest among a few passengers at the rear deck, who looked over the rail. Io crept to the gunwale, to see a massive whale just disappearing under the water.

She heard Leep crying out, "Look, Manas, look at that one!" Io's heart stopped, and she sighed with relief. She craned her neck to get a look at him, but she couldn't be sure. About his voice, though, she was certain. She continued to hear him chatter indistinctly, and her head bowed gratefully. She watched the rising and sinking of the gentle giants for a few minutes more, and the waters shimmering with phosphorescence, then went below to the best sleep she had had in several days.

In the morning it occurred to Io that perhaps Leep was anxious about having left Dastenn and not having a chance to see her. Some days had passed since the scene in the galley, and she felt less concerned about the Steward noticing her presence above. So it was that during her few minutes out of the kitchen in the morning, she went up on deck.

Just as she was giving up and turning back, the Marteague family emerged from the staterooms under the elevated rear deck. They climbed the ladder to the rearmost area, where the lively breeze and far-seeing views were best. She heard Leep crying out about dolphins, but the rest of the family were chatting with the helmsman, who was pointing out some feature of the distant coastline. She watched her brother jumping to see over the high gunwale, and then he was climbing and kneeling on the rail, turning to point, and just then a tug of breeze and a toss of wave pulled him right over the side.

Io didn't even think. Screaming out his name, she vaulted over the side into the sea. Her mother had taught her to swim, but Leep had been too young. It seemed forever between leaving the boat and hitting the water, clumsily, with a slap to the gut that took her breath away, while the boat's bulk moved swiftly past, seemingly just inches away, and with a rush of wake that went over her head. She coughed the salt water and began to paddle and kick toward where she hoped she would see her brother. She didn't hear the shouts from the deck of the ship. She fought the swells, her clothes dragging, while hoarsely screaming "Leep! Leeeeep!!"

A forceful exhalation just beside her startled her. The next wave slapped her full in the face and left her coughing again. A sapphire-blue fin cut the water just ahead of her, joined by others. The *Delphine* had slipped by and its wake fought her even as it showed her what direction to swim in. A long blue body leapt from the water beside her and dove. Then another. Then dozens.

Suddenly she saw Leep, emerging from the waves, clinging to one of the dolphins by the fin. The creature made for Io, while Leep coughed and gasped and wailed incoherently. Coming alongside of her, the dolphin slowed, shoving Leep against Io. She felt the strange, cold, slippery body against her shoulder and wrapped an arm around Leep. He was sobbing now, his lungs almost clear of the salt water.

"Leep, Leep it's me, Io, you're all right. I've got you." Hardly knowing what he was doing, Leep flung his arms around Io's neck. Immediately they were both in trouble, sinking under the water.

But they were surrounded by the strange, smiling faces and sapphire bodies of the dolphins, who thrust themselves against Io and Leep, pushing them up to air. Io grasped a fin, and so did Leep. Then they were moving powerfully through the waves, pulled along by two dolphins while others leapt in and out of the water on either side of them. The ship was a speck in the distance, although it had struck sails and dropped a skiff into the water, and men were pulling oars toward them. It was just a long minute or two before they approached.

The men's and women's faces turned from concern to wonder as they turned from rowing to see the dolphin-borne pair brought to the side of the skiff. Arms pulled them bodily into the boat. Io and Leep wrapped themselves around each other. Leep's face was toward the side where the dolphins had deposited them, and he cried out "Thank you! Bless you!" and waved his little arm as the creatures circled for a moment, and then turned to go their way.

Io pulled back to get a look at his face. "Leep, we're all right, aren't we?"

"Io!" He patted her cheeks for a moment adoringly, and then fell back into her arms. It was then she noticed the hushed boatsmen staring with reverential awe. "Brother of Brightness," she heard one or two of them murmur.

The seaman in the prow beside them gave command in a subdued tone, and the oars turned the boat back to where the *Delphine* had dropped anchor in a bit of bay. They rowed at a gallop until they reached the ship. Leep was hauled up aback one of the sailors who climbed the rope ladder, but Io climbed up on her own. The Marteague family received Leep with open arms, but she stood by herself, still dripping. Her legs were wobbly and she folded them and sat on the deck, head bowed, her face curtained by her hair, which had lost its plait.

Leep burst from the group, almost yelling that this was his sister, the one they were looking for, and throwing his arms possessively about her shoulders. The Marteague family gathered round her, hands reaching. She didn't want to open her eyes, to stand on her feet, for Leep to unwrap himself from around her. She was shivering and he was warm. She could feel the firm flesh that had grown on his limbs, and his embrace was strong. His familiar scent, tinged with salt. But hands were lifting him and her to their feet, and suddenly she was being introduced to the Marteagues.

It was a few hours later that she sat at a large table with Leep's protectors, combed and dressed in clothing not her own, and sipping broth she had no part in preparing. The Marteague children — besides Manas, the child whose bed was next to Leep's in the mansion in Dastenn — were three in number, girls except for Manas. She couldn't have told their names a minute after being introduced, and thankfully was able to call the parents "Mother" and "Father" out of Dastenni politeness.

Free from hunger and uncertainty, Leep had blossomed. He smiled continually and contagiously, and declared his intention to make up a song about being rescued by dolphins and his magical sister who dropped from heaven. He had already forgotten the choking salt water and the stinging cold. But he was also exhausted by the adventure, and after finishing his broth was whisked to a berth with the other children. Then Io sat alone with Master and Mistress Marteague, and their smiles dropped.

Mistress spoke first. "Without a doubt, looking at you, you must be Leep's sister." Io regarded her, her head bowed slightly, deferentially. Mistress Marteague sniffed. "We understand that you are orphans. Help us understand why you abandoned him, and how you have miraculously reappeared."

"At the Ribbon Dance Festival, I was watching the children dancing. Then Leep just seemed to vanish. I spent hours looking for him, but I came to learn he was in your house, being doctored and cared for. I... left him there, because... we had no home. We were sleeping on a tree in Stonemason's Street."

"And how did you know we were on this ship? How did you get on board?"

"Your gate man told me the name of the ship, and I got work as a cook in the galley."

"And what is your intention?" intoned Mr. Marteague.

Io pressed her lips together. Unintentionally, her chin crumpled and tears filled her eyes. "I don't know. I only knew Leep was on the *Delphine* and he is all my family."

"And yet you have allowed him to become part of ours."

"Those with nothing must take what is offered." She quoted a saying of the Brother of Brightness. She was surprised by the effect this had on the Marteagues. They looked affected, and yet frustrated.

"Do you imply that the same is offered to you?"

"No, Father. You offered it to Leep, only. And I am very grateful."

They gazed at one another for a moment. Finally, Mistress Marteague stood, followed by Io. "We understand each other, then. And while we are grateful that you saved your brother's life, we are cautious about strangers. Go back to the galley. We have made excuse to the Cook for today's absence. But we do not assume responsibility for you or your passage."

"Yes, Mother."

"We will call for you when we next have something to communicate. Until then, keep at your work."

Io wiped the furious tears that blinded her, but with strangled dignity said only, "Yes, Mother, yes, Father." Mr. Marteague finally arose to open the door and Io exited. The door closed behind her with a hard pull and a sound of the latch being closed. Io went toward the rear hatch, but before going down, she knelt, her arms crossed on the gunwale, and looked at the stars, floating like snow toward the horizon. The red moon was behind her and the white moon was plummeting into the ocean.

After a few moments, her anger and confusion subsided. Leep was alive! He was on the ship! The wealthy family had truly taken him under their wing. She bowed her head and gave thanks.

She heard water splashing, and peered over the edge of the boat to the water below. A dolphin was grinning up at her, momentarily joined by others, who made the water churn with their cavorting. Io actually smiled back at them, and reached down a hand to wave.

Drawn by the noise, a few deck hands came over to look. They gazed silently down at the dolphins, and then at Io, who didn't notice them. One removed his hat. "Bright's Brother," he whispered. Hands went to hearts around him, a genuflection. They watched in silence, and quietly went back to their tasks.

After the white moon had plunged below the horizon, the dolphins swam away a few at a time. Io yawned fiercely, and crept below into the sleeping cupboard where Cook snored already.

In the morning Cook was called out of the kitchen repeatedly to supervise the stacking of the water casks that were being filled from a cataract on the uninhabited bay near where the ship was anchored. Io prepared the trays of breakfast food, which were snatched up first by servants and then passengers, and finally the plainer trays for the crew of bread and cheese only. When all was cleaned up, the Steward came to the kitchen door to inform Cook that they were going to stay in the bay until the tide turned, and a boat was carrying any who wished to spend an hour on shore.

Cook decided to nap instead, but Io went along to the beach, hoping that the Marteague family would be there, along with Leep. The skiff was crowded but there was a spirit of fun among the crew. She sat between rowers, being small enough to squeeze in between the ends of the oars. Like most of the other crew, she was barefoot so as not to get her sandals soaked as they jumped out of the skiff in the shallows.

Some of the crew were going to hike up the cliff, while some wanted to nap on the sand. Io decided to stay on the beach and watch the passengers. She watched the skiff go and return with passengers. But she did not see the Marteague family. Disappointed, she rose to wander the margin of the shore, where others were finding small treasures at the high tide mark—starfish, seahorses, sand dollars, whelks. She had just pocketed a smooth, pink-lined shell, when someone approached her from behind. She turned and saw the Steward and a sailor, a large, sunburnt woman with short-cropped hair. "Io, come with me. We need to talk."

Io's stomach felt heavy, but what choice did she have?

She followed the Steward and the large woman followed her. They walked down the beach for several minutes until they were out of sight of the beach and the

*Delphine.* Finally the Steward stopped and turned and nodded at the sailor.

There was a sudden *thunk!* in her head and all went black.

She awoke laying high up on the beach, where she had been dragged. There was a knife in her eye—no, it was only the white moon, sailing overhead. She turned her face away from it.

She awoke again later when the sky was paling toward dawn. The red moon was westering and the white moon long gone. Io sat up, slowly. The cliffs were behind her, and the sea before her. Her head thrummed. She slipped a hand around the back, and found a sizeable tender lump, but no blood. She breathed deeply, her hands and feet splayed, trying to clear her head. The change in light showed that the sun was rising behind her, but it would be long before it rose over the cliffs. She stood, slowly.

As she did so, something fell from her lap—her shoulder bag. She stared at it, wondering how it came to be here, when she had left it on the *Delphine.*

The *Delphine.* She needed to get back to it. Footprints led back down the beach, around the bend. She followed them. But when she rounded the toe of land that formed the edge of the bay, she saw no ship. There was only the empty bay. She was confused, and looked up and down the coast. Then she understood that she had been dumped there. Her body felt numb, and she sat back down on the damp sand.

There she sat until the sun peeked over the headlands and warmed her back. As she stared at the endless waves, some gentle, and some almost violent, she saw the blue fins of dolphins rising and plunging, saw their misty exhalations. Some leapt bodily from the water. Some seemed to look back at her. She stared, wondering why they didn't follow the ship and her brother. Her head was dizzy and her mouth was parched, and she shouldered her bag and set off unsteadily toward where she knew the crew of the *Delphine* had filled water casks. There she drank deeply, and washed herself and the clothes she wore — clothes the Marteagues had given her to wear only the night before... no, two nights. The shock was only beginning to wear off.

And just beyond it was a wall of loss and anger she couldn't see her way over or through. She took the fine, soft tunic and threw it in the pool, followed by the silky trousers. She screamed until she ran out of breath.

Then the pragmatic girl from the streets of Dastenn came back, and she collected the clothing. She wrung them gently and laid them to dry on some shrubs, and put on her ratty old tunic and trousers, things she had taken from laundry lines, other people's clothing. Only old, colorless things, nothing anyone would notice.

While the fine clothing dried, she took stock. She emptied her bag and laid out her scant possessions. To her surprise, a small, knotted rag not her own contained a few coins. She restrained the impulse to cast them into the pool and tucked it inside her pocket. There was a bread loaf, of which she devoured half. There was also a corked, empty bottle. This was puzzling to her, but she knew it was best filled with water from the pool before she left the place. There was one spare tunic, also drab and well-used; and one of Leep's. At the bottom of the bag were her sandals. Someone's sandals, that is, that she had taken possession of. Not much else. A piece of ribbon from the festival, of which she had rescued a length that was still bright red and not too tattered.

She stared at her few things. She felt lost, and at a loss. Without Leep to provide for, there was no meaning to these items. She spread Leep's tunic out on the sand. But it was not his, to begin with, and was shaped by another small body. That just hurt to think about and she rolled it back up and looked away.

She could find her way northwest, back to Dastenn until the Marteagues returned from their journey. Or she could go on and hope to find the *Delphine* in some port town. Where was the ship going? She racked her brain, sifting through conversations between crew members. The Marteagues had given no hint, and Leep had not mentioned anything either. It seemed it would call on many ports on the way to some distant shore she had never even heard of. Jahntoll—a name from stories of exotic adventures, not real life.

Leep. Bright's Brother, what would he think when he didn't see her? What lies would they tell him? Sadness threatened, but she couldn't give way. It would overwhelm her, and she couldn't afford that. Nor the deep shame and guilt she felt at abandoning Leep to a wealthy family instead of being able to provide for his care herself. What would her Ma and Da think of her now?

As the sun passed overhead, she collected her things, folded the washed clothing into the shoulder bag, and decided. She couldn't choose between going back and going on, so she opted to at least find her way to a road, and that meant inland.

She drank deeply and filled the bottle the Steward must have added to her bag. She tried not to think about the kind of caring that would give a roll of bread and a water bottle and a few coins and leave her on an empty beach while their ship took the only thing that mattered in the whole world to her far away, out of her life. They left her with nothing.

Those with nothing must take what is offered. She shouldered her bag and began to ascend the headland.

Surmounting the cliffs above the beach left her out of breath, but she followed the watercourse and so was able to drink along the way. At the top of the cliff the sun was hot but a stiff breeze blew her hair in front of her, away from the sea.

She turned to let the wind blow it back. It was dry now and she plaited it roughly as she looked out. From this vantage point, Io could see a few ships like tiny specks inching across the horizon. One of them could be the *Delphine*, with her brother on board. She and Leep had never been more than a stone's throw apart since they came to Dastenn, until he was taken into the Marteagues's home.

The stream divided into tributaries. Io reasoned that the largest would lead... somewhere. Somewhere a road went. She followed the stream as it meandered over open prairie. The grasses grew tall, over her head. She kept on until the sun went down, followed by the red moon, and for a short while the white moon. Then all the lights abandoned her, and starlight was not enough to see. She laid down, spent, among tall grasses.

She awoke to a brief spatter of rain. She drank water and ate half of the half loaf in her bag. Then she walked on.

The prairie spread out before her. There was a mountain range bordering it on her right side, toward the east. To her left, the prairie seemed endless. There was a dark shadow moving slowly toward the west—a vast herd of some kind of beast she had never seen. The prairie undulated in long, slow swells. The grass was going golden as summer was waning, and it rippled like the sea as gusts moved across it. The light squall that had woken her had moved away, and it was a bluish smudge miles away now. In spite of her situation, the landscape was wondrous to Io. She breathed praise to the Brother of Brightness for creating such vast beauties. But it was also enormous beyond comprehension, and it seemed she walked all that day and never covered any distance. The sun overhead seemed like a relentless eye boring down upon her for much of the day. And so the day after, when she consumed the last of the bread, and the day after that, when she found sedge roots in a seep, and thimbleberries, and that was all her food.

But that evening, she suddenly saw a line that stretched from north to south—a road. She was so tired when she finally reached it that she laid down as the sky faded to night, and under the red moon, she slept.

Dawn woke her, together with both hunger and thirst. She sipped from the bottle, having left behind the stream for the road, miles back.

The dust on the road was dimpled from the squalls of two days before. Crossing that were the tracks of one foot traveler, and one cart, pulled by a small horse. Both were going in the same direction. Io started that way.

The road unwound into the endless prairie to the north. Sometime after the sun passed its zenith, the way dipped unexpectedly into a ravine invisible from a distance. Within the ravine, lush shrubs and low trees grew on the verges of a brook. An ancient stone ford crossed the brook. Io drank and drank, washed, and filled her bottle.

Exposed to the sun almost continually from dawn to dusk, Io's skin had browned. Washing the dust from her arms, she was startled by the change. As if the arms belonged to someone else.

She decided to rest in the shade of the trees, and laid in the sandy soil between bunchgrasses, just out of sight of the crossing. When she woke, the sun was westering, and she was woozy with hunger. She decided to see what there might be to eat. She foraged some berries, some sedge roots, some starchy grass stems. Eating them only highlighted her hunger. A bird started from a bush as she passed, and she found a nest. No eggs, only hatchlings, their yellow beaks open and begging, and she had not the heart to rob and eat the little things. She shouldered her bag, crossed the brook, and continued on until the white moon went down on the vast night.

A day passed, or maybe three, in this manner. The dark hills to the west grew incrementally. She took shelter under a stone and tree during a brief shower and was preparing to return to the road, when a small group of people passed. They had an unfriendly look to them and she was grateful that the rain had obliterated her footprints. She waited until they had passed some distance, and around a bend in the trail, and then she hurried on, bent down below the cover of the grasses for a mile or two.

But the next day, her strength gave out. There had been no water the previous day, and several days since the sedge nuts and bramble berries. She kept finding herself sitting down by the way, not sure why she had sat down. Then Io didn't get up.

She was vaguely aware of being held in a seated position, and water dribbled between her cracked lips. There were voices discussing, appraising her. Something about whether she was too young or not. She roused a little when she was lifted on both sides and laid in a cart, which began moving. A bottle of ale was patiently poured into her mouth, bit by bit. She swallowed gratefully. Then she passed out again.

When she woke fully, she was on a cot. Morning sun was pouring through a latticed window nearby, and there was movement up and down a hall outside of the wide room she lay in. She slowly sat up and put her feet on the floor, which was of baked bricks, and cool to her feet. She smelled food. She slowly stood to her feet and looked out the narrow window.

There was a cluster of buildings, set widely apart. Unlike Dastenn, no stone or wood was used in construction; everything was baked bricks and stucco. The ground between the buildings was sandy soil. A few persons and fewer horses or donkeys moved up and down. Workers, hawkers, tradespeople. There was little green in sight, only a few containers with plants, and one mango tree. She returned to the bed where she had been lying to look for her shoulder bag but did not see it. She looked about the room. She turned to the bed where she had lain, and folded the blanket neatly, and tidied the bed. She saw a bottle of water on the floor near a leg of the bedstead and took a long drink.

She left the room. There was a hallway, and noise and smells indicated a kitchen not far away. Io was so very hungry, that unwise as it seemed, she decided to venture to find the food she smelled. She moved slowly down the hall toward the sounds.

First, though, she passed another doorway. Inside, a chunky man, fully bearded, sat at a small desk, writing with ink on papers. He looked up and made an exclamation and gestured with his hand. *"Jebra lada, ma sina. Qene makasi?"* Io shook her head that she did not understand.

Accented, but clearly spoken, he called, "Come, come in, young lady. Come and sit with me." Not knowing what else to do, Io sat obediently on a stool near the table. Her stomach growled, and the man chuckled. Suddenly he shouted a name, and orders to bring a plate.

"You are lucky we found you out in the prairie. You were almost gone, but you look like you'll do, now. Tell me what we call you?"

"I am Io." Her voice was rough from disuse.

"Io. And how did you come to be starving on the Western Way?"

"I was lost. A ship put me off on the beach. I… don't even know where…"

"This is the island of Ara. The city of Pondali. I am Faldan, owner of this house of pleasure."

Io wasn't entirely sure what a "house of pleasure" was, but her questions were silenced by the arrival of a plate of flatbread, goat cheese, a plum, olives, all drizzled with olive oil and sprinkled with sweet marjoram. The servant made to set it before Faldan, but he instructed him to give it to Io. She glanced at him and he gestured reassuringly. Io fell upon the bread and cheese and all else, eating with relish. She knew from experience that she needed to pace herself after a long fast. She ate slowly, but was soon enough licking the oil from her fingers, and wondering what to do with the plate. Meanwhile, Faldan had returned to his papers until she stood with the plate. He gestured for her to leave it on the floor by the doorway.

"Thank you, Father."

"Please, call me Faldan."

"Thank you, Faldan."

"Now, down to business. We are a house of pleasure, not charity, and we carried you out of the prairie and nursed and fed you because you looked a worthwhile investment. How many summers have you?"

"Fourteen."

"Hmm, a bit young. Have you begun yet to bleed?"

She pressed her lips together. "The wide eyes and furrowed brow tell me no, as plainly as if you'd said it. Well, soon enough. In the meanwhile, we have a bit of a mystery. Your clothes, well, my girls would scorn to wipe the floor with them, but in your bag? A Dastenni tunic of the finest make, among a few other oddments."

"Might I have my bag, please, Fath—uh, Faldan?"

He gestured to where it lay against the wall behind her and waited.

"I was sleeping rough, so I dressed poor."

"Why did they put you off the ship?"

"I stowed away."

"Why did you stow away?—no, don't tell, me, I don't actually care." Faldan waved a beringed hand. "What we do need to talk about is what we will do with you."

They were interrupted by a slender woman in a long white kaftan who leaned in the doorway. "*Jebra lada*, Faldan," she said, waving with her hand close to her face. Io stared at her, wondering if it was Faldan's wife, but suddenly several similarly clad women, and at least one man, of varying ages and colors and builds, were passing in the hallway, calling greetings which he returned cheerfully.

Io rather suddenly put the pieces together in her mind. In no way was she ready to become one of those sensuous, doll-like women. She quickly said, "I can tend fires and bake bread and make stews and broths."

"Is that right. We don't burn wood here for our fires like they do in Dastenn, Io. Have you cooked with dung? Or with resin plats?"

"Only wood, and dung." She vaguely remembered her mother using dried animal dung when she boiled soap outdoors.

"Well, then. Take that plate to the kitchen at the end of the hall, introduce yourself to Brennu, who doesn't speak the Dastenni language well, by the by, and get busy. If you want to eat my food and sleep in my house again, that is." His face was sardonic, rather than threatening. Io rose, bowed her head and thanked him, shouldered her bag with just enough jostling to feel the weight and hear the mild clink of her few coins in the bottom; and carried the wooden plate to the kitchen, where Brennu turned out to be a tall and dark-skinned man who jovially cried out stock Arani phrases in between singing incomprehensible lyrics to sinuous, alien tunes. She joined the fray in the kitchen while the colorfully dressed pleasure-workers reclined around a table drinking coffee and awaiting their breakfast.

Days passed in a whirlwind. Io befriended some of the pleasure-workers, while they drank coffee in the mornings and she stoked fires carefully with resin-imbued braids of prairie grass and learned the finer points of baking flatbread, their staple. They told her how to find her way to the docks, for the city of Pondali had a port.

And Pondali was on the great island of Ara. Io had been deposited on its southmost point, and walked across to the northwest point, nearer Dastenn—but still a long journey across the river, across a land even greater than she had walked, and across the Sea of Gulls to the continent of Avann. And there was nothing in Dastenn for her now, unless and until the Marteague family returned there.

There were no days off for kitchen workers, but breakfast occurred so late in the morning while the pleasure-workers slept, that Io often was able to slip out for long walks, even down to the docks, where she wandered along, looking at the boats and observing dismally that most were fishing boats and small ferries—not greatboats like the *Delphine*. At least, not often. But every several days a trade ship docked. Io tried to befriend a worker there, but most of them were too busy moving goods or herding people about to talk to a ragamuffin such as she was, and in her halting Arani. Until she came down one morning in the fine Dastenni tunic and her hair carefully combed, the red ribbon bound across her forehead, a becoming look for her. One of the pleasure-workers had left a pair of elaborate earrings lying about and Io had borrowed them and hooked them through the ribbon which covered her ears. Their dangling made her feel dressed up and confident as she spoke to a ship chandler who spoke Dastenni, who promised to keep his ears open for news of the *Delphine*. She slipped him a coin for his pains and promised more if he sent word to her at Faldan's pleasure house. His brows slipped upwards in surprise, but he closed his hand on the coin and nodded briefly.

Days became weeks became months. Io realized her body was becoming more and more like those of the women workers, and they sometimes encouraged her to take up the life of pleasure, as it paid much better wages than the kitchen did. Io wondered, but she thought of Leep and what he would think of her in that situation. She remembered her parents, her

Da stroking her mother's back as they looked out over the fields in bloom, and she shook her head. With that came motherhood, something she was not ready for.

She learned to speak and hear Arani, the tongue most of the others spoke with each other, and she started understanding the songs Brennu sang to himself when he was not shouting jovially at Io, Faldan, or the pleasure-workers. She learned that he had begun as a pleasure-worker himself, but it didn't suit him, and when the former cook passed away suddenly, he had simply taken over, much to the other workers' joy, as he was an excellent cook.

Io had no plan, other than to save her coins and buy passage back to Dastenn. But coins were slow in coming. She needed clothes that accommodated her changing body— Faldan had the non-pleasure staff wear billowing tunics, generously gathered in front, to distinguish them from the others. She was not permitted to wear them day in and day out, either, for all the workers were expected to smell good— albeit the odors of sweat and drink and other permeated the rooms where guests were entertained, but if she was called upon to bring a tray of food and drinks to guests, she must be fresh and inoffensive.

She kept her eyes downcast and her face blank, so as not to attract the eyes and hands of guests, from whose attentions she had occasionally to make an agile and courteous escape.

Io tried not to think about the goings-on in the pleasure rooms, although she often enough glimpsed more than she wanted to. She understood that it held a strange attraction, even for her. But her parents had shown her the bond of family that was a harbor of safety for the body and the soul, a place for life together, and children. The men who came enjoyed attentions and pleasures that ought to have been part of home life, between a woman and a man. There was no commitment, no consequence to the few hours they spent escaping responsibility with the pleasure-workers.

Most of the women took herbs that caused their bodies not to take in pregnancy, although there were always one or two with swollen bellies, and with customers who were drawn to that. She wondered what happened to the babies produced, and within a few weeks, she knew, for she saw a tiny bundle handed out the back door, and coins change hands.

Brennu saw her staring. "The babies are taken by midwives, who carry them to women who have been unable to bring to birth." He spoke sadly in Arani. "Some of them spend weeks with rags stuffed beneath their belts, and hiding from even their own husbands, and suddenly the baby comes in the night." He shrugged his thin, dark shoulders. "Everyone is happy. Well, most of them. Some of the girls are sad. But they could take their babies and go, if they wish. Faldan is no slave-master."

"If you don't mind me asking, Brennu… why did you leave off…pleasure-work? You don't need to answer if you don't want to."

Brennu smiled, but there was still a sadness. He hummed one of his tunes for a few moments, stripping the leaves off of holy basil stems. "I was poor and desperate, and one of the other boys invited me. He said I was pretty and slim and I would make a lot of money. Well, I did. But so many of the men and women who come here are sad. They aren't looking for pleasure, really. They are looking for connection. Someone to listen to them, to pay attention to them. It didn't work for me because I too, was sad. I had nothing to give them.

"Of course, not all are like that. Some just want to exercise their bodies upon another. That was actually worse. It seemed cold." Brennu held up a stalk of basil. "Brennu is passionate. I knew I would never find a lover in the pleasure-house. The others enjoyed my cooking, so I just inserted myself into the kitchen. The old cook had just died—it was inevitable."

"Brennu."

"Io?"

"Are you still sad?"

Brennu smiled, and the smile was sadder than if he had cried. "Sad. And happy. I love the girls and the boys. I love cooking food. I love you, Io!" Now his smile widened to genuine happiness, and she couldn't help returning it.

"So what is your story, quiet girl?"

Io hesitated. She had never unburdened herself and it felt vulnerable. But she liked Brennu. She slowly told him, sentence by sentence, while she kneaded dough. She left out most of the details. By the time she completed her story until the time she arrived at Faldan's, Brennu looked both sadder, and happier. "You have a brother! You have someone out there in this big, lonely world." Brennu broke off into one of his no longer incomprehensible songs. Io understood the lyrics now:

*Where are you in this world, my darling?*
*I'd travel once and I'd travel twice*
*All around this big world, my darling*
*I'd travel three times to be with you again.*
*I'd wear out a hundred boots across dry deserts*
*I'd cross a hundred rivers with a stone upon my back*
*I'd cross dark mountains, blindfold and broken*
*I'd brave strange oceans to be with you again.*

Io wandered the docks one morning. The chandler had simply shaken his head at her, no news, not unkindly, but too busy to stop what he was doing. She moped down past the docks to a rocky promontory she had wanted to explore.

The cobalt sky was, as many days, riddled with white puffy clouds passing rather hurriedly overhead, some dropping brief showers, which no one seemed to avoid, they were just the weather. Soon enough it would pass by and the continual gusts of wind would dry clothes and hair and beards quickly. The water in the bay was edged with whitecaps, and small but boisterous waves lapped the shore continually.

She followed a thread of footpath where it climbed the rocky outcropping. After viewing the bay for a time she decided to climb down closer to the water. She had seen dolphins playing out in the river, and a few of the huge white birds that plied the beaches on long, stilt-like legs, plying the waves for cockles and minnows. The pleasure girls liked the white plumes they occasionally shed and would pay a coin or two for a good specimen.

She climbed down the hill, which degraded to bare, worn boulders. They ended abruptly and she jumped down onto dry sand. The white birds haughtily turned and worked their way down the shore away from Io. She saw a white plume skipping over the sand and ran to catch it before it became entangled in the wrack at the foot of the rocks. She claimed it and tucked it inside her tunic.

The sand was dry and rough with dried seaweed and larger pebbles, so Io rolled her trousers up past her knees and made her way down to the wet, smooth, firm sand by the water. An errant wave suddenly washed over her feet, cooling them deliciously. She was tempted to swim, but had been told that the shore dropped off precipitously and the tidal current could be strong at the bay's mouth, so she contented herself with wading.

She was gazing at dogfish that came to nibble around her feet, their strange winglike fins edged with gold when a *whoosh*, just a few yards away, startled her. A blue dolphin was gazing at her. Her breath caught and she smiled, scarcely believing her luck at being so close to the delightful creatures again.

The dolphin was joined by three others, and they gamboled around each other for several minutes. One, -the first? -approached Io cautiously. She reached out her hand to touch it as it glided past, then quickly circled around to deeper water, then turned again to face Io and raised its head. It made a sound, like laughter, then waited. Io laughed with joy and realized that she had not laughed in a long time. The joy was quickly followed by a wave of grief. "Go and find Leep for me. And tell him I miss him!" She sobbed out.

The dolphin "laughed" at her again and turned towards it companions. They milled about in the deeper water for a few moments, and then moved away, out toward the sparkling sea.

She felt comforted and disturbed at the same time as she made her way back up to Faldan's. The morning was getting on and fires needed to be stoked for breakfast and baths.

Brennu saw Io come in the door, dejected. He moved quickly towards her and held her briefly, startling her. But after a moment she returned the hug. He squeezed her tightly, then held her away from him. "You've got to get yourself cleaned up and dressed for serving. Don't worry about the fires, they're already lit and the girls are bathing. Io, Jalla died in childbirth, and so did the baby. Faldan is going to be angry and sad and looking for someone to kick for the next few hours. Don't let it be you!" He shook a finger at her.

She nodded gratefully and rushed to her tiny sleeping room with a small pail of warm water. She barred herself in and ran a wet cloth everywhere, combed and replaited her hair, and put on her serving tunic and trousers. Before opening her door, she composed her face into the bland mask with which she faded into the background. She opened the door, and Faldan was in the hall, stroking his beard and gazing out a lattice. He frowned thunderously at her, but she was ready to work and was not late, so there was nothing to fault her in. The tilt of his head changed, and his eyes roamed over her body, evaluating. She dropped her gaze and turned quickly for the stairs back down to the kitchen.

Jalla's death was as a touchstone on the personalities inhabiting Faldan's. Brennu sang only his saddest songs at half-volume, and often was seen standing over his work, shaking his head, his hands resting on the wooden block. Jalla had been aloof, frosty toward Io, and she didn't know her at all, but it was still very sad to die in a pleasure-house with her unborn baby. Shimru, a heavy blond, bawled loudly through breakfast. Jenji lay back, arms crossed across her narrow body, brow furrowed, smoldering at the injustice. Muur shook her head and acted like she knew it was going to happen. And so on. This was all the "wake" the workers were allowed to keep; the house must continue on. Only two, a man and a woman who knew Jalla best, were allowed to go with the body to the burial ground, while the others were expected to smile at customers and laugh at their jokes, listen to their sad stories and fulfill their wants.

When they had a chance, Io returned the embrace to Brennu, who had needed it as much as the one he'd given her that morning. Later, moving through the hall with steamed towels, she heard Brennu's raised voice in Faldan's office. She couldn't stop to listen. She returned to the kitchen to find Brennu switching about angrily. He saw her come in and rushed towards her, whispering, *Tell him NO!*"

Before she could ask or he could explain she heard Faldan's voice commanding her to his office, quickly. She could tell right away this was not the "kind" Faldan who had rescued her from the carrion crows on the prairie. This was the calculating, businesslike Faldan who had evaluated her young body with his eyes.

"Young lady, you are growing up fast. My girls tell me you began to bleed some weeks ago. With the loss of Jalla, I am in need of a pleasure-worker who is young and fresh as she was. You've become a woman now, with shapeliness, good health, and a pretty enough face and very good hair. Shimru could teach you a thing or two about painting your face and you could make very much more money than you do working the kitchen. So let's get you bathed and dressed up, and sent to the front rooms. Your first night will be exceptionally rewarding, as men will pay a high price to be the first to lie with you."

Io's heart was in her throat. "No."

He looked affronted. "What do you mean by this? I am offering you an opportunity here, not to mention that you owe me your life. What are you playing at?"

"It is true that you found me dying and gave me life. I believe I have done my best to reward you by working hard in the back end of the House. I am content in that and do not wish to become a pleasure-girl."

"You've been talking to Brennu too much. Don't allow his experience to color your judgment and lead you to make a foolish decision. Girls come to me every day of the week and I turn them away at the door. I'm minded to put you out on the street for refusing."

"I am sorry, Faldan. I was not raised this way and I am sure it is not for me. I have lived on the street before so that does not deter me. Thank you for offering this to me, but my answer is no."

He looked angry still, but resigned. He waved his hand dismissively. Io crept out of the office and ran back into the kitchen. Brennu was waiting, his hand on his hip. He smiled broadly. "I told him I would leave the kitchen forever if he sent you away." He began singing a happy song, and grabbed her hands and swung her around.

"How did you know I would refuse?"

"This is not your path, Io. It's mine for now, but I know I'm not staying here, either. Not forever. I don't have a brother out there, but I have a dream out there, and a heart in here, and it longs to stretch its wings!" He twirled her again, but one of the pleasure workers arrived in the kitchen, teary-faced, and he instantly began cooing over her, leaving Io dizzy and relieved.

She went down to the docks the next day to view the boats and check with the chandler—no news. She wandered slowly up the street. Peering down a lane that led away from the shore, she saw a House of the Brightness she hadn't noticed before. It drew her in to its pale, quiet interior, where she seated herself cross legged and gazed up at the frosted glass window. In Dastenn, the Houses were round, but Pondali Houses of the Brightness were square. As her eyes adjusted to the dim, she realized another difference. There were painted inscriptions covering the white walls in grey script.

She struggled to read it because it was in Arani, but the letters were very like Dastenni letters.

*From before the lights were kindled, there was the Brightness, and the Brightness was one, and yet not alone.*

*In their love, the one Brightness became many. Can you count the stars? For exceeding numberless is the fruit of their love.*

*Can you number the lights that live in the hearts of humanity? For countless are those who look up to see Brightness.*

*When the Brother of Brightness walked among us, we saw Brightness unquenchable. Look up, and see, stranger, and become the family of unquenchable Brightness.*

She knew there was much more to the teachings. Her parents had taught her well. What was she doing in the kitchen of a brothel? This was how she was to survive, serving a twisted way? *Brother of Brightness,* she prayed silently, *light my way.*

The Longest Night approached, one of the few nights when all were excused from their work, and all crowded into a House of the Brightness—no matter who they were, they were all welcome. Io went down to the small House in Lower Docks Street and slipped in. The songs were in Arani, but easy enough to follow and many of the melodies were the same as back in Dastenn. The service lasted for hours, and many dozed or napped on and off on the piled carpets on the floor. The House was warm with so many bodies. Watered wine was passed around.

When it was time for the Brightness to return anew, the people arose and proceeded to a low hill by the bay. Hundreds from Pondali were there, wrapped tightly against the chill breeze off the salt water. Other groups wandered the night as well, zealots who preached repentance and sang hymns, and revelers who partied the night away unencumbered by religious observance. Among the latter, Io spotted Brennu, dancing down the street and singing loudly a rather secularized version of a song of Brightness, one of those very hymns that the House had raised earlier. She smiled and shook her head and continued to the knoll where light of the new year was greeted, after which the tired but happy worshippers disbanded and straggled home.

Entering by the kitchen, she could hear raised voices from the front room. Slipping quietly up the stairs, she could not avoid being seen briefly by the people in the front room who were evidently unhappy that the usual services were not available, and Faldan was trying to conciliate them.

"You are lying, there goes one of your women right now!" She heard Faldan speak conciliation, but it was only a murmur to her. She padded softly to her room, barring the door.

She had just drifted to sleep when there was a tapping at the door. Soft, but insistent. She stood before it and asked who it was.

"Io, my dear, it is Faldan. I need you to come downstairs."

"Sir, I was given to understand—"

"Yes, everyone is to have the day off. But I have an important client here who deserves our best treatment. He wants to start the new year with some enjoyment. I told him you were just a working girl and he is willing to pay a handsome price for your virginity. You will be well rewarded, so come, now. He is very impatient."

"Sir, I have told you before, I will not do this."

A bang on the door startled her and signaled Faldan's frustration. She heard him stalking away, cursing under his breath. After several minutes of the impatient customer's vilifications, he heard the heavy front door slam shut, and the House finally fell quiet a few minutes later. Io sat on her small bed for about an hour. No one else came back to the House—where had they all gone?

She finally laid down and drifted in and out of sleep for hours. The sun crossed overhead. Finally, towards evening, she arose and crept down to the silent kitchen to stoke the fires. Eventually Brennu came in with several of the pleasure-workers. She did not see Faldan's face in the kitchen all that evening.

Brennu was clearly hung over, which dampened his normal cheerful kindness and made him seem oblivious to others. But later, after the dishes were washed and the fires banked against the night, he poured Io a cup of tea and bid her sit next to him at the table. Without preamble, he said, "It's happened, hasn't it? Faldan made his move, tried to get you working the front rooms?"

She sighed, and leaned her head on Brennu's shoulder. "He wasn't happy with my refusal. Where was everyone last night?"

"Oh, I should have told you, we all stay far away in order to be able to fully enjoy our day off. Someone always comes looking for pleasure and Faldan always wants to please his customers. Money comes first with him. He looks at you, shapely and young, he sees money. But he's not completely without a heart. He'll grouse and grumble and be annoyed with you for a while, but another pretty girl or boy will come along looking for the work, and he'll forget about you."

Brennu squeezed her shoulder. "Forget him. Tell me about your brother."

Io smiled.

"When we first came to Dastenn we had walked for weeks. It was the raining season. We slept in doorways for a few nights. It was hard and cold, and usually someone would chase us off in the night and we'd be wet and cold all over again.

"Leep loved birds, and he watched them fly in and out of the trees. He started talking about, what if we could nest in the trees. Then he saw the tree on Stonemason Street. We climbed up and there was a place where the trunk spread into branches. In the middle, dry leaves were piled deep. The canopy overhead was so thick, it hardly got a drop of rain. We snuggled into those leaves and slept warm for the first time since our farm burned. 'Are we birds?' Leep asked in the morning. 'We live in trees now, so we're birds, aren't we?'"

Brennu threw his head back and laughed, and burst into one of his corny songs. "If I was a bird, I would fly away," he sang. Io sang along.

*If I was a bird, I would fly away.*
*If I was a bird, I would fly away.*
*If I was a bird, I would fly away.*
*Fly to hands, the hands of the man,*
*Fly to the Bright Brother.*

*If I was a bird, I would fly away home.*
*If I was a bird, I would fly away home.*

*If I was a bird, I would fly away home.*
*Fly to the home, the home of the One,*
*Fly to the Bright Brother.*

By the end of the week Faldan had acquired a creature of exquisite beauty, an albino with yellow-white hair to her waist and the palest eyes. She drew all attention to her fair and fragrant self, not even dining in the kitchen with the rest—Faldan himself carried a plate of savories and fruits to her room—Jalla's former room, the best one—which caused small dramas to flourish among the other pleasure-workers. Brennu rolled his eyes in Io's direction, but poured sympathy on the pleasure-workers and assured them that Sylva was the new darling, and so had they all been in their time.

Which made Io think. Her time was also moving on. Her body continued to ripen to womanhood. Regular meals and work made her strong. One morning her ankles, she realized, poked out below her trousers. She had a seamstress let them down as far as they would go but they still required a band of cloth added around the bottom. She needed bigger sandals, and bought new ones. When she wandered the docks in the morning, she was favorably noticed—not something she was used to.

Nothing in her life was settled, nothing familiar. No, she thought, that wasn't entirely true. Brennu was become something solid and settling in her life. A silly young man who had washed ashore in Pondali in a manner not dissimilar to her own arrival in the strange, small city. She was here, now. But at some point she had to go in some direction and find her brother. But only the Brother of Brightness knew what direction that would be.

Faldan appeared in the kitchen to collect a plate for Sylva some days after, but a message arrived and he shoved the plate towards Io with a gesture that clearly instructed her to carry it up to Sylva's boudoir. She was thankful that she had on a clean serving tunic, and her braid was wound about her head in a becoming manner, something Brennu had suggested. She knocked on the latticed and veiled door briefly before entering and averting her eyes from whatever might be happening there. But Sylva was alone, sitting on a window seat, her endless legs folded before her and wrapped by a slender, jeweled arm, her pale hair and white tunic catching a ray of sun. Her eyes wandered idly in Io's direction. Her pale eyebrows lifted slightly.

Io set the tray on a small table near the window seat. She was turning to leave, when she heard a flute-like voice. "Stay. What is your name?"

"Peace to you. I am Io."

"Io." She drew the name out as if she liked it. "Peace to you. What do you do here? You are not one of the pleasure-girls?"

"No, Sylva. I work in the kitchen. I do not wish to be a pleasure-girl."

"Hm." Her mouth pursed thoughtfully. "I wish you to bring me my food and drink, not that Faldan. He irritates me." The statement was so unexpected that Io giggled suddenly before pressing her lips together and looking apologetically at Sylva—who was smiling at her, and then she also tossed her head back and laughed.

There was a knock at the door and Faldan stepped in. He looked as if he were about to order Io out but Sylva, queenly, told him that Io would be serving her from now on. He grunted, frowning, but nodded once. Then he told her, "The man you were to entertain today has been called away on business, but he has paid in advance for the week. Until he arrives, you are at your leisure. But remain ready for him. He paid handsomely, and I promise you will be well rewarded for his satisfaction."

Sylva smiled indulgently. Then she leaned back and gazed again out the window.

Io spoke. "Sylva, is there anything you wish from me now?"

"Not unless you can read."

"I can read."

Both Faldan and Sylva looked mildly surprised. Sylva waved at a book on a low couch—*Stories of the Brightness*. Io collected it and sat down on the carpet.

Faldan cleared his throat. "She'll be wanted in the kitchen in an hour."

Sylva shot an irritated look at him. He took the hint and left the room. Sylva looked at Io and they laughed together, Io smothering her voice with her hand.

"Read the one about the Bleeding-Heart Dove."

Io opened the beautiful book—she had never held one so rich-looking, with a silken ribband for a bookmark which was at the page the story began on. Io read.

"The Bleeding-Heart Dove.

"Far across the Sea of Storms, a guarded island rises from the waves. Narwhals patrol the waters surrounding its emerald heights, their spiral horns gleaming and bitter. Orcas with their great teeth and bodies like juggernauts move about in dark pods. Walruses watch the beaches, and wolves the forest beyond. Jaguars move sinuously through the shade of giant ferns and palms, and even the waters are beset with a kind of water deer, whose fangs are not for show.

"High in the trees, there sat Kirru, a blue-grey dove with a white breast, on her nest. She dared not cry out for her mate because lithe snakes were always twisting about the trunks of the trees, looking for something plump and sweet to devour, and the tree-cats prowled the smooth limbs. So she sat alone, venturing out only to pluck the fruits and seeds in the canopy of the tallest trees, or flying out to the sunlit meadows to forage among the grasses, returning with trepidation lest her haven had been discovered in her absence.

"Kirru sat in stillness one morning when other birds were singing their praises of the Brightness of dawn, when she caught the sound of one of her kind. It filled her heart, and she would have called in response, but her 'coo' caught in her throat, so anxious was she. She heard the dove call from this branch and that, and even glimpsed the flash of his wing, but he soon moved on.

"Kirru listened hard, her heart thumping in her breast, but did not hear the other dove again. Finally she was hungered, and ventured out to the margin of a bright field to feed on seeds and snails. She thought to herself, 'If I can risk the dangers of the forest to feed my stomach, why can I not attempt to find a friend? My stomach is now full, but my heart is still a-hungered.' She turned her dark eyes this way and that, and finally flew for the treetops.

"She lit on a palm tree and called out three times, but a scorpion stung her foot.

"She flew next to teak tree and called out two times, but there a wasp stung her thigh.

"She flew to a mango tree and called out once, but a mongoose darted at her and gashed her throat with his yellow teeth, and she barely escaped.

"The dove Kirru flew to the forest floor, where her drops of blood stained a white stone. As she sat crying, she heard the flap of wings, and soon another dove landed by her. He cooed as he walked around her. Finally she gathered her strength and cooed in response, but her coo was weak. The dove flew away and Kirru's eyes were growing dim.

"But he soon returned with twigs in his beak and laid them out around her on the stone. Again and again he flew and returned in a flurry until he had built a nest around her, and he sat down to guard her. He plucked ruby red berries and brought them to her, and brought the seed heads of grasses from the meadow.

"He told her his name was Kurra, and that he had been looking for a spouse, but had begun to wonder if he was alone on the island. He had heard her call three times, but found only a scorpion. Again he heard her call two times, but found only wasps. He heard her final cry and came but the mongoose had leapt at him.

"He was going to fly back again but saw her blood drops on the white stone and came to see. And thus he found her—not by her calls, but by the blood of her courage.

"This is how the bleeding-heart dove came to have the red blot on its chest."

That was the end of the story, but for a beautiful illustration of the doves in a nest, the female with blood marring the white chest. Io lingered over the picture, then closed the book slowly. She glanced up at Sylva. Sylva had fallen asleep, her head laid back on the cushion in the window seat. Io put the beautiful book down and left the room as quietly as possible to return to the kitchen to help Brennu.

That night she lay in bed, savoring the story she had read to Sylva. She, too, yearned for her brother. It hadn't taken anything like courage to stow away on the *Delphine*—no, necessity was laid on her. Now, she felt herself to be in the meadow, eating seeds and snails, working up her courage. No, she thought, she had already taken flight and been stung, by being put off the ship. And again, her lonely walk across the prairie. Where did that leave her now?

*It's only a story,* she told herself. The book was called *Stories of the Brightness,* a name she had heard—it was teachings of the Brother of Brightness, in story form. *Thank you, Brother of Brightness. I don't know where I am with you, but I too seek the one I love and I am lost and without a voice. Only you can hear me.*

Io returned to the House of the Brightness some days later to find the quiet and serenity she longed for, but found the worship wild and chaotic. The people who had preached so strenuously on the Longest Night had invaded the normally peaceful sanctuary. She decided to leave but chose just the wrong moment—the chaos erupted into the streets directly behind her and she was caught up in the chanting, running crowd. They had linked arms with each other, and two strong older women had clasped her arms in theirs and drew her along, not heeding her struggles to free herself. They ran, yelling repetitively, down to the docks, then up to the High Street where the central judgment hall was located. Io was forced to jog along with them.

From their chants, she understood that they had issue with the lackadaisical morals and loose enforcement of the laws of Ara. Once they had arrived at the broad plaza in front of the hall of justice, the crowd slowed and Io was finally able to loose herself and make her way out of the crowd. The faces of those who crowded the market opposite the plaza were everything from dismissive to angry at the noisy intrusion, and Io received unfriendly looks from more than one. She looked down and "faded" herself, slowing her steps and looking at nothing in particular. Still, more than one person noticed and grumbled about the Dastenni bringing strange doctrines to cause trouble. At home, Io changed out of the Dastenni tunic and put it away.

Sylva demanded her presence for at least an hour each day between the noon and evening meals, when she was not encumbered with customers. Faldan marketed Sylva as a premium commodity so she generally had only one visitor per day for several hours at a stretch. She continued to expect Io to bring her meals, to read to her (her own vision was poor), to attend her baths, or sometimes just to sit companionably. Io often wanted to discuss the stories they had read, but Sylva most often drifted off to sleep, and Io did not begrudge her, knowing that her nights were often long.

One day Sylva insisted that she must leave the house for some air of the river and the sea, and Faldan acquiesced although he fussed quietly and insisted that she be accompanied, and Sylva immediately insisted that Io be the one to go with her. Io wanted to go anyway, as the chandler had told her that he was expecting several larger ships to berth in the next few days as the tides were favorable.

Having nothing else suitable, Io put on the Dastenni tunic and trousers. Sylva draped her with earrings and hair ornaments. Brennu also wanted to come along and he wore a beautiful black tunic and trousers, and let down his hair like so many catkins dangling about his dark face. Sylva wore a voluminous kaftan of pale blue and wound her head with a scarf as well, as protection from the Ara sun.

The three of them walked out into the street, arms wrapped around each other, and headed for the port area to enjoy the fresh air of the sea. They walked down past the docks, to the promontory where Io had seen the dolphins. There were fins in the water but grey, and they were told by other strollers that it was the season when the bay was a retreat for wolf sharks, and dolphins generally stayed away until spring.

They talked and laughed until the sun was high, and then turned back for the House of Pleasure. There was a noise by the docks—the unruly believers were preaching repentance, and the already crowded docks were not welcoming. They veered near the shop fronts but were horrified to see fights breaking out between those screaming that "Those who refuse to follow the light are in darkness, you will go down in darkness forever!" and those who simply wanted them to clear off.

Io recognized the head Mother, Dar, who kept the House of the Brightness—a peaceable, serene woman of many years, she cried out to be heard. Respectfully, those around her fell quiet.

"My brothers, my sisters," she began. "The Brother of Brightness teaches us a different way —"

A resonant man's voice sang out, "Away with the Brother, we seek the Brightness itself! We need no interloper!" Similar slogans were repeated by those around him.

Shouts erupted on all sides, and Io saw the Mother pulled and pushed this way and that. She left the safety of her friends and tried to find her way to where Dar was. When she found her, she wrapped her arms around her and tried to help her out of the riot. She was nearly back to the shops when the resonant voice called out, "See the Dastenni! Whose side are you on? You were with us, now you side with the old ways of the Interloper!"

Io found herself suddenly a focus of attention, pulled this way and that, while Dar was hurried away from the crowd by her supporters. She saw Brennu guide Sylva inside a tea shop. Meanwhile the crowd surged the other way, Dar's supporters running from all directions, Io pushed along helplessly, running to keep her feet underneath her.

She realized they were at the edge of the boardwalk and that the resonant-voiced man and others were being bodily hauled out to the end. To her horror, she realized they were being thrown into the bay, and the plash of their impact with the water met with triumphant cries. There was a moment of release of tension, and Io tried to work her way back to the shops when a voice cried out, "She was with them, at the plaza, the foreigner!" Immediately hands reached out to grab her, pulling her this way and that. She had a free hand for a moment and she took an ornament from her hair and stabbed at the arm clutching her. But where one hand fell away three more grabbed her clothes, her legs, her head. She was being rushed to the end of the dock and then her body was falling through the air briefly and then she hit the cold water sideways.

But she could swim, and after a moment she began to paddle towards a boat, thinking to hide behind it. She reached for a rope and turned to see what became of others. She saw one clinging to a piling beneath the dock, trying to climb out of the water. Another was flailing and looked like they might make it to the dock, when suddenly they were yanked down below the water. A moment later grey fins gathered and the water boiled red for a few moments while the crowd went crazy, the pier swaying and trembling with their movements.

The boat to whose rope she clung to turned in the wind, exposing her hiding place to the crowd. Someone threw something at her, knocking the side of her head so she lost her grip and fell straight down into the bitter green darkness of the bay water. She could see ghostly shapes moving just yards away and seemed to taste the coppery taste of blood in the salt of the water. She came up for air, saw fins, and began swimming for her life. But the long boat to which she had been clinging before was swinging around again, blocking her way. Something hot tugged her leg and in terror, she recoiled, sinking under the water as a rough tail swatted her feet from underneath.

A huge maw, the size and depth of a dug well, but lined with triangular blades, surmounted by eyes dead and black, was coming towards her. She froze, her muscles unresponsive, as it loomed huge before her. There was blood curling around her in the water and searing pain in her right foot.

From nowhere, a blue streak thudded into the side of the shark, which curled away and retreated. More dolphins appeared, back and forth in front of Io as dark blots began to appear in her vision. She needed air but her limbs were still weak with terror.

She was thrust suddenly up from below by a blue, sleek body. Blue fins surrounded her, churning, leaping over her. One broke away suddenly and shot towards a grey fin. The collision was audible, a dull thud in the water. Then the grey fins were receding quickly. Io coughed salt water and struggled to keep above water.

Dolphins were bearing her along as before. She clung to a fin and scrunched her knees on either side of its body while the creatures jumped and dived all around her — fierce, but with a gleeful joy, bearing her away from the now dumbstruck crowd on the wharf, out to the mouth of the bay, towards the sea.

There were boats going in and out and on every one they passed, near or far, faces turned, thunderstruck, genuflecting, pointing. But it was to one large, white and blue caravel that the dolphins were carrying her. They left the sharks behind, and the dolphins began again to leap and cavort. They brought Io right up to the side of the caravel, and she slipped off the back of the one who had borne her three miles or more into the growing surf and bitter salt. The sailors gaped over the side, and a skiff was let down quickly as sails were struck and the massive boat slowly passed her by. From the stern, she heard a voice she loved — "*Io!!* Io, it's Io! Io, it's me, Io, Io!"

The skiff collected her from the water, the sailors lifting her by both arms and placing her in the bottom of the small boat as it turned to catch up with the *Delphine.*

Her eyes and mouth stung with salt, but not as much as her torn leg, which she now saw was gashed deeply and bled freely in the bottom of the boat. She shivered with the pain of it. One of the sailors removed a cloth from his head, and wrapped her leg tightly with it. In a few minutes, she was being lifted by a sling up to the deck of the caravel.

Then Leep was upon her, kissing her and wrapping his little arms about her, crying and babbling. She closed her eyes and once again breathed in his warmth and little-boy scent.

A ring of sailors was standing back, reverently. She heard a mumble or two along the lines of, "I said it were wrong to leave the dolphin-girl behind…We ought to've looked for her…No wonder we were beset by storm and contrary wind…Brother of Brightness…"

She heard the voice of Mistress Marteague, then, screaming in fury at the Captain and demanding explanation. From what she said, it had not been the Marteagues' plan to leave her at the beach on Ara, and they had been told she had simply disappeared. At that, she began to cry. All this time she had thought they did not want her, had stolen her brother from her. Evidently it was the Steward who decided to put her off, without consulting the Marteagues.

In the Marteagues' cabin, while the ship was guided into the wharf, she was fussed over and fed, her foot properly dressed, her hair combed, and Leep would not let her go but clung to her arm, her neck, laying his head on her. Master Marteague alternated between apology and fuming and giving thanks to the Brother for bringing her back to them. She didn't understand their change of heart toward her but it was a relief. It began to make sense the more she saw Leep chattering trustingly to Mistress Marteague, and the way she clearly doted on him and drank his words. Thankfully, the Mistress would not allow any questions until she had been "properly looked after" away from the curious eyes of the crew.

Evening was falling, and Marteague servants hauled out their trunks to an inn in Pondali. Io was carried on a litter over the gangplank and up to a High Street inn. She was grateful for the fresh clothing and a head scarf which she wrapped over her face to avoid recognition. The mob had dispersed from the wharf. She closed her eyes and gave thanks while Leep held her hand and chattered merrily. She did not see the faces of the sailors, and their genuflections, as she was carried away.

She told her story, from beginning to end, to the Marteagues, in the hearing of servants who retold it to other servants, who delivered the tale to the House of the Brightness, from whence it found its way to Faldan's House of Pleasure; where, polished and embellished richly, Brennu retold the story and made it into a song which spread around Pondali until it reached the Golden Wave where it was sung to harps in the finely appointed and light-filled dining hall, by the time the seams of Io's wounds were closed and pinking over. It even reached Dastenn, where the Marteague family returned and gave Io her very own bed and room within the manse whose stones she had climbed. On the Longest Night, they took her and Leep to the House of the Brightness in white garments and spoke their names — Leep Marteague and Io Marteague — to the assembly, who echoed them back, and they greeted the First Dawn as a family — and they never slept in the tree on Stonemason Street again.

## Waken the Stone

My parents had taken me from the land where I was born as a very small child and had lived in self-imposed exile while the land healed from the Year When the Black Moon Set. The city of Bend-in-the-River had been buried under rivers of molten rock that bled from the mountain, the farmlands covered with crumbled stone. Since then, a town of sorts had grown back in the place, and because the river had changed course, it was called simply Bend, or Bend Town.

It was not a pretty place. It was where people went who weren't welcome where they were. It was the place for the desperate and the power-mad who controlled them. But it was where I was now headed.

My parents had spoken often of a hoard they had hidden, thinking that someday they would be able to return and rebuild their lives there. They had had it good, there. We lived in a splendid house overlooking the river bend. I don't remember much about it, but I do remember the rooms filled with the sparkling light of the westering sun setting over the water—something my mother called "the golden hour", a time when we often entertained guests in beautiful clothing, musicians singing and children running around the legs of the indulgent adults. Until one night when the mountain roared, the sky turned scarlet, and in the night we were bundled into carriages and hurried away to Dastenn, where my parents owned a less grand house where they stayed sometimes for business dealings.

So I grew up in Dastenn, a port city where many cultures met and mingled. My parents continued to live well, until a plague burned through the city and all the surrounding villages and took them with it. I had not reached majority, and an uncle from my father's side of the family was appointed guardian. He promptly ran my parents' businesses into the ground, and on the day when I ought to have been presented to Dastenn's finest families dressed in cloth from over the sea, I was instead turned out of my house as it and everything in it was seized for payment of debts.

At least I had been alerted the day before. I had an unexpected visitor in the form of Rodie, a brown-skinned young man among my set and one for whom my parents had begun negotiations for my marriage before they died. He came in the evening and met me in the front hall, speaking the warning low in my ear before hurrying off without saying goodbye. I ruthlessly wiped the one tear I let fall as I watched him mount his tall, chestnut horse.

I judiciously packed a bag with travel clothes and selected what small treasures and coin I could carry and made myself scarce before the Warranters came at dawn to drag my uncle from his silken bed to endure his hangover in the chill of morning. Well, I'm just guessing how it played out.

As I crept out the gate of the back garden, leading Suru, my mother's gelding horse, who was docile, I was followed by a luckless mongrel who hung around the kitchen, hoping for scraps. He had been allowed to stay because of the rats he regularly killed around the storerooms. I didn't want to make any extra noise, so I ignored the dog and focused on coaxing the horse through the narrow gate. Weeping, I cursed my uncle's name as I left my parents' house.

I felt badly at vanishing away from friends I had grown up with, but I also wanted to spare myself and them the awkwardness of my situation. I had seen their parents looking my way as they talked behind their hands, and invitations began to decrease. Some of them knew before I did, and didn't say anything. I won't speak more of them because that was the only thing that really hurt me. Even my older sister, who had married years before and lived in a fine house on the other side of the city, had stopped answering my messages. It was only later that I learned there were rumors about my relationship with my uncle—something that I am sure would never have crossed his mind. I can at least say that about him. But people believe what they believe.

By the break of dawn, I was at the edge of town and headed into the countryside. When I stopped to take a break, I realized that the dog had continued to follow me. He stopped some yards behind, and at my glance, laid down submissively in the road. After relieving myself, I opened a pack of pastry I had secreted after supper the night before. I had sweet-talked the cook into making it for me, and wrapped it while it sat on the sideboard, still warm. It was sticky with jam and goat cheese inside. I looked sidewise at the dog. He was holding himself still as a stone. I knew that if I gave him one scrap, I'd be stuck with him. He was an ugly thing with a squarish face that seemed to have too much skin on it. But not enough hair. What fur the dog had was more like a boar's bristles, and of no particular color. He was ungainly, too large around the chest, and his tail crooked from an old break. Tattered ears, most of one gone. And he smelled.

I sighed. It wouldn't hurt to have an extra pair of eyes. I would have to sleep sometime, and who would watch Suru? Who would guard me? I felt very lonely and sad at that moment, more like an unwanted creature than I would have cared to admit.

I looked directly at the dog and tossed a hunk of the bread in his direction. Hesitatingly, he moved toward me. I patted my knee, and he ran toward the bread which vanished away instantly. After that, as I remounted, he walked more closely behind. I appreciated this on the stretches where the road was lonely, and we met strangers. A look at the mangy and desperate thing following me, and we were given a wide berth. And with him bedded down in the stall where I stabled the horse, I was sure no one would try anything.

With my coins disappearing more quickly than I would like, I began to sleep rough when there seemed a likely place. It wasn't so bad. My parents had taken us girls out tramping a few times. Servants had carried our loads and erected handsome tents, but it was still damp and chilly and exhilarating in the morning. It was just more damp and chilly, and more complicated than exhilarating in the mornings.

I also sang for my supper more than once. I had been trained in singing, and knew a variety of songs. If I stood by the chimney-piece in an inn and sang a few ballads interspersed with bawdy and humorous songs, eventually someone would buy me an ale or two to wet my throat, and if I kept people interested long enough to go an extra round or two, the innkeeper would give me a plate of food in gratitude, and allow me to sleep free in the barn with the dog and the horse.

The dog was hand-shy, but I began holding the food I offered him, and making him collect it from my hand. Then I started touching his face while he took the food bit by bit. When I was finally able to run my hand over his ugly head, he melted into it. The one lovely thing he did have was beautiful eyes, and they looked up at mine with trust and gratitude in their amber depths as I fondled his prickly folds of skin, and his ragged ears. I had to wash my hands in a stream after.

One night, he woke me as he leapt from my side. The dog roared more than he barked. I stood and went to the horse, holding his head, untying it and ready to yank on the bridle and ride away—but it was pitch dark, no moons at all, red nor white.

I heard the savage growl some yards away go on, minute by minute. Whoever the dog was confronting must have changed their minds because the growls got farther away slowly, as I heard sounds of someone or something retreating through the woods. It was a good hour before the dog came back, cringing and fawning as he always did. I told him he was a good dog, and as I lay back down, I patted the space beside me and he immediately lay down. I could sense his tension as he lay with his head up, growling very low in his chest occasionally. I fell asleep, grudgingly grateful.

***

Light rain woke me in the dawn. The dog was missing. The horse's head was hanging down and I felt badly that I had naught to offer him. He had eaten the last oats he carried the night before. I promised him I would graze him at the first open place we passed. As we were just a day or two from Bend, there were abandoned farms that had grown over to weeds and lush grass, between cauls of stone the mountain had coughed out. It was also going to get more dangerous. Where was that damned dog? I needed him, now. I had no more to eat than the horse had, so it wasn't long before I was ready to mount. The saddle was wet, everything was wet. Then the dog came back, his ugly face wrapped around some woodland animal. His crooked tail wagged as he dropped it at my feet.

I knew enough about dogs to know he was offering it to me. I praised him and rubbed my hand over his head, trying not to gag at the blood that came away on my hand.

My woodcraft was limited and I had nothing with which to start a fire, and I couldn't eat it raw. So I made a show of picking up the bloody bag of fur, and offering it back to him. I turned away, trying not to retch, while he tore the hapless animal and gulped the flesh. Thankfully, it was over pretty soon and I mounted the horse and started riding. Confidently, the dog walked beside us.

He needed a name. The way he growled and roared at whatever threat he detected in the woods last night made me think of the mountain cats I had learned of in my tutoring, but never seen nor heard. I looked at him.

"Bobcat." I said it, and the dog looked at me. I repeated the name every time I looked at him that day. It was a bit absurd because bobcats were depicted as beautiful creatures with upstanding ears and pleasing proportions and beautiful fur (I had seen one made into a throw rug); but his tail was bent if not bobbed, his eyes were keen, and he had made it clear that he was not one to back down from a fight, just as bobcats were said to be. I liked the name.

The rain was warm and when the sun came out later, it was hot and humid. At a creek crossing, I decided to go upstream and rest. I was delighted to find a pool deep enough to immerse myself. With myself and my clothing washed and laid out on stones to dry, I turned my attentions to Bobcat. I scrubbed his rough skin with sand from the pool. He submitted stoically. I pulled him into the deep water with me so the dead skin and fleas would wash away, and I could rinse his dirt off of me.

I was shivering by then, and pulled on a woolen tunic over my wet body that itself was still damp. Suddenly Bobcat was standing near me, growling savagely. An armed man was approaching on a horse. He stopped, and called over his shoulder. "I think we found your girl, Master Rodie."

From behind him, another horse rode up. I saw the face of Rodie with mixed feelings—joy over the face of friend, surprise, and not a little anger that my old life had pursued me. It had been hard enough to leave it all behind. My look must have said it all.

Rodie dismounted and gave his reins to one of the others, and approached within a couple of yards. Unaccountably, Bobcat sat down quietly at my feet, his mangled tail thumping.

"Elle. Are you alright?"

"I am just fine. What are you doing here? What did your man mean, 'found your girl'?"

"Elle, you just vanish like the black moon? No word, no message?"

I pouted at him. "What did you think I was going to do? Let the Warranters drag me to the street?"

"We were there in the morning, Elle, my parents and I. We were ready to take you home with us."

"You didn't tell me that."

"I… I wanted to warn you, but I also wanted to surprise you. Be your hero. I'm sorry, it was really stupid of me."

I felt terribly sad all of a sudden and turned my face away. "Make your men back off." They were watering their horses. He turned and signaled to them, then I told him, "Turn around." He turned to face the retreating men. I pulled on more clothes, suddenly conscious of their unpressed appearance, of my broken fingernails, my undressed hair. I kept him turned away while I looked among my things for my bone comb and began to work at my long hair.

"I didn't know you had any such plans about me. I didn't think our parents had agreed on terms before mine died, and negotiations were left unresolved."

"My parents were working a deal with the Warranters. They'll pay off all the debts on the estate. Then the courts will sign it over to them and we'll own it. It was a good enough deal that they said they would consider the marriage. That is, if you wanted it."

My mind swirled. Rodie's family had moved in like vultures to grab my family's home and take possession of me. But another part of me grabbed onto his last words. If I wanted it. Did I want it?

Rodie interrupted my thoughts. "I, uh… might have hinted that there was, ah…"

"You may turn around now."

He turned to face me. His nut-brown cheeks were red. "Your uncle's lips loosened with liquor. My father was regaled with tales of some great treasure hidden in Bend, that your family had had to leave behind in their hurry. I guess I told him I was pretty sure that you knew of it, and where to find it. That intrigued them, and when it got out that you were gone, they hired me these men to find you. Although.... I would have come looking anyway."

I hid my face behind my hair, which I was still combing out. I found myself pleased. I did like Rodie, and we had known each other a long time. But then his last assurance sunk in at a deeper level, and I wondered how much motivation the supposed treasure had been. Well, it had been enough for me to set out on my crazy journey, with little more than a few old letters of my father's that hinted at where it might be found more than ten years ago. I took a deep breath. I put the comb in my pocket and began to plait my hair. I looked at him and said, "Thank you for coming. Are you thinking to take me straight back, or to Bend to find this storied treasure?"

Rodie looked around toward the men, standing fifty yards away among their horses, and then back at me. He spoke low. "They know nothing of that. I did tell them we might be going with you to Bend. That made the price high. And what were you thinking, going there alone? Have you not heard the stories that come out of there? It's not a friendly place. Are you even armed? Brother of Brightness, I've been so worried about you, Elle."

The truth was, I had nothing more than a meat knife with me, and nothing of skill to defend myself. I had to admit, I was trusting too much in the rightness of my claim and not considering that there was no such thing in Bend as the kind of privilege that had protected me all my life.

Bobcat whined, looking up at me, sensing my distress. Rodie gestured toward him. "At least you brought the dog."

"He seems to know you."

"I threw him a bone whenever we had dinner at your house. I'd go out to walk in the back garden, and he'd be skulking around. I felt sorry for him, looking like he does." I chuckled at that.

"That was kindly done. And wise. He's proved very protective of me. He'd have torn your throat out by now if you weren't a friend."

"I wouldn't mind being more than that, Elle." I looked at him with a degree of resentment. He lifted his hands. "But I'm happy to leave it at that for now. You've got enough problems."

I smiled gratefully at him. "Will you come with me to Bend? I can't promise you I will be able to find whatever it is they left behind. But without it, I'm out of prospects."

"You'll have a place in our house, Elle, prospects or no. I'll see to it, whether you consent to marry me or not. We don't have to go to Bend."

"I need to go. Whatever is there is all I have left from my parents."

The sun was getting low, so we made camp there. The two hired men soon had a fire going and were boiling pulses and salted meat. One of them foraged some wild garlic and herbs and added that. My stomach growled intensely — I hadn't eaten since the night before last. They gave Suru oats and one of them rubbed him down in turn with all the others. One checked his hooves and cleaned them. I felt badly that I had neglected to do so. The other man constructed a lean-to of brush and boughs. With my horse's blanket thrown over it, it gave me privacy.

We ate in silence from tin cups. I gave a portion to Bobcat. No longer stinking, and free of caked dirt, he was no longer quite so repulsive. I petted his head and could feel his tension, as he looked at the hired men, keeping an eye on them. After eating, I felt suddenly exhausted and though it had only been dark for an hour or so, I laid in my shelter with Bobcat just outside and was dead to the world until morning, feeling safer than I had since leaving home.

***

Even recounting it now I feel keenly the chagrin that I faced when I awoke. Yes, I had heard about Bend and I wondered why on earth I thought I could just walk in there and access my inheritance, pretty but penniless and unarmed. Well, here we were. I was lucky to get this far, and very lucky to have a friend like Rodie—whatever his motivations really were. I determined to be kinder toward him. He likely saved me from a nightmarish situation.

We arrived at the outskirts of Bend in early afternoon. The men rode one ahead and one behind Rodie and me. Bobcat kept close to my horse, his head low. I saw women as well as men bustling about in the muddy street, preparing food, doing normal things. One woman smiled at Rodie broadly, leaning in a doorway, with far more of her chest bared than was customary. When Rodie averted his eyes, her smile swung between Ridd and Sull, the men Rodie had hired. Ridd responded with a half-grin, Sull with a sigh. We were to see many more such women, some old enough to be my mother, some younger even than me, many of them gone with child.

Bend wasn't much to see, but as the land fell away on one side of the road, we caught glimpses of what used to be the bend in the river backed by the Burned Mountain, which seemed to have bled its innards over the surrounding landscape, covering much of it in solid rock so hot it had incinerated everything it didn't bury. The forests and crops had burned so hot it was said that the farm fields that weren't covered in stone had melted to obsidian glass. The river had changed course, and now lay miles to the south, except for a bit of a stream. Even from a distance one could see that the water was slow and malarial.

We stopped before an inn one of the men had picked out. The horses were led away, followed by Sull, who grunted that you had to watch what kind of mash they would feed them. Bobcat stuck to my side. The innkeeper, a large and red-nosed woman, glared at him, but Bobcat rumbled back and she shrugged her shoulders.

"We've got but two rooms. Two silver each. Or your girl can earn it on her back, it makes no difference to me. Baths are half a piece each. Dinner comes with."

"May we see the rooms, first?"

"I don't have time for that. Take it or leave it, young puss."

Rodie looked angry as he paid, and there was a hushed conversation which I assumed was negotiating. We were shown up to the rooms, each with odd-sized beds scattered about, and no linens, which didn't surprise me. Sull and Ridd went into one, Rodie and I into the other. He set my little bag down on one bed. "Look, Elle, I better sleep in here with you. I mean, not *with* you…" He flushed again, his brown eyes full of embarrassment.

"I get it, to protect me. Bobcat will probably protect us both."

"I've trained in fighting, you know. I've been riding along with the caravans from the docks this year, and I'll go on shipments with my father next year. There's pirates and thieves all along the way. I'm competent for that."

"All right then. Show me."

"Show you what?"

I made him give me pointers on defending myself with my meat knife, which was, after all, sharp and fit my hand better than the daggers he carried in his belt. There was a wood post in the room which I'm afraid we left nicked and scarred a bit more than it already was as we pretended it was an assailant. I had told Bobcat to stay by the door. He was unhappy with the arrangement and whined loudly. Finally when Rodie pretended to grab me from behind, Bobcat sailed through the air, landing on Rodie's chest and pinning him to the sad rag of carpet, snarling.

I shouted at Bobcat to stand down, which he did, suddenly meek and apologetic toward Rodie, fawning as Rodie stood up and brushed off. He stood over the dog, glaring down. Then he told Bobcat, "Good dog. You protect her. No matter who it is." Bobcat's tail thumped the floor tentatively, then hard as I petted his block-like head and thanked him. I actually bent over and kissed the prickly top of his head — surprising even myself.

"Maybe that's enough knife-training for one day. I'm smelling food and I don't even care what it is. Shall we go down?"

"Elle, the innkeeper asked me if she could buy you. She assumed that a pretty thing like you who clearly hasn't had to work a day in your life, judging by your perfect skin, and in a place like this, was already my property. When I told her you weren't for sale, she told me I was wise, that there was good money to be made with fresh stock, but warned me that girls didn't keep their beauty long in this country. I was thinking maybe we'd get dinner sent up?"

Of course I had heard of such dealings, but I shuddered to think that this was an assumption. I wasn't hungry, suddenly. I told him it was all right. The men brought us up plates of stew and hunks of gritty bread within the hour. Things got louder and wilder downstairs, and Bobcat rumbled almost continually.

I told Rodie that Bobcat should probably go out and urinate before we slept. I wrapped up in my cloak and we crept down the stairs unobtrusively. Bobcat stayed close, and all the way out and back, kept his head high and his ragged ears up.

"Your dog against mine, stranger!" We heard the call and tried to ignore it and the enthusiastic cries that followed the suggestion. The dog beside him barked and stood at the man's whispered command. Bobcat turned to face the other dog, his amber eyes fixed on him. His face became even uglier than before in some way I can't explain, his eyes burning yellow. The other dog whined and sat down. A woman at the table hissed, but Bobcat just turned and ambled up the stairs. We followed. The noise downstairs died down surprisingly fast after that, and I actually slept a little. Bobcat lay before the door. Rodie and I talked quietly for a long time, mostly about childhood memories. Then his breath became a slight snore.

I looked over to Bobcat, whose head was still erect. In profile, with the wan light of the red moon from the small window high in the wall, he didn't even look like a dog. The proportions were all off. "Bobcat," I said. His face turned to me. "You are a good dog. Thank you for coming along."

He yawned then, with a contented moan, and laid his head on his paws, watching me. I closed my eyes and dreamt of something I cannot recall.

\*\*\*

We left early and headed toward where the river bend once was. From an overlook, it appeared a wrinkled, black plain, but as the trail descended to it, it became clear that there were deep fissures that ran parallel to each other. We dismounted to have a look into one that was particularly wide—about two yards. There were pale plants trying to find light, and a distant sound of water moving, and darkness swallowing whatever lay at the bottom. We remounted. The fissure came to an end, and we followed where there were already trails etched into the surface of the stone.

Although I had been a child, I felt I knew where the house once stood, although we were perhaps ten yards above it. When the stone was flowing from the mountaintop, it had obliterated everything. They said the stone was still hot a year later, but now it seemed like dead stone. It was dry and windy. They also said that the mountain's line had changed considerably; now it walled off rain clouds coming from the northeast, and in the summer months the stone baked in the sun and animals died of thirst trying to cross it. In the winter, freezing winds howled down the slopes and living things froze in their tracks.

I dismounted Suru and walked to the top of a ridge and looked around. It was eerily beautiful in its way. The mountain was a blue wall, and the land sloped down from there for miles until it met the plain where the molten stone had come to rest. All that timber had burned up to the slopes of the next ridge of hills to the south. The land was rough and stony, not suitable for farming, and had gone to endless brambles and brush coming up through the deep-piled ash. The river had found its way to the next valley, where it formed a long lake before flowing out its other end and rejoining its old pathway to Dastenn.

I stood in one spot, turning around carefully. The line of the mountain had changed, but not the line of southern hills. I remembered my mother telling me that the ridge was called the Shining Hills because their slopes in winter reflected the setting sun just so. I had spent many afternoons waiting for the golden hour when not only the waters, but those hills, fed light into our home. I walked my horse about a furlong to the south, keeping my eyes on those hills, and met one of the furrows just where the hills looked the most familiar. I peered down into the void.

It was both deeper and wider than the others we had encountered, but to my surprise it looked like a treetop was reaching for the light. The leaves were turning yellow in the autumn.

Sull had procured a length of rope, Rodie having told them that we might be descending into one of the openings in the stone. Whatever he and Ridd thought of our venture, they kept their own counsel. He led his horse to within a few yards of the edge of the canyon and doubled the rope around the horn of his saddle. Sull stood holding the horse's head. Rodie took the doubled rope and crossed it behind his back, brought the ends forward and down between his legs, and took the ends in his right hand, and the rope to the horse in the other. "Sailor's trick for a quick descent from the masts," he told me. He backed to the edge of the ravine and began walking down the wall. My heart was in my mouth. After a few minutes, he called up, his voice strangely muted. "I'm at the bottom. Pull the rope up."

For me, they formed a sling. I sat in it and held the rope. They had backed the horse up and walked it very slowly toward the ravine, lowering me down. I wanted to cry out with fright as I walked backward until I was hanging free among the branches, descending into the twilit canyon. Rodie caught me and helped me get my feet under me. I was pulling the sling down around my feet, when the rest of the rope came tumbling after me. It was heavy rope and it thumped down bruisingly on my head and shoulders.

Rodie began shouting up at Ridd and Sull. We heard nothing from above but the snarling and barking of Bobcat, mixed with men's voices shouting, and finally hoofbeats receding quickly. Then the silence of the ravine.

Rodie was still hollering when Bobcat's face looked over the edge. He whined and moaned, walking up and down the edge, trying to find a way down.

Rodie began to fret and curse the hired men. I was stunned by this twist of fate, and sat down, dizzy, on a ledge of stone. I tried to catch my breath. I remembered something my mother had taught me: a prayer, and a practice. I spread my hands on the damp, mossy rock and bowed my head.

*Brother of Brightness, I touch the earth. Brother of Brightness, I breathe your breath.*

*Brother of Brightness, I look for your face. Brother of Brightness, I come to myself.*

It was something I hadn't done in a long time, but it dissolved the panic I felt. I stood and looked upward, just in time to see Bobcat leap into the void and land on the upper branches of the golden-leaved tree. He fell from branch to branch in a shower of leaves, landing on his haunches with a yelp, and immediately running toward me, limping slightly. He circled my legs before sitting down on top of my feet. I bent over and touched his head. He looked up at me, pain and fear in his amber eyes.

Rodie was the one to sit down next. He shook his bent head, his black curls falling over his face. He looked lost and full of regret. I sat down next to him. After a while I got up and decided to explore.

Dark, undulating walls rose on all sides fifteen or more meters. There was some dampness in the black soil at the bottom of the ravine, and pale and leggy vegetation trying to get some of the light. The ravine walls were studded with mosses and ferns and other plants trying to get a foothold. I walked down slope. The bottom became squishy and then a rill appeared, dribbling over edges into puddles. The ravine widened considerably. The water flowed a couple of feet wide and I was surprised to see what looked to be old paving stones. Not street stones, but circles and diamond shapes. The kind of pavers one would see in a courtyard or a garden. I stopped and looked more carefully around me. Bobcat stayed by my side.

I saw a child standing in the shadows. I gasped and stared, but it wasn't a child — it was a statue. I approached it. It was of a small boy, holding two birds in his outspread hands.

I remembered that statue. It stood in the center of our garden. But now, it stood a few feet from a wall of black stone, and was cracked and leaning. My sister and I had chased each other around that statue. I recognized the edge of the round bed where hollyhocks and mallows and roses had run riot. Their ashes had surely washed away long ago. What pale growth found a foothold there now must have grown from seeds blown on the wind or dropped by birds.

Beyond this, the ravine narrowed. I had seen enough for now. I bent and drank of the slightly mossy-tasting water where it dribbled over an old garden curb, and then found my way back to where Rodie still sat, head in hand. He sat up as I approached, his face pale with shock. He wore a small waterskin and he drank from this and offered me some. I told him I had found water farther down the ravine.

"We'll have to find a place to climb back up. Did you see any place like that?"

"No. But I found our old garden. Come, let me show you."

"All right. Let me get this first." He reached for the rope and coiled it with practiced hands, then put it over his shoulder and neck so it hung across his chest. He took a deep breath.

Bobcat had recovered from his limp and led the way down the ravine. I brought Rodie to the statue and we sat on the curb. I took out my father's letters and spread them on my knees.

"My father always had copies made of his correspondence, so there would be a narrative of all his business dealings. He wrote this letter to the Warranters in Bend-in-the-River before the disaster.

"'Greetings in the Brightness.

"'I am requesting that you add a few items to the deed to the house on Riverfront Street. I am attaching a list of improvements to the house that need to be added to its description.' So on and so forth, but here is the interesting part.

"'The contents of the cache hidden on the property are strictly for the benefit of my wife and or my daughters; lest any trouble befall them and they find themselves without resources they should be given access at any time. Otherwise the contents should remain concealed and proprietorship transferred to their progeny. The location remains a secret between my wife and me; if something happens to us,'..." I choked up then. Rodie rubbed my shoulder.

"Well, anyway. My father says to refer to another letter… I am pretty sure he means this one here." I shuffled the letters so the one I wanted was on top.

"In this letter to my mother, he talks about a 'stone of light'. If you were just reading it through and not thinking, you would assume that he's referring to something to do with spiritual things. I think he did that on purpose. My Mama and Papa were faithful in prayers and took us to the House every worship day, but this stands out because they were very orthodox, and here he is talking about a 'stone of light', like some fringe teaching."

"Like one of those 'deeper light' people." He referred to a cult of wild-eyed evangelists who were given to things like trances and ecstatic frenzies and claimed some secret knowledge. My mother felt sorry for them. She said they were mostly the poor, driven to desperation and vulnerable to unfounded teachings. But some rich and gentry were part of them, too.

"Right, but they weren't attracted to that at all. So that makes me think that this is what we are looking for." I handed him the letter. He read out the couplet that made up the whole body of the letter.

"'Deep below you will find the stone of light, in the shadow of the white moon of an autumn night.

"'Deep, but unburied, awaiting the tone that will waken light from the hidden stone.'"

Rodie finished reading the couplet, staring at the paper. He turned it over, and back again. "This is it? Elle, we came all this way to…" He closed his eyes, visibly frustrated. He took a couple of breaths. "Do you understand our predicament? What we need to do is find our way out of this hole, not chase poems in the houses of the dead." He pushed the paper into my hand and strode off. He was looking for some egress from the ravine. My throat hurt badly, but I decided to follow him.

If we found a way out, perhaps I could talk him into returning later to our old garden.

We circled around the widest open part of the ravine. Then we entered the tunnel at the farther end. For a while, we followed it. There was a tiny bit of light from where the sun, now at about nooning, reflected behind us and ahead of us. The roof of the tunnel opened again to the sky and closed again. I knew we must be right where the old riverbed had once been. The tunnel widened. Eventually we would reach the end of the flow of molten rock, beyond which I had seen from above were acres of crumpled and broken stone. Some of the stone was dressed blocks from buildings, even carved moldings and gargoyles. I didn't look forward to crawling over that.

But suddenly the tunnel branched into different directions. One was open to the sky, the others descended to blackness. We spent hours going down these, the open one first. It ended abruptly in a pool of water. We splashed our faces and drank from Rodie's waterskin before going back upward to the place where the tunnels joined. We went down the largest of the dark tunnels. It became so dark that we were afraid of falling into a hole, even with Bobcat sniffing the way ahead out for us; so we returned again. The light by now was fading.

Rodie did have an iron and flint and charred flax in his coat pocket. We gathered what leaf trash and dead twigs we could find and looked for a likely place to spend the night. We found a dry recess under the black stone wall.

I realized that we were going to sleep alongside each other. The damp chill of the canyon and the lack of blankets made it a necessity. Rodie took the rope coil off and arranged it for a pillow. He started the fire and it was a comfort, but it wasn't long before the few twigs were burning down to ashes. Rodie laid down and bade me curl into him. Bobcat laid on the other side of me, a respectful distance between each of our three bodies.

In the night, I woke to find that we were tight together and I was surely the only warm one.

\*\*\*

The next day was a repeat of the afternoon before. We explored the tunnels as well as we might. The first one was long, riddled with small openings high above that allowed us to see. But it ended at a rock face. In happier times, we would have enjoyed the beauty of the serpentine rock shapes, the small plants that found purchase on even the tiniest shelves of rock; as it were, it was just a barrier between us and salvation. Silently we turned away and retraced our steps.

The second tunnel we explored dwindled in height and width. We could see light ahead but there came a point where Rodie—thinner than I—could not even crawl ahead on his belly. We gave up and went back.

We rested awhile in the cavern from which all the tunnels exited, and then went down the final tunnel. This one descended for some time, like the others. Then it rose slowly over several yards. It opened widely to the sky, and revealed something we didn't expect.

There were ruins here, a stone jetty, and above that, a domed folly of white stone, six columns, walled in between, and a cap that had shifted and fallen slightly askew. Most of the columns were also cracked.

"I remember this place. My father built this in the river. There was a bit of island here, and he added the pavilion. We used to come out on a boat and picnic. But it became a nuisance, people treating it like a public landing, fishing and drinking and leaving their trash about. He had the folly bricked up to discourage visitors." Rodie and I climbed all over and around what used to be the little island. Beyond it, the tumbled scree of broken stone of all sorts began—scrolls and rolls of molten stone that hardened that way mixed with bricks and capstones and whatever wouldn't burn or melt from the intense heat from the mountain's bleeding heart.

The ravine was deep here, and already the light was growing dim. We didn't really decide to stay there, we just sat, somewhat defeated as the sun went down. We were dizzy with hunger and discouraged to the heart. Bobcat sat with us for a time, and then went off to explore more.

The red moon peeped into the ravine. We heard Bobcat whining and yapping. Finally we bestirred ourselves to see what he was interested in. "It could be dinner," observed Rodie, and we chuckled weakly. We went to the ruined folly and found Bobcat emerging from a break in the wall. He whined, turned, and went back inside. First I, then Rodie, crawled in after him. The red moon's light revealed what had been a dome-shaped space, now collapsed on one side. We hadn't noticed until then that there was a round opening in the top of the dome that let the moonlight in. In the center of the floor was a well mouth.

The white moon made its sudden appearance, the circle of white moving across the floor visibly as it fled across the night sky. I went to the raised edge of the well mouth because when I was a child, I was forbidden to lean over it and look into the depths and perhaps fall in; but there was no one now to warn me away. I knelt by the edge and rested my arms on the lip and leaned my head over, gazing down. The white moon's light passed over and pierced the darkness of the well. To my surprise, it was more like a cistern, much larger below than above. And the waters were low, and still. I saw the circle of light reflected, and the shadow of my head. I saw Rodie's shadow appear at the opposite edge, looking down.

The white moon traced a circle across the still waters, and then we saw something else. The moon caught the shape of some object in the center of the cistern. It was unclear and reflected strangely as the moon passed over. Did we catch a gleam of something? We asked one another what we were seeing, but had no answers. In the light, there seemed to be nothing, but when we leaned over and shadowed it there seemed to be some object reflecting back. The white moon's light traveled on, and waned as it passed the circle in the dome. Soon only the red moon's light wanly illuminated the space.

Eventually, we laid down and slept. When we woke, the sun was pinking the clouds. Hunger no longer dominated my thoughts. I had heard that after three days' fasting, the hunger would diminish. But we were both very thirsty and had to make our way back off the island, down the jetty, and climb back up a ways to find clean water. By the time we made it back to the island the sun was shining full into the ravine.

We discussed finding a way out of the ravine, but we both had a sense that there were answers yet to be found in the broken folly. Bobcat managed to catch himself a huge water rat, which he offered to us but which we respectfully declined. I sat thinking for a long time while Rodie wandered the island. It wasn't more than a stone's throw long, and somewhat less wide, so it didn't take much time to explore, but he did so twice before I joined him for a third round, just to stretch my legs.

On our way back up to the folly, Rodie discussed using the rope to climb down inside. But when we looked into the cistern, we could see nothing. There was a dim reflection of the oval of sky that showed through the roof of the dome, but that was all. The still waters below rippled occasionally as we disturbed bits of grit from the lip of the well. Afternoon passed. The white moon came up toward evening, before dark. I happened to look down while it passed over and called Rodie. We again saw a shape and gleams, as if off of glass or porcelain. Once the moon passed, we couldn't see it anymore.

During a lull in our desultory conversation, I started singing. It was just some romantic ballad, nothing special, but it had a pretty melody. It was almost pitch-black in the folly as the red moon was low. The chorus of the song went high, and when I hit the highest note, there was a flickering of light. I looked up at the hole in the dome. "Lightning?" I said.

"It's late in the year for a thunderstorm, isn't it."

I began to sing the chorus again, and the same happened when I hit the highest note. I stood up and went to the lip of the well, singing down into it. When I hit that particular note, there was a glimmer of bluish light from far below. I called Rodie over, and did it again.

"There really is something down there, Elle. How did that couplet go again?"

"'Deep below you will find the stone of light, in the shadow of the white moon of an autumn night.

"'Deep, but unburied, awaiting the tone that will waken light from the hidden stone.'"

"Bright Brother," whispered Rodie. "It's an autumn night, and the white moon's shadow reveals something...deep, but not buried. I need to go down there, Elle!" I rose up from where I had been sitting on the coil of rope and he picked it up and began looking around for a place to tie it off. There was a large block of stone that had tumbled from the collapsed side of the folly and he wrapped it double, crisscrossed it around himself again, and was climbing over the edge. My heart was once again in my throat as he descended into the blackness. Rodie told me to sing that note again, but I was anxious and it was hard to find the tone again.

Bobcat was clearly unhappy about the arrangement and stood with his paws on the edge of the well. He began to moan and whine. I had just found the right note, when Bobcat turned his face to the sky and let go a full-throated howl. The cistern was suddenly blinding, as if the sun itself had been bottled in it. I had to turn my face away. Bobcat howled on, and on, and on, and suddenly the light was moving and dimmed. "I've got it, Elle! But I need an arm to hold it, I need you to help pull me up!"

My arms were only as strong as regular horseback riding and vigorous dancing could make them, but somehow, I managed to pull Rodie back to the edge. That was the most difficult part because he had to get the urn he held over the lip of the well, and after dropping it carefully to the pavement, he had to heft himself over just as my hands were going numb and my arms were like a couple of dead eels.

He rolled over the edge, gasping. I sat up and massaged my hands. Bobcat fussed over both of us, sniffing and smacking his lips and whining. Finally, I crept over to Rodie and we leaned together against the lip of the well. In the dark it was difficult to know how the hours passed, but I woke as dawn was showing through the roof. The object that lay on its side was a glass urn. It was stained by dirty water and dust, but these wiped away. Within the urn was a brilliant blue, many-branched crystal.

"Rodie, look at this, it's amazing!" Rodie was sitting up straight, passing his hands over his face.

"It's pitch black in here, Elle. What time of night do you suppose it is?"

I looked at Rodie. His eyes seemed swollen and red, and he rubbed them again. Even his face and hands looked scalded.

"Bright Brother, Rodie, are you all right?" I put a hand on his shoulder and waved the other before his face. "It's morning, can't you see?"

"It's every bit as dark as when we brought the urn up. Maybe if you sing that note again, it'll light up. Go ahead, try it."

I hummed a few notes, and at a certain pitch the blue gem shone again with inner light. I looked at Rodie. I sang louder and the light swelled, but nothing like the blaze of glory that Bobcat's howl had elicited. Rodie's face betrayed nothing. I fell silent.

"Keep looking for the right note, Elle."

"I had the right note, Rodie. And it's full morning now. Something's happened to your eyes."

He looked toward me, his eyes searching, stricken.

"I was looking right at it and it got so very bright, but I couldn't look away, it was so... so glorious. I can still see it when I close my eyes." He palmed his eyes. "They really sting."

I didn't know what to say, but I held his face in my hands and looked into his burned eyes. "Rodie, we need to find our way out of here and get you to a healer."

I cut a length of rope and tied it round the neck of the urn, and hung it over Rodie's shoulder with the rest of the rope, coiled. I took his hand. We went down the far end of the island and slogged through the murky waters between it and the tumbled scree at the other end.

It was hours and hours of climbing out. I had to go ahead, Rodie pushing me up in places, and me pulling him after, and sometimes even Bobcat needed help. Bobcat's claws were broken and bleeding, and Rodie and I both considerably worse for the wear, by the time we emerged onto the black surface of the molten stone. We were miles from town. Every step of the way, I had to guide Rodie, who fell silent as the gravity of what had happened to him sunk in. And we were a long way from home, carrying a dangerous treasure of inestimable worth.

It was dawn of the next day when we stumbled into the beginnings of Bend. I hung the urn round my own neck under my tunic, and by tying my belt and sash in a certain way, I could pass for pregnant. Rodie had his moneybag still with him, and I took it and paid for a room off the street with a kind landlady. I led him to it. He sat the bed and Bobcat sat in front of him, his dear ugly head on Rodie's knees. When I came back from the kitchen with bread and eggs in broth, Rodie's hand was roaming over the dog's head over and over.

He took the stew from my hand but just sat with it. I told him to dip the bread in the stew and he did, mechanically. Meanwhile I was practically inhaling my own food, but I left some for Bobcat and put the bowl on the floor for him. I helped Rodie eat some of his, but it was work, and I ate some and gave the rest to the dog.

Rodie was pale and his eyes dull. The skin on his face and one hand had blistered and broken, and was scabbed and peeling. I sat by him and took his hand, and recited the prayer.

*Brother of Brightness, I touch the earth. Brother of Brightness, I breathe your breath.*

*Brother of Brightness, I look for your face. Brother of Brightness, I come to myself.*

"Say it with me, Rodie."

He knew of the prayer and recited it mechanically. I made him repeat it until it sunk in. His color returned and his shoulders drooped. He heaved a deep breath. "I won't leave you, Rodie. You came after me. I'll see you home."

"I'm so sorry about the men. I had no idea—"

"Rodie, Ridd and Sull—they're dead. We passed near their bodies out on the stone. Someone else took the horses." I didn't mention the ravens picking over what was left of them. Even their clothes had been taken. It was awful to see. I had prayed that their souls would find the Brightness.

He sighed again, and he turned toward me. He even smiled. "We found your treasure."

I smiled back at him, although he couldn't see it. I was thinking about what was really precious, and it was the kind of thing not easy to put into words, so I just squeezed his hand. "Yes, we did."

Let me not dwell too much on the difficulties of our journey back to Dastenn. The glass urn had the property of concealing what was inside it in daylight, revealing it in the shadow of the white moon. I could have gotten a sack of silver for it in Dastenn but instead traded it for thick blankets and healing salve, and the remaining good rope for journey bread, and I hid the crystal under my clothing. As delicate as the branches of it were, it was unbreakable.

Nights were cold and damp, although we were able to sleep in an inn here and there. We feigned poverty and I continued to sing for plates of food—the gem well hidden in Rodie's emptying money bag. Rodie was up one day, depressed the next. My boots, not meant for the hard use they were getting, began to disintegrate, and my long plait matted. By the time we reached Dastenn, Rodie had recovered his good spirits for the most part, and his skin had healed. We arrived at his home and were welcomed in with open arms and with mixed grief and shock and joy.

The crystal was put on display. I was dressed in satin and caused to sing in dimmed rooms or on night verandas, lighting the gem just a little. Bobcat stayed with Rodie and was not permitted to sing along. Eventually the King took the gem into his collection. I was well-compensated.

I had an overflow of suitors at this point but wed with Rodie in the spring. After our honeymoon, he did go out on the ship with his father, and Bobcat and I went along with him as his eyes. We lived in the house where I had lived with my parents and we filled it with children.

## Sylva's Dream

I, Sylva, am too old to be wallowing in such memories as those that haunt me in the evenings, when I sip a glass of gooseberry wine and gaze out the windows at the sun lowering into the Sea. I would rather just see *this* sunset, taste *this* wine, listen to the plucking of the demilute by the boy in the corner who will play until the red moon sets, and silently hang the demilute on the wall, and go his way. A demilute I once played myself, before my fingers became to slow and clumsy to form the chords.

But ah! I do remember so much. The way I was sold into prostitution by my father to pay his gambling debts. I was traded from hand to hand until I came to the city of Pondali, to the house of Faldan, who told me that although he had paid a great sum for me, he did not own me, and I was free to go if I no longer wished to live that life—although he would be grateful if I did work for a time, seeing as I was so attractive to his clients.

So I stayed. I made friends, and even lovers within the House, but none lasted. Few stayed in the pleasure-house for more than a handful of years. One day I found myself looking in the mirror at how those years were written on my face and my body, and soon demand for my attentions would begin to fall off. I turned at a sound to find Faldan gazing at me. He offered simply to be my husband, and I could stay with him. I had known for years that he adored me, from the way he looked at me when we sat and talked together, that he was only waiting for me to turn to him. I was deeply moved by the hope and pain in his eyes, and knowing how good he had been to me for so long, I consented.

Faldan was older than me, and himself ready to retire from his endeavors, and so he handed off the management of the House to another, and we moved into a home with a garden courtyard, the inner walls painted pale blue, with a fountain in the center; and an upper story that looked out to the Bay of Ara. We had one sweet child together, our son, Beam. Faldan was a loving father, and in the end, I loved Faldan for that, and his own brand of integrity. Then in a few years, Faldan passed down the spirit road.

I sold the pleasure-house off to those who managed it. I no longer wanted any part of that life. Living only with Faldan, and our little boy, and having actual friends who honored the kind of boundaries that show respect, was a revelation to me. It both brought me back to my childhood in my parents' house and memories of sisters who had been older and escaped before my father ran afoul of the gambling house; and helped me feel that my life was something that could become new. My friendship was no longer a product with a monetary value ascribed to it. Instead it accrued a worth intangible, better than gold.

After Faldan passed, I decided to travel. I had plenty of *lunas*, but had seen nothing of the world. Beam and I first took a luxury caravan that toured around the vast prairies of Ara, south of Pondali. Beam was transported by the sight of the vast herds of wild beasts, the eagles that kettled overhead, the prairie cat that screamed in the night and frightened him — but yet he cried when one of the caravan's guard brought him the salted pelt of one he had shot. He slept with his head on that fur for the rest of that journey.

"I'm sorry I was afraid of you. That made them want to put arrows into you. I won't be afraid anymore, I promise. I hope your kittens will be fine."

"Beam, dear heart, it was a boy cat. They don't help the mothers raise the kittens."

"Even so, Mama. I hope he fathered some kittens and they are out there somewhere, hunting in the night. I won't be afraid of them when they scream. I hope I won't, anyway."

Boys grow so fast.

We sailed to islands where the narwhals played in the surf, and sable, tall-legged birds plied the forest floor, looking for the phosphorescent larvae of glowing moths, while owls *whooooed* from the canopy above the treehouses where we laid with our faces hanging over the edge, watching by the red moon's light the pageant below — the panthers prowling, the black mouse deer eluding them.

We sailed to the far north where the ice bears dragged the pale seals over the edges of floes and the snow gulls cried for their share and the white elk passed in uncountable herds over the frosted tundra. We trekked back to Pondali through the Arani desert, where even Beam wrapped his face against the brutal sun, as we passed the Crystal Plain where salt stood in pillars shaped by the wind into shining blades.

Sooner than soon, Beam was a young man.

My friend Io, who lived in Dastenn, had written that her brother had sat his examination after studying at the college, and was now a doctor. But instead of leveraging his well-placed connections with wealthy merchants and nobles, he was looking after men, women, and children who lived on the streets, as he and Io once had. I decided I wanted my Beam to study at the college. He had read every book he could get his hands on in Pondali — which isn't saying much, Pondali in those days was a frivolous city where no one seemed to have the presence of mind to sit reading. I didn't read well as my eyes were weak, but I always had someone to read to me.

All I see now is lights and shadows, although the setting sun cuts through the mist. And the white moon. And sun on faces or flowers. There are colors, but as through sea glass. But I never miss a sunset, or a moonrise, if I can help it.

That is when the best things happened—when Io would read to me and I would fall asleep, or pretend to, free for an hour from the pleasure-seekers who came to my room. It was at moonrise that Beam was born. All my infants came with the white moon, and fetched a high price, and went to only privileged families, good families, followers of the Brightness—I made Faldan swear that much to me. Others in the House whispered that it was the white moon that gave me my albino skin and silver-blond hair and lashes. I knew it was only a family trait passed from my parents. Even my father shared this trait with me, something he tried to cover by dyeing his hair and beard and even his eyebrows, which only made him ridiculous.

But I am wandering from memories of Beam. He and I took a ship across the channel to Avann, and followed the coast to the great city of Dastenn. It was so different from Pondali—the stone and wood houses, the great trees in every street, the Houses of Brightness distinguishable from most other buildings by their round shape and fantastic windows. It was chilly, too, and thick clouds hid the sun so that I could walk without the heavy veils I wore in Pondali to keep the sun from spoiling my skin. Anyway I no longer had to preserve my beauty as if my life depended on it. My heart was free as a bird as Beam and I rode a palanquin up the ways of the city to an inn.

That night I lay in the lavender-scented sheets and slept fretfully, the feeling of being rocked by the sea returning to me although we were on land. Toward dawn, I awoke from a dream.

Beam was leaning over me, waking me from sleep. "Mama, Mama, wake up, everything is okay, it was only a dream."

But as I rubbed sleep from my eyes, Beam's face grew dark as though shadowed, and larger, and farther away. Voices rang, shrill, deep, strident, muttering, echoing all around. Beam's hands were pulled this way and that by many other hands. Vines and tendrils grasped his many limbs, and nameless tentacles. I reached for him but he was far, far away, and vast, and dark as night. I screamed his name but I couldn't breathe.

It was then I woke up truly, and it was just before dawn. Beam lay across the room in an alcove bed, dead to the world.

I wrapped myself in a shawl and went to the balcony. The morning was cool but the sea air was refreshing. Still, I couldn't shake the feeling of the dream. A bell rang from the House of the Brightness, and I could hear the chanting of the worshipers.

I splashed my face, pulled on my veils, and went down to the street. The House of the Brightness was a short walk from the Inn, so I made my way, pulling the veil from my face. I had forgotten that I did not need them here, for the streets were shaded by trees and the sunshine was gentle.

I walked slowly up the few steps and entered with trepidation. I had missed perhaps half of the worship, but I inserted myself among those gathered and stood, taking in the unison voices and the string drones, the bells, and the beams of light through the white glass. It was in Avannese, not my mother's tongue; but I understood it well enough. Then a prayer began that I had learned long ago from a friend:

*Brother of Brightness, I touch the earth. Brother of Brightness, I breathe your breath.*

*Brother of Brightness, I look for your face. Brother of Brightness, I come to myself.*

I came to myself, even as I looked for the face of wisdom, of Brightness, of peace. I stood still as many other worshipers turned to leave, some talking quietly, a few remaining. When the place was nearly empty, I folded my legs and sat on the carpet.

Even as I sat there, the peace slipped away. I shook my head after a moment, and rose to leave.

"Funny, how quick we are to run back to our worries."

An old man with short, grizzled hair and whiskers stood nearby, gazing up. It was as though he had said it to himself.

"The peace is so hard to hold. Worrying is easier," I replied.

He turned to me, smiling gently. "That's just it, though. Peace isn't something you can grab a hold of. It lives in that space between our reaching for it, and our receiving it. The space between the breaths. Between looking for the Face, and coming to ourselves." He smiled. "Hungry?"

I realized that I was, and nodded. "Come to the refectory. I think I can get you a seat at the table." I followed the old man through a door at the side, down a hallway, towards a low-ceilinged hall where long tables were crowded with women and men in white robes like his.

We were served tea and oranges, followed by bread and goat cheese. I pulled at the warm bread, my thoughts to myself as the old man chatted with others at the table. There was no way he could know my former way of life, and that helped me relax. Today, I was only a mother about to leave her only child at university. Finally, he turned to me. "Soben. My name is Soben Doney. And yours is?"

"Sylva al-Faldan, Father."

"Please, call me Soben. Now, tell me what dreams have weighed your spirit this morning?"

I was surprised, but not too surprised. I described my dream to him. He listened and nodded. I finished, and he continued to look at me. "Are you not going to interpret the dream for me? Or tell me it was only a dream?"

"Dreams can say quite a lot. But tell me, how did you *feel* in the dream?"

"I felt anguish. Loss."

"Loss of control. Over your son."

"Yes, Soben. I have been his red moon and his white for several years now, since his father passed. And he has been my sun."

"And now he will hearken to other voices, be pulled in other directions."

A tear escaped my white lashes. "On the day he was born, I knew this. But here we are. Knowing I would have to let go, and doing it, are two different things."

Soben's hand reached as though to close over mine, but he merely touched the edge of my sleeve, and withdrew. "May the Brother give you the grace." He smiled, but sadly, and stood. "Peace to you, Sylva. I have duties to attend to."

"Peace to you, Soben."

I wandered back to the Inn, but found that Beam had gone out by himself to explore the city, and left word that he would meet me for supper at the Inn. I sent a message to Io that I was in Dastenn, and told her I would visit tomorrow. But an hour later, she burst into my room, throwing her arms around me. We talked about our families, people we knew from our many letters back and forth. Io had married and was a mother of five children, but she was also a shipowner and often went herself out on trading excursions. We ate a midday meal together and made plans for the following day. I walked with her halfway to her house. She tried to convince me to stay with her, but I knew her home was a turbulent, albeit joyful, mess of children and dogs, grimalkins and parrots, songs and tumbling, and I was accustomed to having much of the day to myself.

Beam returned in the evening, full of adventures and having got hopelessly lost and finding his way back by returning to the river and following the route the palanquin had carried us the day before. After the colored adobe houses and rooftop gardens of Pondali, the granite and brick and timber-and-wattle houses of Dastenn were a new world. He had tried street food and made new friends and had ample practice for the Avannese language we had learned together from a tutor while he was growing up.

And he had met girls. Of course he had. I had deftly steered him away from Pondali girls, feeling there were greater things for him than a well-placed marriage to a merchant family and a dreary counting-office.

I took him to Blackmoon Schola, the institute where Leep had so successfully studied, and by day's end he was sitting an interview with three of the academicians who tested his foundational knowledge and took copious notes while I sat, veiled, in a waiting room, idly perusing a book. The words were a blur, but I had all the stories memorized and the book was a good distraction.

After what seemed hours, Beam emerged. He smiled, anxiously, and told me they asked him to walk about the grounds and come back in about half a bell. So we went down to a garden with a path that stretched to a bell tower and we walked the path between long, rectangular ponds and fan palms. A bell rang in the tower and we turned back. Beam went back into the examination room, but moments later he reappeared, gesturing that I should come with him.

The academicians told him that despite the gaps in his knowledge in a few areas — Avannese history and botany, and some theological principles, it was clear that Beam was intelligent and studious, and they took his Arani upbringing into account. He was accepted into the Schola with stipulations that he would have remedial classes to address those minor shortcomings, which they were confident that Beam could easily accomplish.

Beam and I celebrated by ordering an expensive dinner on a floating restaurant, and went to the theater. The next day we found Beam a room in a student boarding house, and brought his few possessions there so he could settle in. Despite the spareness of the small room, he was excited to spend the night there, and I went back to my lodgings alone. For the first time in many years, I spent the evening in my own company and no one else's. It was a strange sensation, but not unpleasant. I listened to a musician in the great room of the Inn and told myself one of the Stories of Brightness.

*The Bright Brother walked on high mountain paths when he was young. One day one of his sandals broke, and he walked without them, his feet on the earth, which was a carpet of mosses, grasses, low shrubs, flowers, berries, lichens and fungi. As he walked, he realized that he had trod on a bluebeetle. Sorrowfully, he sat on a stone and lifted the shattered creature in his hand. He wondered how many beetles and other creatures had been crushed beneath his sandaled feet without his ever thinking on it. How many tiny insects had he inhaled, swallowed, or drowned as he washed his body? To live, he realized, was to accumulate a load of the world's brokenness. There was nothing for it.*

*The Brother blew on the bluebeetle, restoring it to wholeness before he set it back down. From that day he sought those who were ill, or crippled, or diseased, that he might breathe wholeness into their bodies as well.*

*Years later, the Brother healed an old man of numerous crippling and disfiguring boils. But just a month later, the man walked the spirit road. The people muttered about it. "Why did he heal him, only to have him pass away of old age so soon after?"*

*A Day will come when the breath of life will restore all the broken to wholeness, but this is how the Brother gave the world a picture of that hope. Sometimes words are not enough – and yet, no act of compassion is ever wasted.*

Storms set in after that, the streets littered with leaves and the skies dark. It was novel to be indoors all day, windows shut and rattling, and rain dripping down the panes. The inn was able to provide me a reader, who huddled by a lamp and read from books I had brought. I often paced the room while listening, wondering what Beam was up to, and knowing full well he was busy reading his remedial material with his tutor, and hopefully making friends with other students. The storms prevented me from going to see him or anyone else, or from thinking of sailing back to Pondali any time soon. The seas would be roiling for days after the skies cleared, and no wise shipowner would risk it. During a lull, Beam came bursting in, soaked to the skin, but exhilarated and full of stories. I had to send him back after a dinner in the room, because darkness fell early. That was the highlight of the week before the clouds relented and the sun finally came out, revealing a disheveled but cheerful city, scrubbed clean and open for business.

In the wake of the rain, every nook and cranny of the city came alive with rainflowers. Reds and yellows and oranges and every shade in between crammed the verges, emerged from cracks in walls, even populating rain gutters that needed cleaning and cropping up in potholes in the street. There was a bit of a festival as street hawkers and vendors came out from hiding and people enthusiastically walked around eating street food and gazing at the short-lived flowers. I had never seen anything like it and by the time I came back from visiting Beam to see how he was getting on, I was half in love with Dastenn. To make a long story short, I consulted with Io and in a few days had bought a small apartment on the top floor of a house that overlooked the Neck, where the Bay of Dastenn narrowed on its way to becoming the river that flowed from the Burned Mountains. I was busy for a couple of days buying a few furniture items to make it comfortable, and long, white curtains, and cases for the books I would buy, and a chair for the reader who would open the paper worlds to me.

I also did not neglect to visit the House of the Brightness, and spent time talking with Soben. Eventually, I divulged my former occupation to him. He just nodded and asked how it started. I told him about my father selling me, but that Faldan had set me free.

"You did not choose that life."

"But I chose to stay in it when offered a way out."

"By then, it was all you knew."

"Still…"

"Sylva, you chose a path that seemed right to you at the time. And eventually, a better way opened up. The Brightness never stops shining for any person. The Brother is always seeking to kindle the Brightness into every life. Even now, he pleads within your soul for you to renounce your old paths, and let Brightness by kindled in you."

I closed my eyes. I took a couple of ragged breaths. I did not open my eyes when I said, "I want that."

I heard Soben murmuring prayers. I could barely hear the words, but they gave voice to what was in my heart and took from me the burden of forming my thoughts into sentences, so I just listened and whispered "Yes…yes." Tears flowed down my face and dropped on the silk veil I had bunched in my lap. I don't know when Soben rose and left me in the sunlit hall, but when I opened my eyes I was alone.

I walked home alone, slowly. I did not veil myself, and unlike before I did not feel the eyes of men upon me. Like a shed cloak, I no longer carried the burden of men's desire. It was not my burden to carry. I walked with the Brother, and all was well with me.

I wanted to see more of Dastenn, so I bought a horse — a gentle, middle-aged mare. She was lovely, but in the end I took her back and asked for an animal with more spirit. The dark gray gelding I ended up with, I rode down to the beaches just west of the city and galloped him up and down the strand. A couple of thieves tried to waylay me but I only urged the horse on and found him game — the highwaymen jumped away before being run down. But had the horse shied,

I always dressed with my daggers on my thighs, and had some skill with them, for try as Faldan did to vet the clientele of the pleasure-house, more than once I had to slip a blade from beneath my pillow to a whiskered chin. I knew the ways of men.

I rode confidently through the streets of Dastenn to the Schola Quarter, beyond the great dome of the main House of Brightness. I left the horse with the gate man and asked after my son at the receiving post. Beam was surprised to see me looking windblown and flushed. His friends stared at me — something I am acquainted with, as an albino, so it did not bother me. I looked frankly back at them and their gazes soon dropped politely as Beam introduced them. Feeling carefree and generous, I offered to buy the lot of them some supper. What young man would refuse a good, free meal?

I showed off my new horse, who was called Arvo, to Beam and his friends, and then we walked together to an eatery. At some point, a couple of pretty girls joined us. After, I bought them all pastries sticky with honey, and they tore at them while walking back to the Schola.

Without really meaning to, I settled into life in Dastenn. My apartment had a small kitchen, but I did not enjoy having hours of my day in the company of a Dastenni woman who cooked my meals, although she was pleasant enough. I rented the adjoining apartment, and she cooked my meals there, and often slept there. The apartments shared the chimney-piece and her cooking kept my rooms warm enough most days. I was exhilarated by the cooling weather. I learned to wear woolen tunics in the Dastenni style over trousers trimmed with embroidery and belted with a wide, woven sash.

I was really beginning to enjoy Dastenn, when the Schism began to cause trouble. The same had almost cost Io her life as she was mistaken for one of their followers; now a score of years later, they had become more organized. What is more, the Old King was in his final days.

Io invited me to visit the palace for the equinox festivities. It was fine to wear my best silks and cashmere web stole, and wear the jeweled headdress Faldan had given me for our wedding, and roam the gardens and aviary, the gorgeous rooms in the palace gazing upon treasures old and new, listening to ancient tales of the Stone Folk, harrowing accounts of the Night the Mountain Bled, and stories of sea journeys both real and fantastic. A woman sang to a large, delicate blue crystal that produced an otherworldly glow when she hit certain tones. Timbrels played and dancers swirled; the finest singers spun their ballads.

The entire company crowded into the great hall to greet the King and raise a glass to the success of his reign. Even I was moved by the tribute spoken by a gifted orator, for the King's time was indeed blessed with peace and prosperity, albeit marred by the tragic loss of Bend-in-the-River. But when I caught a glimpse of the man, I saw him, already half a ghost. He hardly seemed to know what was going on about him, and his courtiers made him disappear as soon as could be gracefully done after the official toast, as the music and conversation resumed.

I saw it on Io's husband's face—he frowned in the direction of the podium after the attention had turned away. "Baradan," I said, and he looked at me. No fake smile wiped away the ponderous look—something I appreciated. "Who will take the throne after King Chaldenis?"

He leaned in, bringing Io with him, as his arm was about her shoulder already. "His eldest daughter, Chaldeene; but she is notorious for entertaining sun-gazers and other lunatics."

"Sun-gazers?"

Io explained that it was a popular name for the fanatics who believed there was no need for the Brother as intercessor with the Brightness—the same breed as those who began the rioting in Pondali all those years ago, an incident which led to

Io being reunited with her brother, and revered by sailor-folk ever since. "Many are saying that the King's advisors are dead set against her becoming queen, and are in favor of her sister, Kamchala, who is far more orthodox. Although in my experience, she has ideas of her own."

"You know her, personally?"

"No, I've only spoken with her a couple of times. Likely she wouldn't remember my name if we met tonight. Oh, look! Leep is just coming in!" We made our way through the crowd to meet her brother, who had grown tall and had an open-faced smile, quite different from his introverted, albeit adventurous, older sister.

It was well into the morning when we left the palace. Io and I followed Baradan as he wended his way down the picket line of horses to find the young man who watched over our three. We chatted about this and that, suppressing yawns and then laughing about it. We found our horses and mounted, but Baradan disappeared into a group having what seemed an urgent discussion. He came back after several minutes during which time Arvo had become agitated, bored with having been picketed for hours. I was about to get down to hold his head, when Baradan strode back, mounting as he talked. "Apparently the Royal Road is full of rowdy fanatics. We're going to have to wind our way down the back of the hill and along the River Road."

Arvo was only too happy to take the longer road, but I made him follow Io's horse because the way was dark and unfamiliar, and who knew if there was a cobble askew? There was a downside to having a high-spirited horse, like when you were tired and just wanted an easy ride home. But Arvo was again to prove his worth before the night was over.

It took most of an hour to wind around the back of Royal Hill, through an area of orchards heavy with plums and pears, back to the River Road, the main street that ran from the wharves all the way to Bend Town and beyond. We were nearing the turnoff to my street when we met a multitude of people, and reined the horses. We were about discussing an alternate route when the crowd rushed at us. I swear I heard the words *"Pondali whore"* shouted by more than one person, but however we offended them, a group broke off and charged at us. Io cried, "Follow me!"

We turned up a side street, but it was slow going because it was a market street and although dawn was only a hint of a blush in the east, many carts and persons and livestock were already jumbling the lane. I found myself surrounded suddenly by schismatics, and I was the object of their attention.

My past had caught up with me, and my judgment was certain.

Hands reached for Arvo's bridle, but he bared his teeth and nipped at them, one side and the other, yanking the reins from me. I clung to the pommel but other hands were dragging at my clothing, my legs and arms. I heard Io shouting, and screamed at her to run. Baradan was close by, using his rein-ends to whip the rioters while urging his horse toward me, shoving bodies out of the way. Arvo bucked, his legs kicking out behind, and I heard a man scream. He reared, his hooves flailing, and the crowd drew back. Somehow I managed to hold the pommel—I had lost the reins—and Arvo leapt forward through the crowd. I was slipping, but Arvo did not let me fall. He slowed as soon as we were clear of the riot, and I righted myself, clinging to his mane and telling him, "Home, Arvo, good boy, *home!"* Belatedly, I drew a dagger and looked behind me—no one was following; the market people were now shouting and shaking fists at the retreating mob. I slumped over my horse's neck. My clothes were torn and I knew the bruises would show on my arms this day.

Arvo trotted, stepping high, tossing his free head, occasionally cantering a step or two, but Io and Baradan were both back with me and the horses seemed to want to keep together, so he didn't break into a run. Baradan managed to lean over and grab Arvo's dangling reins and hand them to me.

Io stayed at my apartment while Baradan went home to the children. We steeped tea from chamomile and lemon verbena, sipped it silently, and slept in my bed huddled together like two children.

In the evening Baradan came for Io. I had told the housekeeper, Dene, not to come until afternoon, knowing I would be at the palace all night. She arrived and cooked a meal for us. Io was eager to go home but felt, it seemed, genuinely anxious about leaving me alone. I told her I would be fine. I went down to check on Arvo, whom I had simply given a perfunctory wipe-down and blanketed the night before, knowing the stable boy would waken and see to him shortly—which he had. The horse was fidgety and I decided to ride him down to the beach again. I borrowed a crop—not for Arvo, but in case of unruly crowds. And I veiled myself well, hiding every inch of skin and hair.

Stretching his legs on the sand was good for both of us. After an hour I returned him to the stable, where he seemed more ready to relax. I fed him chunks of sugar cane I had bought from a hawker, and all seemed right between us before I went upstairs, bathed, and slept through the night until pale dawn.

But morning came with red light as the sun rose over smokes and noises arising from the inland, ragged edges of the city. Dene, the woman who kept house for me, arrived looking fraught and windblown. She told me the Old King was dead, and the Sun-gazers were stirring up a commotion in the poor sections of Dastenn and within the Schola.

While she was sweeping I went out on the balcony. It was clear, but chilly, and I could see the brown smudge to the east, drifting out over the mouth of the river. I could hear distant crowds. My stomach clenched and I dressed in a hurry and rode Arvo upward toward the Schola quarter. At Dene's advice I had not veiled myself—it made me stand out too much as a foreigner. Instead I plaited and scarved my hair and wore a Dastenni riding cloak whose hood I could pull up if I felt the need. It felt odd to be out among people without my veils, but I was trying to get used to it.

At Beam's rooming house, I asked the patron at the door for him. I was told he was out with friends; the man wouldn't meet my eyes.

I fixed my gaze on him. "Where do *you* think I might find my son?"

He began to wring his hands. Finally he looked at me straight. "A big group of them went down to the Eastern Common. There's something on there. I told them not to go, but they wouldn't hear me over all their shouts of excitement. They were all out the door before I hardly knew what was what."

I was alarmed. I wanted to ask more questions, but I was sure it was useless with the old man. I stalked back to Arvo, tied at the gate, and rode toward the eastern end of the city to see what was going on.

I never got there.

The street was fairly quiet, until a sudden swell of sound made me pull Arvo up short. The street I was on fell steadily away toward the east, but undulated back and forth around small hills. About a quarter of a mile away, the street was filling with people. I strained my eyes to see—it was a multicolored, swaying mass to my eyes, but my ears heard the chant getting louder each second.

A gate opened to my left. A woman gestured and shouted that I should come inside. I and a few others on the street rushed in gratefully and she closed the gate and latched it. I dismounted Arvo and patted his twitching neck. There was a hitching post near the gate and I tied him there and went back to peer through one of several slits in the gate. The crowd arrived and swept by, chanting loudly. I couldn't see individuals, just a mass of arms and faces and clothing. And clubs. Lots of clubs. Where did they get the clubs? I squinted and recognized that most of the weapons were tool handles with the iron removed. Shovels, rakes, brooms, hoes; innocent of their blades, they looked somehow impersonally brutal. I shrank back from the gate, feeling faint. None had had weapons the other night.

The woman who had opened the gate for the several people was beside me. "My lady, will you step inside? You look as if to pass out." I nodded.

"Peace be with you," I said, by way of thanking her.

In the warm and steamy kitchen it took some moments for my eyes to adjust. A cup of water was placed in my hand and I drank it off gratefully. Another woman in a fine dressing gown stepped down into the kitchen from the house. She saw me there and eyed my fine riding habit and clothing momentarily before greeting me.

"Peace be with you," she said.

"The Brother's peace to you and your house." She nodded.

"My lady, will you come upstairs? We will be above the heads of this mob, and we can have a cup of wine." I accepted this invitation, hoping upstairs was cooler and brighter. Which it was.

She showed me to a room bathed in sunlight, and poured wine into two small funnel-shaped, bulb-footed glasses. She sipped hers, and then put it down to pull sheer curtains over the blazing windows. I was too restless to sit, and I drifted near the windows and pulled the curtain aside, slightly. I could only see a multitude of colors and shapes passing.

"Look at the Schola students," she remarked. "Those heretical teachings have caught on with them recently. There must be a hundred or more of them." I squinted, but the faces were flowing by too quickly… but a mother knows the movement and form of her son. I put the glass down on a table lest I drop it. Then I sat down on a small chair beside the table.

"My son…" I put my hand over my mouth, to keep from saying more. I breathed deeply and prayed, my eyes closed, for several long moments. By the sound of it, the crowd was trailing off. I had only whispered and the woman did not seem to have heard me.

There was another small chair at the table, and the woman joined me. I inhaled sharply and forced myself to sit straight. "Forgive my manners, I am new to Dastenn. I am Sylva al-Faldan, a widow from Ara. I am so grateful for your hospitality."

"It is nothing, Sylva. I am Eridit Bendmirk. I am sorry you have to see our city at its worst. I can't recall things getting this out of hand. But with the Old King passing, and the throne in dispute, I'm afraid it will be some time before Dastenn is its old self again." She stared at my pale eyes, but I was used to that.

"Thank you again, Eredit. I should be going… can you direct me to a safer route back to the Queen's Bridge quarter?"

Eridit described a route that would avoid the Schola quarter and the palace, where she ventured the crowd was going. I made Arvo walk and trot most of the way home, with my ears strained for disturbances. He tried to turn towards the beach, and finally I relented. We went for a short run before going home, which cleared my head as well as Arvo's. From there we went up to the House of Brightness where I tried to meet with Soben, but I was told he was out.

I then headed for Io's house. It was quieter down near the river, but I remembered the suddenness of the crowd both the other night and this morning. It was mid-afternoon when I reached there. Io pulled me in the door and hugged me, before I could remove my cloak. Then we spoke as I removed it and handed it off to a servant, and we moved through the house towards the kitchen.

"Where is Beam?"

"I tried to find him this morning. He was marching with a group of Schola students. I took refuge in a kind house until they passed. I'm afraid to go back there."

"Don't go to the Schola quarter. Hopefully things will calm down in a day or two. Leep is actually going up to the House of Brightness—"

"Not the Great House—"

"Brightness's sake, no, there is one off the green a couple of blocks away. He is arranging for any injured to be treated there. And Baradan is at the docks. We have the small schooner almost ready to sail for Kandhara with a load of goods, and we might just go to get out of town. You are welcome to come along, we can easily divert to Pondali."

"Thank you. I must know what Beam is up to before I think about that."

"Of course."

We stepped into the kitchen, where Io poured tea for us and offered me some cold lunch. Before I could say yes or no, she was loading a plate with cold chicken, grapes, olives, cucumbers, flat bread, a small bowl of olive oil; then still talking, she carried it into the dining room and set it down on the table and waved me to sit down with my tea there. She sat next to me. One of her children, a boy of seven named Benbo, wandered in and asked if he could have tea, too, and something to eat. Io went to get him a cup of tea, and I took a piece of flatbread, spread it with cheese, stuffed it with dates, and gave it to Benbo.

"Thank you, Aunty Sylva," he said, his voice already muffled with a mouthful of the rolled flatbread.

Io returned, looking askance at Benbo, but I just smiled. She bade him sit down to eat his food. He polished it off in a few bites and made to run out of the room, but a look from Io and he sat back down until he had chewed and swallowed. I sipped the herbal tea, tasting lemon verbena and knowing it would help calm my nerves. Benbo excused himself politely and ran from the room.

Io and I looked at each other and suddenly, I began to cry. I felt her hand on mine on the table. "Bright One, protect us and our children," I heard her whisper.

It was well after dark when Beam burst into my apartment. I had dismissed Dene early so she could get home safely. I was sipping warm broth by a small fire. I almost dropped the broth as I surged up to embrace him. He was excited and talkative and his eyes were shining.

"Mama, you should have seen us. We marched from the Eastern Common right up Hill Street to the Great House of the Brightness. There were hundreds of us, thousands by the time we got there, the front line armed with clubs in case they met with opposition, and when we got there the soldiers tried to keep us from the House but they fought them and got the doors open and everyone ran inside. The place is huge! Some ran to the Library and—"

"Beam, wait! Why were you with them? What is it about?"

"It was all about finding out the truth. You see, Mama, the Houses have been telling us so many things that have twisted the teachings of the Brightness. A lot of the High Scholars are questioning the House and they demanded access to the ancient scrolls. Only a few of the priests have access, and it's unfair—"

"All this fuss and noise and burning and fighting, over some old scrolls? Were people hurt?"

"Mama, the truth is important! Why would they hide the ancient scriptures away, if there is nothing to hide? The fighting was justified. The scrolls have been carried to the Schola library where the High Scholars can read them out to the people. That's where many of us ended up, in the big courtyard, hearing the reading from different steps, from the scrolls so old, they were falling to shreds even as they read them out."

"Well, thank the Brightness you are unhurt. What did you hear of the old scriptures?"

"Well, it was—I mean, a lot of it was in the old tongue, and the Scholars were reading it and interpreting it. Most of it sounded like the stories you used to have read to us in the evenings."

"*Stories of Brightness*." I waved my hand at the mantel, where the few books I had brought with me from Pondali were stacked. "I have it right here. All that danger and noise, to hear that? No one is hiding that away, you can buy a copy at any bookseller."

Beam looked frustrated. "The point is, they were limiting access, and now they are on the wind, where everyone can hear, and read for themselves."

"And in so doing, the old scrolls are falling to shreds, so no one can read them again after today."

"Well, it's more than that. The High Scholars want to go back to the oldest scriptures and interpret them anew. They want to understand the true place of the Brother in relation to the Brightness."

My heart felt heavy.

"Be very careful, Beam. Those people tried to kill your Aunt Io. It's good to ask questions—never stop asking questions. But, Beam, it's a short distance from asking 'what is truth?' to making it up on your own. And that is a dangerous place to be. That's why humility is so important in the Stories of Brightness."

Beam stared at the fire. He looked suddenly exhausted. I could see he was thinking, but perhaps too tired to think well. I decided to change the subject and I suggested he spend the night. He assented, but went out to buy street food, brought it back and ate an astonishing amount of it in a short time, and then went to sleep in a spare bedroom.

I awoke to the sound of Beam slipping quietly out of the apartment. I tried not to think about why, but he soon returned with Dastenni pastries wrapped in paper, and a jar of fresh yogurt. He told me he had hoped for fruit, but the vendors on the street were scant. I added honey to the breakfast and we sat at the table, picking at the pastries and dipping them in yogurt and honey.

"I was thinking about what you said last night, Mama." Beam looked almost apologetic. "I know Dada wasn't deep into the Brightness and all. But he did teach me to take careful account of those around me. To ask myself, what do they have to gain from me, and what might I have to lose?"

"Your father was a good father to you. He had his own kind of wisdom. And kindness."

"He certainly kept a sharp quill to his investments. Always evaluating profit and loss, costs and returns. Not a lot of thought left over for things of the Brightness. But he did tell me one thing I remember well, and that was that when it comes to the Brightness, he knew there were no bargains to be struck. That the only transaction with Brightness was already satisfied in the Brother. That we have nothing the Brightness needs, and bring him no profit. Brightness asks only to shine into all our shadows. And in that way, the Brightness was unlike humans because when it comes to people, everyone wants something. Including us."

I was struck because I never recalled Faldan having so much to say about soulish matters. Yet it seemed to me that what he said to Beam would have resonated with Soben.

The plate was empty soon enough and Beam carried it to the other side of the chimney-piece where the food was cooked. I heard the sound of splashing and he came back scrubbed and pulling on his cloak. "I'm going back to Blackmoon and see what's happening. I want to know what the Scholars have found. If I'm going to ask questions, I want real answers."

I looked at my son admiringly. Afraid. I wanted him to stay with me, perhaps to take the ship to Kandhara. We had talked about it, but he felt it was overreacting. I wasn't so sure — there were yet bruises on my arms and thighs and my breath froze if I thought on what the crowd might have done to me if Arvo had not been so valiant a horse, and my friends had not been with me to help.

Still, as I looked upon him, I knew I could not cage the bird of his daring, his intellect. I slipped a hand along the side of his face. "Be careful, my son. You are my sunbeam." He smiled crookedly, collected his few things and kissed my cheek before leaving. I felt the few bristles that were emerging along his upper lip and cheek. I whispered prayers long after he was gone.

The streets filled with people as the morning went on, but it was for mourning the passing of King Chaldenis. Small groups wended their way towards the Royal Hill, talking somberly with one another. They wondered what the new Queen's reign would bring. There was an undertone of discontent mixed with the genuine sorrow for the end of the King's long and prosperous reign.

I watched from the balcony, where the sun shone warmly; it was at the rear corner of the building and looked down over the small courtyard and the street it abutted. I took out the great crystal lens I had bought recently and tried to distract myself with a book, but I was restless. I heard my name being called and looked over the edge of the balcony. Io and Baradan were there with a bodyguard. Baradan wore a sword belted over his dark coat. I called down "Peace" to them. We tried to have a conversation but ended up mostly gesturing—they wanted me to join them. I waved them upstairs and they waited while I finished dressing to go out, plaiting and scarfing my hair in a fashion similar to Io's. I again wore the riding cloak and pulled it up over my head. We went out and joined the throng, walking unhurriedly in the general direction of the palace. My daggers were strapped to my thighs.

One of the guards walked before us and one behind. I walked with Io at my side, Baradan just ahead of us. The crowd surged peaceably up the Royal Hill. We ended up on the broad avenue before the palace where the crowd came to a stop. At first people were standing sociably, a few songs catching voice in the crowd. But as time went on, the crowd pressed tighter and tighter. The bodyguards stood firmly to each side of us. Io found a curbstone to stand on so she could see; Baradan and I were both tall.

The palace rose before us, pale grey and weather streaked, arced and domed and crenelated, although most of it had been purely decorative for more than a century since the last time it was under any real attack. The royal banners flew high above, crisp silk on the sea breeze. King Chaldenis's banners were triangular, pale blue with a stylized yellow cormorant spreading its wings. Suddenly there was a drum tattoo and the crowd fell silent.

The tattoo went on for some minutes. The palace fence walls were high, but the bars were slender and the grounds quite visible. An honor guard was spread across the battlement within the iron barrier. They had already removed their blue and yellow tabards and were in bare armor. At a signal, the drums rolled, the cormorant flags descended their poles as one—I counted three dozen of them. They reached the bottom and were received into the arms of the honor guard, who rolled them up neatly. One of their number marched from pole to pole, her arms stacked with the rolled, obsolete banners. This was done with great gravity while pipes played a solemn air.

Meanwhile the honor guard who had taken down the Old King's banners were turned away from the crowd, concealing with their bodies and armor the new banners they clipped to the halyards. The solemn air came to an end, all the flagpoles bare. There was a moment of stillness.

The drums tattooed again, and the pipes began to shrill a rousing anthem. The honor guard pulled the halyards and as one, the banners of the new reign rode the wind up the flagpoles.

They were white, with a yellow sun emblazoned on the silk with gold sequins and crystal beads, sparkling and blazing in the morning sunshine. They were so heavy with gilt thread that they hung stiff unless the breeze stirred them momentarily. Mostly they drooped, but for the white triangular points that flopped crazily about. The honor guard was donning new tabards over their armor, white with not gilt, but yellow suns appliquéd to their fronts and backs. The strident anthem played long and loud and I was getting a headache. Io and I were looking at each other like we were both thinking of going, when the crowd began suddenly to stir, and then to roar.

The palace doors were opening, and the new Queen was emerging beneath a silken canopy carried at each corner by a servant. Her tunic was white, with a gilt sash wound around and around her middle, the lower part of the tunic belling out to each side dramatically. The embroidered slashes up each side revealed golden-yellow satin wide-legged trousers and gilt shoes. Her head was wrapped in folds of cloth-of-gold. No crown; the coronation would take place after a month of mourning the Old King. Mind you, I could not see this well, despite the bright sunshine; Io later filled in details for me. In my eyes she was a blinding glare. I had to pull my hood low over my eyes and wished I had brought at least one veil.

The anthem ended with a flourish. Chaldeene was handed a huge conch shell which apparently had property of amplifying the voice to be heard over the crowd, because it was as if she were standing next to us and speaking into our ears.

"My people," she began. A jubilant roar arose from a group we hadn't noticed, white-clad and yellow-sashed, to the far-right side of the palace. They had appeared to be part of the honor guard, but now it was clear that they were not in any kind of uniform, just wore white clothing of various kinds. The sashes were cheap cloth, hastily wound about their middles—men as a belt, women winding it to cover from the chest down to the waist; similar to the Queen's styling. Almost all were youths.

"My people," Chaldeene began again, "My father reigned long and well, and his reign was prosperous. I am sure that all peoples of Avann are grateful for the wisdom and the strength Chaldenis brought to our land. It is with the greatest solemnity and gratitude that I accept the mantle of rule. And yet."

She paused. There had been silence, but the slightest murmur seemed to run through the crowd as the pause drew out. She scanned the crowd as she waited, and tension built. Suddenly she threw her head up and cried, "'*From before the lights were kindled, there was Brightness, and the Brightness was one, and yet not alone.*' So you have heard it preached in Houses of Brightness on all the continents and isles of the West of the world. So, my good people, have we been taught to believe.

"In the Year the Black Moon Set, a dread pall arose from the east and covered all this land, blotting out the sun and the moons for many days. Ashes fell on the land, on man and beast. Houses of Brightness filled with worshippers, crying for Brightness to return. 'Bright Brother' was on every lip and every song raised to his mercy. During that time, I chanced to meet a mage of great power. He had the power to create light that did not dim with the turning of the days or seasons. His light-globes are undimmed to this day, and light many inner chambers of this palace. In those days, they were the only light sufficient to dispel the gloom from the east. And yet, this great man of light scorned to revere the Brother, teaching instead that the Brightness in each of us is sufficient.

"I felt I had heard the truth speak to my soul. In that encounter, I found the key I had sought. That very night, I prayed to the Brightness without the intercession of the Brother, with whom, I now understood, I was coequal. As are each one of you, my people!"

The group to our right side now roared ecstatically and began to chant, "We are the Brightness! We are the Brightness!" Io was peering toward the group and I saw her lips part, her chest rise with her intake of breath. I touched her arm and leaned close, but she glanced at me and her face changed, her lips smiling slightly but not her eyes. She directed her attention back to the Queen.

At a wave of her hand, the chanting ceased. "I prayed then that the Brightness would come back to us. But I prayed not to the Brother. I stood before the Brightness itself and called. No interloper, no intercessor, just myself and the Brightness. Within the hour, the wind turned and blew the clouds and ashes back to the east. The Brightness returned!" Ecstatic screams. Io scoffed. Baradan glanced at her, open-mouthed. I was shocked by the Queen's audacity as well.

As the Queen's speech went on, it sounded more and more like a refined and high-brow version of all we had heard in Pondali. At a point, Io pulled Baradan's arm and spoke into his ear. He looked at her, and me, and tipped his head, asking if we were ready to leave. We had all heard enough.

The bodyguards had their work cut out for them as the crowd was now packed tight, but there was uneasy movement, and we were not the only ones trying to make our way out. It took some time during which the Queen's monologue still rang in our ears, punctuated by youthful roars and chants, but more and more by protests. I wondered when we would reach the end of the enchanted conch shell's range, and had my palms pressed to my ears which only muffled the sound.

Fights were breaking out by the time we reached the corner and forged our way, more quickly, down the hill. As soon as we were out of line of sight from the palace steps, the Queen's voice was silenced at last. I removed my hands from my ears and heard many, many voices crying out. We hurried, almost running down the hill at this point.

My apartment was closer than Io's house and we rushed in to the cool, dim stairs and I locked the door behind. The bodyguards saw us up to the rooms and then insisted on placing themselves at the front door and rear, stable entrance. Baradan had several gulps of water and after conferring with Io, left to run home. He said he would send horses for Io and the guards as soon as he got there. He looked at me.

"Sylva, we are shipping out this evening. You should come with us. You and Beam."

"I have to find him and persuade him, first. I can't leave him." He nodded, then headed down the stairs. Io followed him partway. I heard them talking on their way down, Baradan telling Io "She needs to come with us…"

For my own safety, yes. But not without my son.

Io came back up the stairs and closed the door behind her. She looked at me. "You're not coming, are you."

"I will, if I can bring Beam."

For a moment, Io wouldn't look me in the eye.

"You saw him, didn't you. In the crowd of sun-gazers." Io looked at me then, sadly. She nodded her head.

I sat down. Io opened the balcony door and went out. There were people moving hurriedly away, the same that had moved so solemnly up the hill just an hour before. I went out to join her. The air was still cool but the sun was warm. I had to shade my eyes.

I had given thought to the new ideas when back in Pondali. It seemed exciting and fresh. But just as I had to veil my eyes from the sun's strength—even when it was gentle—I knew that before the Brightness, I needed that covering the Brother provided. I needed an intercessor. Because of what I had been, I could not fool myself into thinking there was only light in me. There was light, to be sure. But there was darkness, too. Places where my girlish dreams had been poisoned, where I had denied myself the dignity to protect my body from being used for pleasure. I had sold my infants for a few gold *lunas*. I despised some of the men who came to use me, but I submitted myself to their pleasures all the same. I knew there was darkness in me which my own light could not suffice to dispel. And if I stood before the Brightness himself—should I walk the spirit road and come before him— I would burn up in his brilliance. I needed the Brother to stand forth for me.

Perhaps I had not shared these thoughts with Beam clearly. I was loth to reveal to him all about my and Faldan's past and where our wealth had come from. I was sure he had figured things out over the years, but if I had only been clearer… Io and I conversed about these things. She reassured me that I had done the best I could with the choices I had been given.

She urged me again to come with them on the ship. I promised I would pack a bag and be ready, but that if Beam was set to remain in Dastenn, I would most likely wait it out and hope it turned out for the best. The horses arrived for her and the bodyguard, and Io embraced me warmly. "Brother of

Brightness, protect you," she said, and rode away, looking back once before turning the corner.

My housekeeper did not arrive that morning. I made good on my word to Io and folded my clothes and items I valued into the small trunk I traveled with. The books and furniture, perhaps even the demilute I still played would have to stay. I ate cold chicken from the night before, yesterday's bread, a bit of goat cheese, a juicy apple. Then I put on my boots and cloak, had Arvo saddled and bridled—thank the Brightness the stable boy lived downstairs—and went out into the streets.

It was quieter now, but a skulking, uneasy quiet. I could hear there were still crowds of people and did my best to avoid them. I wove my way about the city to the Schola Quarter. And as I drew near, I smelled burning.

Arvo smelled it too and I felt him twitching with apprehension. I tightened my grip on the reins and patted his neck reassuringly. His nostrils flared but he did not slow his walk. He tried to toss his head but I wouldn't give him an inch of rein.

It was just too hot for the hood and I had tossed it off. My plaited hair was wound with a linen scarf from my forehead to my thighs, and I had lined kohl around my eyes to conceal the whiteness of my lashes. I avoided returning anyone's gaze and sat tall in the saddle on my dangerous horse. A broad avenue led up to the green around which the blackstone Schola buildings stood—today, they seemed to huddle. The trees were bare, and the sun was gone. Rain spit briefly and the breeze fanned whatever flame was built in the center of the green.

I tied Arvo near a few other animals at a corner across from the green and mounted a set of steps so I could see what was happening. The green was crowded with students chanting. I saw armloads of what I assumed was firewood being brought to the flame—but soon recognized the fuel as scrolls. Hundreds of the ancient scriptures were being thrown gleefully upon a bright fire.

Religion had not been a major component of my world at any point. So I was surprised at my own reaction. I felt the loss as love's labor over centuries turned to ash, their words and pictures and messages lost—words and messages that meant something, pictures that had opened the door for healing in my life and given me hope in spite of my wrecked life. Without realizing it, I stalked through the crowd of students towards the flames, drawn like a moth. When I felt the heat on my face, I stopped and gawked. Suddenly, my arm was grabbed.

It was Beam. "Mama, what are you doing here?"

I could only stare at him. Whether it was from the smoke or my heart aching, tears were pouring down my face. Or perhaps it was the rain that was beginning to fall. Beam put his arm around my shoulder and guided me to the edge of the green. "Oh, Beam," I sobbed. "The heavens are weeping."

"It's only the rain, Mama," Beam said, but I saw worry on his face.

We reached the steps where I had tied Arvo. The other horses were gone and he was now alone in a sea of people, although there was a wide space around him and he was tossing his head and his ears were back. I called his name as we approached and he turned to look our way, people backing away from his lurching hindquarters.

"Ride with me, son," I told Beam as he helped me mount. He untied Arvo's reins and was handing them to me when brilliant light filled the green. Arvo reared suddenly with a neigh, and just as suddenly stood calm, now facing the fire.

The flame that now burned there was without smoke, and the increasing rain did not quench it. More brilliant than the sun, yet I could gaze upon it without discomfort. The crowded green was utterly silent for a moment that stretched out, yet within the silence there was a note, pure and clear. I could smell rain, grass, orange blossoms, white ginger, and oud. The light was pure and yet color seemed embedded within it. There was no darkness anywhere within the green.

"Mama—" whispered Beam at my right side.

All the love I had ever known seemed to find form in the shape that was now coalescing within the fire. It stepped from the flames, leaving them guttering and smoky. It walked through the silent youths, who backed away as though scorched. A few, though, came forward to follow the brilliant shape which I could now see was child-sized, with eyes forming within the brilliance, which itself was becoming golden.

Forward the bright child came. Beam was on his toes, trying to see over the heads of the crowd. But the people were parting before the Child anyway, and soon was approaching us and passing before us, turning towards our left—Schola Avenue, a broad street which wound through the hills of the city and ended at the Great House of Brightness. Arvo followed after the Child, the reins loose in my hand. Doves flew from roof to roof overhead, collecting in great numbers. Dogs, collared and stray, padded beside the people. Squirrels ran along tree branches to follow. Even the few leaves that remained on the trees seemed to bow down, and tore themselves loose to swirl in the breeze with the butterflies among the ones who followed the Child. We were singing. How the song began or what it even was, I could not tell you. The sun had come out. We walked together to the Great House of Brightness and entered together. Did I tie Arvo, or did he simply wait for me outside? I couldn't say.

Beam had stayed behind.

He later told me what happened there. When the Child arose from the burning scrolls, most of the people thought that someone had poured liquid fuel on the flame, for it burst out so suddenly, blinding and hot, scorching the skin, hair, and clothes of those nearby. They had to cover their eyes and huddle away from the searing light that separated itself from the flame and moved across the green, drawing a few souls in its wake but leaving most of them coughing and wiping their filmed eyes. Water was brought to quench the flame completely.

Some of the High Scholars tried to rally the group. Some shouted that someone had accelerated the fire; that those who mocked them as "Sun-gazers" were to blame. Further, as no trace of the scrolls was found where the fire had burned, they had used the flame to divert attention so they could run off with what they could salvage. To Beam, that had seemed contradictory—why would they throw fuel on the fire when they did not want the parchments to burn? But he was shouted down, and the crowd became increasingly angry and self-righteous—and vindictive. High Scholar Daisan called them to march to the Palace, where the Queen would surely take their side and enact justice.

Not all agreed, but many turned at once to follow the same road on which the followers of the Bright Child had gone only moments before. Beam told me that they marched furiously, shouting hoarsely—and yet they did not overtake those of us who moved solemnly with the birds and the leaves toward the House of Brightness. Which they passed on their way to the Palace; but none dared approach the building as it seemed itself consumed with unburning flame. They passed onward up the Royal Hill.

Inside the House of Brightness—how can I find words for what happened there? And yet, it was words that was happening. The Child ablaze in the center of the House, and all around him murmuring serenely. Scribes knelt among the people, feverishly writing. I was amongst them, praying in Arani, and yet a scribe close to me was writing my very words in Avannese. For hours, we chanted and prayed and praised the Bright One, until we came to ourselves. The parchments were filled with words and pictures, fresh and crisp, and although the Child was no longer visible, we knew that the words and illuminations limned on the new scrolls had come from the Brightness that shone there, and still shone within us. How did we know? We just *knew* that we knew.

With serenity on every face, we flowed out of the House, also *knowing* that the peace we felt was the only peace in Dastenn.

At the palace, Beam and his companions were met at the gate by guards in their sun-blazoned tabards. Their message was carried into the palace and the Queen heard their complaint—an assault upon the Scholars and students while they carried out the work of reform. Soldiers were sent back to the Schola, and to clear the House of Brightness and bar its doors, and those of all the Houses in the city. But when they got to the Great House, it was empty. They locked the great doors on echoing silence.

The city erupted. By now the sun was going down and I was almost to my apartment. I was walking, leading Arvo. Suddenly there was a noisy crowd rushing down the street behind me. I mounted Arvo and cantered him home.

The apartment gate was unwontedly closed and I had to wait a few moments for the stable boy to open it for me. I rode Arvo in and he locked and barred it behind me. "Peace to you, ma'am. The other residents bid me lock up but I was waiting for you to return. You're the last one home." I thanked the young man and went up to my apartment, locking the stairs door behind me. I was happy to find that my housekeeper had arrived late and made up a lamb stew. I ate hungrily, then brought a bowl down to the stable boy and asked him to open if my son should come. He was grateful, as he was unable to leave to buy food. While I was there, another resident brought him a ball of cheese and an apple. I spoke with my neighbor for a moment. He had another apple for his horse, who was turning around in his stall, kicking at the door. He told me they had had a harrowing ride to get home from the market as it suddenly filled with a mob shouting about he didn't know what. People had grabbed at the horse's bridle and struck him. He went to talk to the upset animal and give him quarters of apple.

Back in my apartment, Dene pointed me to a paper that a messenger had delivered an hour or so before. It was from Baradan, considerately written in large letters I could read: "WE SAIL AT THE TURN OF TIDE, ABOUT 4TH HOUR OF THE NIGHT. PLEASE COME WITH BEAM, BRING YOUR HORSE AS WELL, WE WILL TAKE CARE OF ALL. SLIP #34, THE *SILVER FIN*. BARADAN"

But I wouldn't be on the *Silver Fin,* I knew.

The city was in chaos for the next several days. I did not see Beam, nor receive word. Leep Marteague looked in briefly the second day — he had decided to stay in the city as well. The Houses of Brightness were barricaded shut by the Queen's orders, but many of them were broken into and occupied by followers of the Brother. There were too many of them throughout the city for the soldiers to enforce closure everywhere. Leep occupied one as a treatment center of sorts going for those injured in the fires and fighting that broke out all over. Dene was not always able to come nor I to go out; it depended on listening from the balcony, meeting with neighbors, surreptitiously looking into the street, and deciding it was safe to go out and find food and fuel — or not.

On one such outing, I returned from a particularly successful visit to a market where I had been able to purchase fresh foodstuffs and a bundle of firewood. These were tied to Arvo's sides. I had also been to the depository to withdraw some gold *lunas.* I kept my crop at the ready — there was plenty of desperation in the city. I took a detour down an alley, and skirted a midden. A filthy little girl was picking through the trash, looking for something to eat. Her feet were bleeding. Her limbs were sticks. Her hair was matted. She wore nothing. She found something—I don't even know what it was—and tried to bite into it, but it was too hard. I stopped Arvo. The stench from the midden made his nostrils flare, but I just looked at the little girl. Her eyes were dull and her hair pale and dry from malnourishment. She didn't have the energy to draw away as I rode Arvo near her, reached down and pulled her from the pile by her bare arm and placed her on the saddle in front of me, and pulled my cloak over her nakedness. She struggled only momentarily. As we moved down the alley, she was already asleep, her head sagging over my arm.

Dene helped me feed the little thing and scrub her clean. She was listless and slept until the next day. She urinated in her bed and the urine was blood-tinged. I didn't want to think what had been done to her. I wordlessly washed her little body as gently as I could, and fed her. She didn't speak and I wasn't sure she could. I called her Ulan—"peace", in Arani. She ate continually, but slowly, as if she had to make it last. When she slept again in the afternoon, I went to find clothes for her. Shops were closed and I had to rely on a fripper, raking through piles of discarded tunics and trousers and guessing what would fit the girl.

A woman watched me from a doorway. I didn't have to guess; it was a House of Pleasure—not the pretty and pretentious kind Faldan ran, but the kind of dark and dirty warren Faldan had found me in and redeemed me from. "You love your little girl," she said to me. "How about a boy? I'll let you have mine, for a silver *luna*." I came home with that child, too.

My eyes were opened then and I began to see other discarded children, children enslaved, children for sale at bargain prices because Dastenn was become a desperate place. I filled the apartment with a flock of children. I put my eyes on the Houses of Pleasure and saw what I needed — a young woman who, like me, had been sold into that life. After speaking with her, I bought her from the proprietress and brought her home to help shepherd my little flock. She stole my best dresses and ran away. I didn't need the dresses, but the next helper I got was sent to me by Leep, who found an orphaned girl of about 14 who had been impregnated; I didn't ask how. She was called Vindra. She was as dark of eye and skin as I was pale.

She was good with the children. She reminded me of Io, who had also been orphaned and on the streets. Her story had changed, as had mine. I realized I could offer that chance to others, and I no longer minded the huddled-down existence Dastenn offered. Beam's ongoing absence was an ache in my heart nothing quite erased. But the children filled it up so that it didn't take up so much space, anyway.

Dene advised me to have a daily routine, that children needed that structure. So in the mornings after breakfast, we read stories. I taught them letters and sums and songs. I took the children out to the courtyard behind the apartment. There wasn't much there but a few trees, a pavement for slaughtering and for washing clothes, and a broken-down cart, which I paid the stable boy to demolish to firewood and scrap iron. I had a rope swing hung from a tree. The children loved to be held up to pet the noses of the horses and give them a carrot. We brought Arvo out and gave them a few turns in the yard astride his back. The other residents complained a little about the noise but when they found out what I was doing, I began to find stacks of folded children's clothing, nappies, little hats and sweaters, baskets of oranges, even an old wooden elephant with wheels, left at my door.

After, we came in for milk and bread, and a lie-down. Some did not want to rest, but we were strict about it. Vindra and I needed the break. The older children learned more letters and writing, on a good day; on a difficult one, if it was raining outside, then they all played hide-and-seek and built blanket forts and generally plagued one another until supper, baths, and bed. I embraced and kissed each one before they piled in their few beds, and told them they were loved, then I told them stories of Brightness in a lulling voice.

Leep came by once a week to see to their health. I was busy in the kitchen with Dene when he came in and told me, "Ulan allowed me to look down her throat with the mirror and the light."

"Yes? And?"

"Her vocal cords are normal. She can speak when she is ready to. Poor bird, I am sure the story she could tell is not a happy one." I thought of the bloodstained sheets of the first night; I had told him about that. I had had a look myself when she was sleeping. She was healing well.

His face brightened. "Io and Baradan are back. They've anchored in the bay and sent me a message. They would love to see you. I've already messaged them back that you are doing well. What do you hear of Beam?"

I shook my head. It had been weeks. Just then a wailing toddler, Po, entered the kitchen and I lifted him up to kiss where it hurt. Besides Vindra, who was oldest, and Ulan, the youngest, there was Po, Primrose, Arbrey, and Delsey. These last two were twins of about ten years old. I had caught them being sold at the back door of the House of Pleasure whose alley I used as a shortcut and offered a better price. Neither spoke either Arani or Avannese. But they were learning fast.

I marched them all, scrubbed and dressed as best as we could manage, to the House of Brightness. Soben blessed them all and advised me to bring them all for naming at the next worship day—this would start the process to make them legally my children.

To my surprise Io and Baradan came that evening. "Leep told us about what your situation is here and we figured we had to see for ourselves!" Io cried. "Tell me about each one!" Baradan and Io were accustomed to children climbing and tussling so I didn't at all feel uncomfortable talking while the children bathed and dressed for bed with Vindra's help. The freshly-bathed ones came running out, making Vindra chase them and capture them and pull nightdresses over their heads with plenty of giggling. As each came through I managed to name them and tell how I had found each one.

Finally I was wanted to kiss them and tell stories. Io and Baradan graciously waited in the sitting room until the children were settled.

Back in the sitting room, Io told me, "This is ridiculous. The place is too small! Bring them to the house."

"The children have just found a home here. I'm not sure moving them is the best thing. We're fine here. You and Leep managed in a tree for some time, didn't you?" I teased.

"What if you find more children? You don't have room."

"I am sure I will find more. And I'll figure it out."

"Do you need —" Io stopped herself. "Can I help with money? I would love to help."

"Recommend for me a good cobbler who will come to the house, and we'll call it even."

"You know I'll pre-pay the cobbler."

"I wouldn't dream of stopping you."

A woman and her teenaged son showed up a couple of days later and the day's entertainment was watching them work outside on the pavement in the courtyard. Each child was fitted for shoes and by evening the following day the shoes were finished. I liked the woman, who was kind to the children, and asked if she would go over Arvo's tack as well.

She returned the following day and had her son clean and check all the joints and seams and buckles while she greased the children's shoes against the winter wet. She did the same with my boots and any other leather things I could think of.

When I went back to the apartment, Beam was there.

He was in the sitting room, looking rather dazed. Vindra had shepherded the children to the other side of the chimney piece, in what used to be the other apartment. I could smell Dene's cooking. I knelt before him and put my arms around his neck. I could feel his shoulder blades, sharp as they moved under his skin to return my embrace. He began to weep.

The door opened, Dene peering in. I looked at her, shaking my head slightly. She withdrew, closing the door softly. I could hear plates clanking on the table.

Beam told me his story. I sat across from him on the low settee.

It had all seemed so glorious, this quest for truth, for the pure words from the Brightness. The scrolls were said to have been corrupted with copying over, the pictures were pollutions of the pure Brightness. Purity and clarity were everything. The Queen supported the movement, providing white robes to all who renounced the Interloper. She had heard of the newly-written scrolls that came out of the Great House on the day of the Bright Child's visitation. Only, she characterized the Child as a demon who had stolen the scrolls so that the priests could continue to control the narrative. The priesthood was condemned, and Scholars and Mages were now the ones in authority. But the new scrolls eluded them.

But soon enough factions developed between them. The Scholars pled belatedly for caution, that the remaining ancient scrolls be carefully indexed and studied.

The Mages wanted total revolution. They were led by the so-called Prophet Eradis, a man said to be older than all living, and yet youthful in appearance and strength. He and a handful of followers had emerged from the hills northeast of Dastenn, where they were known for their accomplishments in creating gold and jewels, silks and dyes, and other items of value that had enriched their community. They came bearing such gifts as Dastenn had never seen.

Beam was with the Scholars, feeling that a grave error had been committed on the day the scrolls were burned, and that was why the demon had emerged from the flames, scorching those around it and drawing away many gullible followers. But Beam had watched his mother following after, and it had set him ill at ease. So after a few weeks unable to resolve the hypocrisy and the dissonance in his soul, he had gone to the Mages with his questions.

After some days of gaining their trust and recognition, he was finally allowed to see Eradis himself. Eradis spent hours with Beam, talking him through his doubts and questions. Spinning his lies slowly and patiently as the orb-weaver spins its web to trap the unwary moth. Beam's unease grew even as Eradis's words grew more and more irrefutable. His tone more gentle, his smile broader. He drew near Beam.

Days later, Beam awoke in a small, dark room in the back side of the Palace. He was weak and lethargic. His soul was lower than it ever had been. He dragged himself to a friend's flat, where they helped him clean up and eat some food. He didn't know what to say to them. He slept there and the next day came to my home, still so weak it had taken him most of the day to walk across the city.

He sobbed out that he was sorry. I told him it was all right. That he should eat, and rest, and then we would talk about what really happened that day — and in the weeks since.

The next morning, I left Beam still sleeping. All the children wore new clothing and shoes. We held hands in a line and walked to the neighborhood House of Brightness. Soben seated us near the center. The worship went as customary, except that when the Reader read from the scrolls, almost everyone there seemed to know the words by heart — even me. I held up the smallest children one by one, and the community chanted their names. The twins, and Vindra, I laid my hands on.

"Ulan... Po... Primrose... Arbrey... Delsey... Vindra..." All were given Al-Faldan as a surname. Soben invited my now much larger family to the refectory to eat. I was offered a number of gifts for the children; apparently Soben had alerted other families. I took them, although I had no need; it was good for the children to receive love from the community of the Bright One.

It was midafternoon before we trooped upstairs. The children were all tired and sleepy and laid down quietly. I opened the door to the guest room where Beam had slept.

He was not there.

Instead, I found him sitting on the balcony, paging through my *Stories of Brightness* book. I sat on a stool next to him. We talked for a long time. I told him all that had happened from my perspective from the fire on the green to filling my life with children. I told him about how I came to be in Faldan's House of Pleasure, and even told him that Io herself had kept her and Leep alive on the streets for some time before the Marteague family took them in; and that I wanted to be part of changing the story for a few children, as Io's and my stories had changed. And that this was because of the words and pictures I had seen in the *Stories of Brightness*. He wept again but I told him all was well.

Dastenn, however, was a terrible mess. The Schola was in chaos. Trade was at a standstill. Markets were furtive and bare, and prices high.

Some few days later, we had had enough. The *Silver Fin* had taken Io's family to safety a fortnight before so I booked passage for my seven children and my beautiful horse and the cat who had somehow found its way into our number on a small schooner for Pondali where our house by the sea awaited. When we arrived at the house with the courtyard fountain, Ulan, who was seated before me on Arvo, tugged my sleeve and pointed. "Home?" she said.

"Home."

I often think about the Bright Child that came from the fire, and how we sang as one in the House of Brightness. Dastenn went through terrible times after that, until Chaldeene was finally overthrown and Kamchala crowned Queen. Dastenn went back to being Dastenn after that. The rainflowers bloomed in season, and the Ribbon Dance filled the street in high summer, and trade throve. The Mage Eradis escaped back to the hills with his followers.

I wondered how something so holy and miraculous could seemingly come to nothing, but then I remember how my own life was so very different after that. Even after settling in Pondali, I added lost children to my home. Beam brought home a wife and they added more children. My joy was in indulging them in the love I myself had missed out on as a child, and giving them the boundaries the Brother taught us to uphold. And my life is all I can speak of, I don't know how the Burning Child changed others.

This new life was not without its heartaches. Not all the children I raised returned blessing to me. But that is the way, is it not? Children grow to be their own persons. Some bring grief while others are a continual joy to the heart. Most are a mix of both.

So I sit here of an evening sipping pale gooseberry wine and looking out over the sea, recalling our adventures, of which this story is only a beginning. Often enough my lap holds a child or grandchild, and I tell them stories. Stories of Brightness, stories of life. Some are true, through and through, and some are tales I allow my mind to spin. But this is not one of those. This is my story.

## Solace

It was solace and a clear head I sought as I climbed the ridge, toward midnight; the wind growing blustery as I reached the top. Still, the sentinel pine there had withstood much greater troubles, so I climbed the spoke-like branches and sat near the top, watching the stars and idly trying to wipe the sap off of my fingers onto the bark of the trunk.

So it was complete chance that a dark shape interrupted the stars long enough to catch my attention, and I saw within it a pair of eyes. In surprise, I reached my sticky hand up and it was grabbed by a grey-wrapped claw of a hand, while grey eyes clawed for a hold in my own.

A face formed around the desperate eyes while we stared. My arm had snaked around the trunk while the wind buffeted the rest of the body of the figure about, but there was no weight or pull beyond the pressure of the hand that warmed in my own.

"That harshbag, Eradis!! He turned me around so I've been anchorless and lost to the world for, how long? Seven winters or seventy. Please, your other hand. *Please*," she begged as I hesitated, then released my arm from the tree and held it up toward her. Another arm formed from the shadows and a cold, grey hand grasped mine.

Then she was swinging down to sit on a nearby branch, gasping. Further shadows formed in the night but I couldn't tell where she ended and the tossing pine boughs began.

I could sense she was very, very tired and the fever-bright eyes closed slowly. She leaned slowly toward the trunk and rested her head. "How is it you saw me?"

"I was a follower of Eradis. I *am* a follower of Eradis," I corrected myself, but the eyes had opened and fixed on mine again, wild.

"Was, you said. Was? What happened? You said 'was'. I think you meant it." She looked me up and down, and then sat up. There was frantic curiosity in her eyes, which I realized were blue, not grey. Color was returning to her lips, as well. "You no longer trust him, do you."

I hoped my voice was indifferent as I said, "What's between me and Eradis is none of yours. What about you, why did he send you spinning?"

I realized, though, that she was no wraith, but a girl; not much younger than myself. And she was shivering. If she didn't get out of the tree soon, she would fall out. Eradis might not like me pulling her out of the sky like that, but it was already done and I may as well find out what I could from her before sending her back. If that's what I was going to do.

By the time we reached the bottom branches I had to carry her pig-a-back, but she was thin as a twig on a dead sapling. I kept her aback as we descended the ridge as it was easier than trying to support her as she stumbled along. The fire was embers in my hut and getting out of the wind, it seemed almost cloying. But the grey girl huddled up to the hearthstone and shivered there a long time. I lit a lamp and put one of my two stoneware cups, full of lukewarm tea, beside her. I drank cold water because the trip down had warmed me. Also, I didn't trust her and I was on high alert. I had no idea what she would do, but if Eradis had warranted her offenses great enough to toss her over the side of the world, I had best be on the watch.

I went to the rill and filled the small, black cookpot with sweet water. Inside, I added knots of wood to the embers and placed the pot on the three stones. I had washed barley and set it to soak earlier, so I added this to the pot with a knuckle of a wild boar and a good pinch of salt. It was simmering before the girl decided to speak. Now that she was almost warm, she smelled of icicles and smoke and summer storms and lilac and falling leaves and cold death, all at once. Her skin and hair remained grey, and I noticed that her lips had faded again to the color of old bone. I was surprised to see them color as she spoke in cold anger.

"It was in the year that the Old King died, that Eradis discarded me. Of course, kings had little to do with us. But that was the news, and the people in town were celebrating the new Queen's reign. Eradis had got close to the new Queen. Or that was the excuse to have a party, anyway. I was surprised when Eradis insisted we go down and enjoy the music and the cider, maybe dance or play a game. He warned us to take care, but it seemed like he himself didn't have a care in the world." Her voice rasped and she picked up the cup and drank deeply.

"Oh, but that's good to feel going down." She eyed the cup gratefully, then glanced at me. Her eyes again fixed on mine, and tears formed in the lower rims. "So cold, so lonely..." I squeezed her shoulder. The skin was cold in the rent at the shoulder of her ragged garment, but warmed under my touch immediately. When I pulled my hand away, the creamy color remained for a few minutes. I could even see freckles.

She relaxed visibly and returned her gaze to the fire, her hands idly playing with the cup. "You went to the fête," I prompted. The bitter aspect returned.

"We danced, we drank, we ate roasted meat and pears and fried bread, and we laughed and danced some more. Then we started disappearing, one by one. I asked Eradis, 'Where's Paloma?' He would," the girl shrugged in illustration, "'Oh, she went back tired.' From the six of us, only myself and Tury remained and it was getting dark and then he was gone and I saw him, trudging back up the path, like a ghost of himself. I started after him to ask what happened and Eradis was there, holding my arm in a grip like a bear's jaw."

My mind was turning over. I had never heard of Paloma or Tury. And what old king and queen was she referring to?

I thought of the last harvest festival I had snuck off to. I knew Eradis looked the other way sometimes so I wasn't worried about missing a few evening chores. The big house itself had plenty of places to hide, and he could assume I was playing in the hay with one of the girls.

I had my fun and came back after dark, full of cider and music and the smiles and kisses of one particularly sweet and pretty girl. Suddenly, Eradis had been on the path in front of me. He grinned broadly at me and drew me to himself as I passed out... I awoke in the dawn, clothed on my bed, shivering and down in spirit as I could ever be. The cider had been sour, the music harsh, and the girl unkind in my memory, although none of that had seemed right.

I dragged myself about my day, but Eradis was full and strong and seemed younger and more kind and happy than ever. I was grateful for his patience with me as I fumbled about my lessons and went back to my bed to sleep rather than practice.

The girl continued her story. "I asked Eradis if Tury was all right and he started laughing. It was like he couldn't help himself. He let go my arm as he doubled over. I ran to Tury to walk home with him, but it was like Tury couldn't hear me or understand anything I was saying to him. He told me he felt so empty and cold. But I had seen him not a half-hour before, smiling as he taught a little girl the steps of the summer reel. I had eaten roast meat and plums with him.

"Eradis was there again, and the same smile I had seen on Tury's face as he encouraged the little girl was in his eyes. A lot made sense all at once. The others. The waking up cold and hungry of a summer's morn after feasting. But his grip was on me, and this time after draining me of light and joy, he simply said, 'Too bad. Now you know,' and flung me into the summer wind, spinning and turning."

She looked down at her arms, and slid her hands up and down the thin biceps as if to warm them.

"Summer wind doesn't stay summer, does it?" I murmured. While she had been speaking, I had added wild leeks and thyme to the pot, and now I filled two gourd bowls with the steaming soup and set the half-full pot on the hearth to cool. I added the pig's knuckle to her bowl.

She could barely wait and in a few moments had picked up her bowl and was blowing on it to cool, slurping tiny mouthfuls. My mind was a-roil and I couldn't eat just yet.


I had so much more to ask her — who she was, to begin with — but a warm, full belly was too much for her and she was asleep in a heap almost before setting the bowl down with the clean-gnawed bone. I covered her with a blanket and took the bowls to the rill to wash. I returned and banked the fire. I covered the stew, of which there was enough to break our fast.

I was still very unsettled, and it was already deep in the night. So I decided I would ask her dreams a few questions. I curled up behind her on the floor mat and pressed my forehead into her hair. Her body grew warm against mine and I stilled myself long enough to sleep.

In the morning, she was sitting up, rubbing her face, before I woke. She looked askance at me, then shrugged. "I suppose I would have done the same," was all she said as she unfolded her tiny frame and went outside. I also needed to go outside but gave her a few moments to herself out there. I poked some life into the embers and put the stew near the fire.

Suddenly I wondered if she had left, and I grabbed the blanket and went outside.

She was just standing in the first beams of the morning sun among the dead barley straw. Her hair, I noticed, was gold at the back where I had pressed my face into it; or was that the morning light? I shook out the blanket and began rolling it tightly.

I realized what she was doing. Just standing still in one spot on the earth. Savoring that. I left her to it.

Some time later she returned to the hut. She glanced at my things, which I had tidied into a bundle for traveling. There wasn't a lot. She herself spooned out the warm stew into the bowls.

I told her, "We can't stay here. Eradis will come looking by tomorrow, if not today. I've been away for a few days. He knows about this place. It was my uncle's. He died a few weeks ago and I told Eradis I wanted to make sure the place was in order for selling. But I really just needed to get away for a few days."

"I know all of that, you realize. Luken." She looked at me significantly. My dreams had been hers as much as hers had been mine.

"Sidoney," I said. Saying it, I realized how much I liked the name.

"I don't know where you want to go, but I'm heading up the river, to Gloswin. I have a couple of relatives who might want to buy this farm from me. At least, it's a place for me to go. Maybe Dastenn after that." I looked up from my bowl. "What about you?"

"If some time has passed, I think I can go back to Bend-In-the-River. He won't come looking for me." I must have been staring at her, because she stared questioningly back.

"Do you mean Bend Town? You don't want to go there. The Redhands would grab you and make you one of their thralls in a heartbeat." She frowned, and I explained. "The whole city burned in the Year the Black Moon Set. That was a hundred years and more ago. The mountain bled molten rock that covered Bend. The land was ruined. It's only outlaws there, and the Redhands dominate the local trade in slaves, brew, gambling, and murder."

Sidoney drank the last of her stew and sighed. "I have been gone a very, very long time, it seems. All my people would be gone." She looked at me suddenly. "How old is Eradis?"

We both realized that Eradis was unnaturally well-preserved, and we didn't have to guess how he accomplished his continued vigor. He sapped it from his young followers like a spider drinking the blood from its prey. Whatever misdoubts I had about Eradis became firm disillusion. And resolve.

Sidoney took my empty bowl with hers and stood to take them to the rill to wash. "Go down stream a hundred yards, and there's a pool for bathing. Use one of the bowls. I found some clothes. You can't show up is Gloswin in those rags." I handed her a bundle containing a tunic and trousers and a woolen jacket, with a small pot of the musk herb-scented oil that my uncle had used on his skin. My uncle hadn't been a big man, and had been fastidious about his linen. I myself had changed into his old clothes just so Eradis wouldn't spot my familiar red tunic. I had left that hanging from a peg in the hut.


I walked backwards, saying goodbye to the farm. Even bare in the late fall, the place had charm, and I had always liked visiting when I was a child. The water was sweet and the exposure of the barley fields was favorable. The land went up to the ridge and the wild boars were plentiful on the hillside in the forest past the plum trees. My uncle had brought in his barley, dried his plums, and cut his wood; but it would go to whoever decided they wanted to live up there. It was a little far from town but a good living situation at that.

Sidoney had come back from the stream with her hair dripping. I loaned her my comb and she worked at the tangle as we walked. Her skin looked soft from the grease, but she still appeared pale as a corpse, and as her hair dried and she plaited it down her right shoulder, it was clearly going to remain colorless as well. With the blue of her eyes, it gave her a strange beauty, like a stormy sky with a single patch of blue, a sapphire among ashes.

Her gait seemed slightly unsteady at first and I imagined that after being tossed about the sky like a feather for however many years, she needed to get her land-legs back. I was eager to put some miles behind us, especially if Eradis decided to come sniffing around. He would have his beautiful brown horse to ride. Only he would expect me to go downriver, to the town, not upriver. I had never mentioned any connections there. I wasn't even sure my shirt-tail relations were still alive, or in Gloswin. But my uncle had spoken of them many times; his cousins.

We passed numerous small farms and traded stories of Eradis and how we had come to be his followers. I told her my "gold-skill" was spinning silken thread from mermaid's hair growing from rocks in the stream. She laughed and told me in her day all the money came from forging implements for the old king's insatiable appetite for the hunt. She herself could make a mean spearhead from the icicles that hung from the caves on the mountainside. Too bad it wasn't winter, I thought.

Our shared dreams had given us a sense of intimacy we both knew was false. Neither of us knew what the other would do in the real world. I knew her name, what anxieties entangled her, and the cold tug of the wind for a hundred winters over the land until it blew her over the sentinel pine on the ridge. In her dreams she flew over and over that pine, never quite catching my uplifted hand. She also knew a little too much about my fear of drowning, and that I still missed my twin brother who died when we were five.

We slept the first night in a woodshed, in exchange for stacking wet wood almost to the ceiling. I could see she tired quickly and told her to collect twigs instead for our bed on top of the wood. The next afternoon it began to rain and we entered a small public house. As Sidoney huddled by the fire, waiting our food, I noticed again her strange scent. It was natural and lovely and repulsive all at the same time. I wondered if she were actually human, or genuinely alive. But I had been inside her dreams and there was nothing unexpected there, in the least.

I paid for hot baths, something I had been some days without, Sidoney for who knows how long. After a hot meal it was like taking a sleep drug. So we were both dead to the world and who could blame us if we didn't hear hoofbeats come up the road. It was the subterranean smoothness of Eradis's voice that pulled me suddenly from sleep. I shook Sidoney's shoulder and we both arose. I pulled on my uncle's shoes and Sidoney my uncle's sandals, and were out the window in a few heartbeats.

We were out of sight of the inn, hurrying down the wagon track in the meager light of the red moon, when a claw-like hand gripped me around the upper arm. "Harshbag!" he cursed me. "What dried-up husk have you found for me? No sweetness left in this one." He cast Sidoney aside to the grass at the edge of the road. "But you still have something of summer left in you, boy. Don't think I don't know how you poisoned the others against me. All my fair ones saw the look in your eyes before you flitted off, and they did the same; I find myself short of the liquor of youth. I will drain you to the last glint of your eye."

Eradis closed his arms around me—even starved for the nectar of youth, he was still powerful—and my consciousness began to flicker. But before it faded away I felt something else. Something pulled his head back and his grip loosed me. I staggered, shaking my head. The beams of the red moon between the trees were just enough for me to see Eradis, struggling to loose Sidoney, whose arms were wrapped around his neck from behind and her legs around his waist. She was groaning with the effort, almost croaking.

I was still woozy and it was easy to fall into the semi-trance in which Eradis had taught us to do our various transformations. In this state I could see that the more Eradis struggled, the stronger Sidoney became. They tumbled in the wagon-tracks and into the grassy margin. Eradis grunted and choked while her death-grip only tightened. Her limbs glowed with vitality. And she laughed musically.

By the time he fainted onto the grass, a shriveled man impossibly old, Sidoney was no grey girl anymore. When the white moon leapt suddenly over the treetops in its hurried transit, her cheeks glowed and the dead grass stood out white against the golden brown of her hair. Her limbs were pink. I reached out to pull a twig from her braid. I saw that she was smiling.

But her mouth crumpled and I realized there were also tears brimming over and trailing down her fair cheeks. Without thinking I brushed one away, and Sidoney fell against me. I circled my arms around her. She was laughing and sobbing, both. We walked back to the inn some time later, and climbed back in the open window through which we had left.

I curled myself behind her on the bed, and together we dreamed of Eradis's ancient body crumbling in the ditch, the mead of a hundred summers drained from his bones. We dreamed of faces we had known who had mysteriously vanished from our lives, Eradis saying "When they're ready, they leave". We dreamed of dances and cider and roasted meat eaten on autumn afternoons, of winter fires, of spring's multiform burgeoning. We dreamed of slow aging, and even death come welcome after a life fully lived and surrendered. We woke, and she no longer smelled of smoke or lilacs or death. Just soap and skin and a hint of musk-herb. I was awkwardly aware that the grey girl was a young woman with me on the bed. I arose, and stood over her; she was blushing and pulling the blanket up to her chin. Her lips were rosy and smiling.

There was nothing left to do but buy her a proper dress and visit the village priest, who tied a red cord around our wrists and waved us away as we walked back to my uncle's farm, where the water was sweet, and there was barley and dried plums for the winter, and wild leeks blooming in spring by the bathing pool.

# The Stone Folk

## Chapter 1

Among her kind, Sintramalala was known for her love for green and growing things; for the way their hues pulsated across the land with the passing of seasons from browns to greens to many hues; through golds and russets and back to brown. For this, she was regarded as somewhat simple, but dear—although none would say so. In fact, no word had passed between the Stone Folk in millennia, there being no need.

For they had wandered the length and breadth of the world a thousand times over, and a thousand again. There was no hurry in them. Their pillar-like forms had grown slow and craggy enough for mosses and mushrooms to cling about their shoulders. They had forgotten all the ambition and exploratory spirit that led them to cross rivers and mountain ranges; it seemed to them hubris, now. Still, they walked in gratitude, for their wanderings showed them how brief and fragile life could be.

And so they had slowed to contemplate the passing of time. It could take fifty summers to cross a meadow, five hundred to wander up one side of a great mountain and down the other.

On a day, Sintramalala roved a tall-grass prairie. In the hissing of the wind in the grasses, she heard symphonies. In the placid nights, the silence was a profound balm. She had left the shadow of a wood not a score of years before and had miles of symphonies before her.

Until an acorn dropped into her path.

She ceased her great, slow movement, and regarded the object, so strange to see here. A shadow passed—without looking up, she recognized the silhouette of a squirrel in the clutches of a red-winged hawk. The question was answered. A drop of blood was even now drying on the acorn.

As she watched, rains fell, dawns and dusks passed. The acorn sprouted tender green leaves; the pale root searched downward through the woven stalks and the sod below for good soil. Sintramalala marked the moment when the rootlets began to draw nutrient-laden moisture, and the withered nut dried as the green leaves became bold and unfurled. Sintramalala smiled lovingly upon it.

By chance, another of the Stone Folk approached from the other side of the prairie. Over the centuries it had entered the plain from the West, crossed rivers and creeks, and seeing Sintramalala from afar, made his way in her direction. For it was true that seeing one of the Folk set for another a course to follow in a world that had long since lost any sense of destination for them.

The tall grasses waved around Sintramalala's waist and whispered of Mehanaba's coming. She wondered if he would share her joyful regard of the oak, which now quivered among the grasses meter high. Mehanaba saw the oak tree and stood gazing.

Winters passed into summers and the leaves of the oak were innumerable. From bare, to green, to gold, and back to brown again. Great was Sintramalala's delight when owls populated the tree, and when one perched upon her head she saw Mehanaba's glance brighten. And then he did something no Tall One had done in many long years—he laughed, and she also laughed with him.

The sound carried on the wind, and three more of their kind appeared over the next few score of years. By now the oak had cast its own acorns, and its children had also borne saplings, and Sintramalala and Mehanaba stood in a glade where chickadees and robins swooped, and leaves cascaded in the Fall, and winter silenced everything but the insistent wind and the footstep of the deer who bivouacked beneath the windbreak of massive trunks.

So they were five who stood in a circle regarding the tree as the stars wheeled overhead, until a storm bullied its way across the prairie, and with howling winds and stinging hail and roaring thunder, tore the grove apart while the Stone Folk nodded slowly.

It would have been their way to then turn away and wander off. But that time was past. Standing in their circle, they were joined by a few others. But like them, most of their kind now stood, unmoving, gazing up at the inexorable pageant of the sky, or away to the unending horizon, or down to the humble earth.

As for Sintramalala and Mehanaba and the others, they watched the ancient oak become again a part of the earth while its children grew old and multiplied around it, joined by other trees whose seeds the wind and creatures carried there. Ferns and mosses clothed the Stone Folk, lichens bejeweled them, vines encircled them.

But deep inside each of them, a soul still listens and watches, delights in beauty, rages at injustices, sorrows at the brevity of lives, and drinks in the ongoing life of the world. They are not hollow, they are not dead, they are not cold stone.

\*\*\*

That's what my grandmother told me, anyway, about the circle of standing stones in the Plainwood. I might have added a detail or two in retelling, but what storyteller does not so, even to themselves? She often told me mysteries that I drank in as gospel as a child, dismissed as a young woman, but came to respect grudgingly and later gratefully as the years laid their silver cloak on my head and I was no longer young and proud, and needed somewhat to hold on to. I was fast approaching the time when the manner of women would cease with me, and I had no better explanation for the stones, nor for other mysteries she held up to the lens of story.

But this is my story, Lylaba's. And I have mysteries of my own to hold up to the lens. Like Sintramalala and Mehanaba, my name is not yet forgotten — if those were indeed their names, and if the Stone Folk indeed wandered the earth and formed the circles in the woods. As for the others in the circle, their history and names may or not be details altered in the retelling; may also be forgotten. I know mine will be, as well, in time. But I still have a story to tell, and a name.

Lylaba Davey is as good a name as any. I'm not beautiful, nor tall, and I don't attract friends easily. But I am strong and loyal, and true to my word. I work as hard as anyone. And I remember everything.

In a clearing in the Plainwood, I was raised by my parents and grandmother and several brothers and sisters to boot. But the plague took all but my grandmother and me, and more than half the town of Sheaf, which we lived at the edge of. My Da had taught me how to carve things from the wood of the trees around me, and this I did since the tools were there. Many caskets of all sizes were required for the victims of the plague. This kept body and soul together for myself and my grandmother for almost three years. Then the plague finally stopped taking people. I was making cradles again, among the yokes and ax handles (things which wear out; there were plenty of empty chairs and bedsteads about, even in my own house).

I loved a man and invited him in, but he was no good. One night when he struck my grandmother in a drunken rage,

I broke his skull with the ancient, dull sword that hung over the mantel. The Sheriff was called, and he only nodded as if he expected it from the man. We buried him in the back, and that was that. There was a hearing, but I came out of it all right. The marriage had lasted just a year. I won't even mention his name. His grave bears a blank stone.

I bore a child a few months later. I gave her the name Onna; my grandmother's grandmother's name. In the House of Brightness I held her up and spoke her name to the community, who echoed it, called it, sang her name. She grew up with wood shavings in her silvery hair, and could split wood with a hatchet by four years of age. By nine, she was making lovely boxes with carved lids—there were birds and deer and trees in relief, and she gave them gemstone eyes with the carnelians and quartzes she discovered in the rocks of the gorge at the far edge of the Plainwood. This she did on her own, while I was carving my endless cattle yokes and plow beams. She picked the prettiest pieces of wood and made the boxes according to the size of what she found. She sharpened her tools fastidiously by the fire at night while grandmother—or Gama, as Onna called her as a toddler, and it stuck—told her stories and spun goat's wool, and I washed the wooden bowls and spoons and iron pots and pans.

Unlike me, Onna was pretty and charming. Besides the boxes, she was also making candy from maple and birch sap, and would enclose a bit of it, wrapped in birch bark, in each of the boxes she made. If she really liked the buyer, that is. Rather than coin, she mostly traded for things we needed or wanted about the place- cloth, nails, emery, salt; or the occasional luxury, as she loved to give gifts. I wore a necklace of blue stone beads she had traded for, and my grandmother one of rose quartz.

But being women alone in a clearing attracted, at times, the wrong sort of visitor. When a knock on the door sounded at night, grandmother would wordlessly pick her bow from the corner behind the chimney piece and nock an arrow. If it was a male voice, she drew the bow. If the door opened, it was kept trained on the visitor until she recognized him, or his business was concluded and he was on his way. And she would follow him out, standing on the doorstone, until she couldn't hear his footsteps.

No one would guess she was blind as a mole. Her eyes followed voices and sounds, and she still practiced her shot with blunt arrows by having Onna toss wood scraps at the side of the barn where we kept a few goats and pigs and the cart pony, and she would hit where it hit — more often than not, splitting the chip of wood before it bounced and fell. The sound of the repeated *thwaps* was reassuring. The Brother of Brightness taught that we should be like the water deer — peaceable and gentle, but sharp of fang and hoof when we must be.

Still, she was asleep the night a voice called, "Peace to the house." Onna was curled, asleep, on the settle by the fireplace. I was reading a broadside, trying to memorize the words, to a tune I was humming. It was a mild night, and a small window was still open, cheesecloth hung over it to keep out the insects that would be drawn to the light. I spoke through the window.

"Peace to you."

"I'm sorry to disturb you so late. I'm a weary traveler, looking for a night's shelter, is all. I mean no harm."

"The house is locked; the barn is shut tight. There's a heap of clean straw under the lean to, left side of the barn. You're welcome to sleep there. Move along in the morning."

"Thank you kindly. Perhaps I could trouble you for some water? My bottle's empty."

I went and filled a pitcher from the urn and lifted the cheesecloth to pass it through. I saw a decent, old face with tired eyes. I heard the water gurgling into his bottle. He drank some off with an "Aah" of satisfaction, then topped off the bottle before passing the pitcher back to me. "Water's sweet. Thank you kindly."

"Wait a moment." I wrapped some cold meat, cheese, and fruit in a cloth and passed them through. He received them with gratitude, blessing me many times over.

"Rest well, travel light." I closed the wood shutters on the night and prepared myself for bed. I carried Onna to her cot, laid her down, and covered her with a light woolen blanket. I washed my feet and greased my callused hands and slept well.

\*\*\*

In the morning, the traveler was seated on a stone at the end of the walk to the lane. He stood as I emerged into the already balmy morning, turning his hat in his hand. I walked toward him and stopped a few yards away, asking a question with my face.

"I didn't like to disturb your night. But I thought you ought to know." He gestured towards the road to town. "There'll be more where I came from. Most'll branch north at the bridge, take the river route through to Dastenn. But I was feeling crowded, and so were many others who might take this route. You take care, now." He put his hat on and turned to go.

"What's driving you?"

He stopped and swung his head back, his eyes haunted. "Shadow. In the south. That is, something's blighting the land. Growing." He looked even more tired than he had last night. "Can't stay in that shadow."

I was puzzled, but not used to asking a lot of questions. But I felt sorry for the old man.

"Where will you go?"

"I had people beyond Dastenn, in Till. I'm hoping they're still there."

"Will you take something hot before you go?"

"I thank you ma'am. But I'd rather get going early. I had some journey bread." He nodded. "Thank you again for the shelter, the food, and the water." He marched up the lane to the right, away from town. The lane was once a trade route, until the bridge was built on the other end of town. It still ran the fastest route north, if you had good legs. Much of it was washed out, just a footpath now.

"I'm Lylaba," I cried after him, on a sudden impulse. He turned with a half-smile, but didn't miss a step.

"Campo."

I waved, but his face was already set like flint on the path ahead. He moved well, for an old guy. I turned back to the house, collected a few pieces of wood from the neat stack, and carried them into the kitchen.

Gama was shoveling the ashes from the fireplace, finding a few embers to blow up the fire for breakfast. I told her what Campo had said. She frowned. "I heard talk of a shadow to the south, last time I went to the House of Brightness. I thought it was people finding fault and I paid it no mind. Guess I ought to've listened in."

Onna came running in to my shop some time later. "Mama, so many people!"

I walked to the open door and looked toward the lane. A group of a few dozen was just passing by. After them, a few strays. Then some minutes later, more. They passed all day, mostly family groups. Only a few returned my greeting. I told Onna to stay clear. I pulled my work pile outside and split my flitches where I could keep an eye on things. Gama put a full pail of water by the stone at the end of our walk, and a dipper, and filled it a few times that day.

By evening, I had to know. I messed around with the goat tethered near the front until I spotted a family heavy on small children and old folks, and asked them if they'd like to stop for the night and sleep in the barn. They hesitated and I offered baths and told them I was nervous and looking for more people in the place to feel safer. At that, they assented. I didn't have but a few goats in the barn and I kept the chickens in their own place because I didn't like the hay a mess. There was an empty horse stall piled with bedstraw I was collecting to fill the ticks fresh before winter. I helped them spread their blankets over it and went in to make bread for supper, and told Gama to fill the large pot and add another old layer hen who wasn't earning her keep.

The chairs were full that evening, and every lap with a child in it. We ate the stew and the fresh bread. They offered dried apples they were carrying. They were tired and the children were ready for sleep after eating, so the older children shepherded the younger to the privy and the barn. I asked the adults to wait behind.

When the door closed, I sat back down at the table. There was a couple, a girl who looked the wife's sister, and three older ones — the parents of both the husband and wife. One of the older women, Rhu, spoke first.

"I'm sure you've heard why we're moving."

"I've not heard much. Only rumors." I poured more water into my wooden cup from the pitcher on the table. "I can see it's something no one wants to talk about."

"You might have heard of the ancient ones, the Stone Folk. Children's stories. Well, that's what people say, anyway. They're saying that the stories we scare our children with are coming to life."

The wife, Selde, broke in. "This is real. This is no story." She looked at me. "It's like stones are growing from the ground. Or like a mountain. But it's...black. So dark. And tall... it blocks out the sky. And everywhere it touches, the land dies. Turns black. And it's so dark, everywhere around it. Dark like it's sucking the light out of your eyes." Her expression, which had begun frank and pragmatic, took the same haunted look I'd seen on Campo's face.

Rhu spoke again. "It started at one of the old standing stones. Someone noticed it was turning black, that the moss and everything growing on it was dead. Someone else said it was larger, but people poo-pooed that at first. Then it was like it was growing in every direction."

"Not solid, like, but as if more stones were growing beside it, but they were...connected with the first," Rhu's husband, Dern, put in. "Black vines, or roots between them. And everything near them was dying off. No one would go near them..."

Ivy, the other mother-in-law, said, "Until my cousin Jeth. He was curious, and took tools to the stones. They..." her face crumpled. "bled black on his hands. It poisoned him. Took him four days to die. In agony the whole time."

There was silence as we grieved together for a moment. "Peace to his soul," Gama murmured after a moment, and the phrase was echoed by the rest of us, each lifting a hand into the air.

Selde's husband, Tu, finally spoke. "They just keep growing. Whole farms have been consumed. The king sent envoys. They stared and mumbled for some days, and went back. It's sending out runners, and it casts its darkness all around."

"The shadow," I murmured. There were nods.

"Bright Brother, spare us," said a voice, and the blessing was echoed. I said the words, but my mouth was dry. I drained my cup of water.

We spoke for a short while, but they were exhausted, so they went to the barn to sleep. I put the big copper pail by the hearth and filled it with water. In the morning, the fire would heat it. Gama and Onna and I went to bed, silent.

\*\*\*

Over the next days, the ranks of refugees swelled and shrank. I invited a few to stay in the barn each evening. These were folk who had passed through the village of Sheaf and kept on going, desperation driving them. My bedstraw would be beaten to dust, but there was more where that came from. Many paid for their supper with work, some in kind. A baby was born in the barn. An old man breathed his last there and was buried behind the house.

Someone left a sore-pawed young dog behind, tied to the fence and yelping. One less mouth to feed, for them. He became Onna's immediately, and she combed its short, pale hair after giving him a good delousing bath and putting grease balm and socks she had outgrown on his feet. He sat, drinking in the attention. That night he curled up at the foot of her bed proprietarily, looking askance over toward Gama's bed (for I still slept in the marriage bed Gama had surrendered to me when I married, and Gama's cot was on the opposite wall from Onna's).

"What'll you call him?" said Gama.

She gazed at the pup, who gazed back. "Mehanaba," she said.

"That's a lot of name for a little dog. He'll have a lot to live up to."

Onna giggled. "You mean he'll have a lot of standing still to do, to prove himself?"

Gama smiled. "Mehanaba was much more than a tree-gazer, before he came to be part of the standing stones."

It had been long since I heard this particular story, so I made sure to get ready for bed quietly while she told it.

***

Of all of the things of the world that the Stone Folk loved, -- the roaring oceans, the placid valleys, the mighty forests—it was the mountains they revered with almost holy awe. They believed that in the dim past, they had emerged from the rocks of the tallest mountains. And of all the things in creation, it was perhaps great peaked stones they resembled more than anything—but stone with sight, and voice, and faces.

When they were young in the young world, they lived together in families. They had songs and dances and stories of their own, which grew in the telling, until a tale could take a night to tell, a saga could last months. They loved each other and bore children. They built homes the like of which the world has not seen again, for they had immeasurable patience, and did all things beautifully. They would grow their houses from trees which they planted, and trained, and shaped over patient decades into marvelous things of woven branches, living and growing, tall and green. And always, within sight of mountains.

The habit of standing and looking long may perhaps have started with the mountains. To gaze upon them filled the Tall Ones with gratitude for their beauty, for their soaring majesty, and for the fellow-feeling of eternality. They had many long talks on the topic of whether they had emerged from mountains, or whether in fact, mountains were some of their own folk who had stood long, reached high, and ascended into a greater form. For the Stone Folk had some gift in this—they were able to grow themselves larger if the need occasioned, and become hard as old stone, cold as the grave.

One named Boonjeh was seen standing unusually long, gazing upon snowy peaks far away. Mehanaba came and stood beside him for some time, gazing, worshipping. But when he turned to look upon Boonjeh, he saw him cold as old bones, hard as young stones, staring with a dark aspect toward the mountain peaks.

Mehanaba looked long upon him.

"Friend," he said. "What are you seeing?"

Boonjeh grunted, and it was long before he spoke, and his voice was rough from disuse. "I see the high mountains of our ancestors. And I wish, like them, to become something greater. To ascend. To be mighty. To be above." Even as he spoke, he grew larger. Within the passing of days, as Mehanaba looked on, he surpassed the height of the tallest of the Stone Folk. Then he paused to rest. He was dark, and rough, and slivers of him shivered the air around them. He was stooped with the effort, but his eyes were two coals. A foul suppuration ran down his body.

"Friend," spoke Mehanaba, concern in his voice, "Cease now this untimely increase. Let the mountains be mountains. Be what you are. You are admirable and strong as you already are."

A day and a night passed while Boonjeh breathed deep and hard, and as the next day dawned, he readied himself. But Mehanaba was also ready.

As Boonjeh clenched and creaked, Mehanaba moved close to him. Boonjeh's waist was now the height of Mehanaba's shoulders. "Cease!" Mehanaba cried. "Before you become something incondign." But Boonjeh was all consumed in his struggle and heeded him not.

Mehanaba stretched his arms around Boonjeh's waist. He also began to grow, but lither, his arms lengthening like vines to meet around Boonjeh's body, and around again and again; braiding together stronger and stronger.

Boonjeh could grow no larger. He groaned and writhed. Mehanaba's embrace was inexorable.

They strove together like this while a score of years passed overhead and underfoot. Many of their kind came to look on. Most moved away after a time, shaking their heads.

The ground beneath them trembled. Over the years Mehanaba swelled in might; Boonjeh also, but his appearance became strange; brittle and dark. Finally one night, Boonjeh's heart burst with a dry *Crack!* sound. He began to diminish, a hollow and desiccated thing of stony splinters bound together by Mehanaba's knotted arms, which he had held so tightly for so long that he was unable to let go. As years passed, the slivers shrunk and fell away until there was room for Mehanaba to move. But something kept him holding on, gazing down at the sheaf of splinters.

Mehanaba's family had decided to intervene. On a day they came close and began to pull the dead shards out of his arms, gently, laying them together in a cairn, one by one. When a few fragments remained, Mehanaba drew his arms to himself. He could not unbind them.

But there, in what remained of Boonjeh, as the final shards were removed, was a child. He was dark, as Boonjeh had been. He was silent, and curled small. Mehanaba tried to pick him up. The child climbed into the circle of his arms, and went to sleep.

\*\*\*

"What happened to the child, Gama?"

"That's a story for another night."

"Mehanaba is a lot of name for a dog, I suppose. Let's call him Ba."

"A sensible name," I said.

After a pause, Gama said the blessing. "Brother of Brightness, protect us."

We joined in, our hands uplifted. "Brother of Brightness, bless us. Brother of Brightness, lift us to yourself." I always felt like a little child, reaching up for the embrace of a parent who never reached back. But Gama and Onna's faces shone with contentment at the words. I tried to curl into them, like the child Boonjeh, and find what comfort I could there.

\*\*\*

As the summer wore on, the number of refugees dwindled. I cleared out the ruined bedstraw. I'd had a windfall from the latter travelers, whose loads tended to be more, and who brought old folk and the lame and maimed along with them. They needed their carts repaired, or realized late that they needed conveyance even if it were just a travois. One small family had me create a yoke for two goats to pull their little cart. With the proceeds, I purchased a sturdy gelding, and made wheels which I had the blacksmith shod with hoops. I built the chassis and a flat bed for hauling wood and whatever finished items I had to deliver.

Meanwhile, a boy had insinuated himself into our lives. He was lame, and an orphan, and after setting out with fell sick with fever and was left behind. After he was on the mend, thanks to Gama taking him under his wing, he went about the place on his twisted, unequal legs and did what he could to earn his keep. This he did without asking or being asked. He carried wood from the pile to the house and split it. He set traps in the woods behind the house and brought rabbits and squirrels to the stew pot. He harvested dogbane along the creek and twisted strong twine, presenting fist-sized balls to Gama, who seemed to find uses for them. I noticed how smooth and regular the twine was twisted, and asked Gama to put him to work spinning the flax that had would have awaited the winter snows, when Gama would have been each evening with the spindle by the fire — when she had been able to see.

I asked the boy his name, finally, finding myself growing used to having him about, and even taking pleasure in his ever-useful presence. He dropped his gaze, his long, dun-colored lashes shading his green eyes. "The family I stayed with before called me Boy." His mouth twisted to one side.

"Is that your name, or what they called you?"

He shrugged.

"Do you like being called Boy?" His eyes met mine for a moment. He shook his head. "Well, then, Boy, we'll have to find you a name you can live with." He smiled, and sniffed, and reached into his pocket. He held forth a ball of twine. I smiled, and accepted the gift. He ran his twisty run out of the workshop.

Some days later, Onna and Boy were out late into the afternoon. They came in breathless, cheeks shining, with a string of trout and wild leeks. They seemed to share a secret, and Onna begged Gama to tell Boy stories about the Stone Folk. Gama was never shy about her stories, but she was poorly and wanted straight to bed, so I recruited their help getting the dinner things washed and put away and we sat by the fire. Boy got out the spindle, but I told him to let it rest for the evening. It was important to me that the stories be told, and listened to well, and learned by heart, and it occurred to me that sleeping with the goats offered few opportunities for this betterment.

I told them the story of Dancer.

\*\*\*

There was a Stone Folk who was not tall. The girl moved quickly, and many said this was why she did not reach stature — she did not stand long enough to receive the nourishment the earth, rain, and wind provided. So they called her Little One, in their slow tongue.

Little One tried hard to listen to the sagas. But many days and nights together in the same place grated her soul. She had to move away from the circle of listeners. Thus it took her many long years to learn even the shortest of sagas, for she missed great long stretches of them out in the spaces away from the rest, moving this way and that to work out the restlessness of her soul, before returning to the circle leaner than ever, and being ordered to rest and ground herself before she wasted away.

One night as she slipped away from the crowd, she carried in her heart the story she had heard, of the first Stone Folk to cross the great ocean to the west. She lifted her arms to portray the wind that called them, the clouds that passed overhead, the birds that cried along the shore. Then her feet moved with the waves, as her people had stridden into the water, and felt the currents move over their heads. The hair of their heads streamed, and as they moved slowly across the ocean floor, small fish found refuge in it, and kelps wound around their bodies, waving gracefully, back and forth.

It was almost without realizing it that Little One found herself back at the circle, moving her lithe limbs with the story. The circle opened and soon she was at the center, the eyes of the others shining on her. She moved and swayed, telling the story with her body.

When the story was finished, she had a new name. Dancer.

***

When I had concluded, Onna's face shone even more than before, while Boy looked thoughtful. "We found the stone circle, Mama. I told him some of the story, but I don't know it well yet."

"I haven't been out there in years. How did you find the place?"

"We crossed the stream and headed toward the hills. We were looking for a good place for traps, but found the circle."

"I wondered if it was still there, or if the stones were all tumbled."

"Stones?" Onna cocked her head.

I felt a bit flustered. "Well, much as I love the stories, they certainly behave like stones, don't they?"

"I suppose. But one looked at us."

Flames crackling was the only sound for a few moments. Then I leaned forward and cocked my head at Onna. "Truly?"

"I *saw* it looking at me. I saw an eye."

"I saw it too," Boy chimed in. "Two eyes."

"Did it wink at you?" I said, and we all laughed. Then Onna looked thoughtful.

"Finder," said Onna. "It was you found the stones. Can I call you Finder, Boy?"

A slow light grew behind his eyes, and his lips pressed together.

I tried it. "Finder." Boy smiled broadly.

\*\*\*

I was surprised by a secondary flood of travelers passing by us some days later. The leaves were beginning to color, but harvest was not yet in. The pace of them seemed fearful, desperate. Gama came out onto the doorstone. "Is there a storm moving in? It doesn't seem bright as it ought to. I can hardly feel the sun on my face."

The sun was peeping over the trees to the southeast, but towards the east a cloud bank seemed to loom. Although the rest of the sky was clear, the sun seemed thin and weak. It seemed to be fleeing the storm.

Finder was leading the pony out of the barn. As he entered the paddock, he snorted and kicked nervously. I felt the chill in the air, not the fresh chill of autumn, but something that raised the hairs on my neck and caused me to wrap my arms around myself.

A woman stopped to drink from the dipper which still hung on the edge of the pail by the lane. I approached her.

"Peace to you."

"Peace to you and your house." Even as she said so, her eyes slid to the east from which she had come.

"I recognize you. You had me make a door a few months ago." She lived not far from the center of town, but on the other side, at the edge of the farms.

"Aye." Her eyes remained on the eastern sky.

"Storm's coming."

"It's no storm." She shook her head. "Crops wither in that shadow. No bird that flies into the shadow flies out again. Strange fruit grows on the pale vines that strangle the trees. Livestock that eat them lay down and die." She looked at me. "Children, too." A tear cut the dust on her left cheek as it rolled down. I reached out and squeezed her shoulder, speechless.

"Brother of Brightness protect you." She sniffed as she turned to go. I watched her for a moment, then turned toward the eastern sky. I saw now that there were no clouds. Just a cold darkness like a pall over the morning.

Onna came out, trailed by Finder and Ba. They joined me in staring at the east. I took a deep breath and turned to face them.

"Today we're going to the circle."

Chapter 2

Joben's land was among the first to be encroached by the cancerous darkness that rose from the grove on which his wheat field abutted. The crop loss was not devastating to him, as it was a sideline — his cobbler's shop fed him. The field had been his late wife's and he kept it in cultivation to honor her and gave most of the produce of the land to her parents to help them in their old age. For she had passed without bearing any children, and Joben had lived alone these seven years, making boots and saddles and leather bags.

The boots had been many of late, as travelers needed strong new ones, or their old ones repaired. All his stock of leather bags was sold out. He hired a boy to help him with the stitching and the nailing and still had a crowd about his door as soon as the sun was up. Until the shadow overtook his shop, and no one would come near, except a local boy who told him his wife's parents sent word that they were going east to some relations there. Even his apprentice didn't show up, and the cat was nowhere to be found. There was a strange chill on the wind.

He walked to the back field and saw the blackness spreading, the jagged vines with their strange fruit dropping and splitting, already rotten, on the blasted soil. It rose, a broken wall, brooding, grumbling, hissing, blocking out the sun. The mist of stone-like splinters landed on his face and stung his eyes. Where he wiped the back of his hand across his face, it came away bloody. He kicked the spreading, root-like stone, and the cold of it stung, even through his own boots. He saw the leather dry and curl away, smoldering, and backed away, kicking off the boot. He left it there in the field. Thank the Brightness it wasn't his best pair.

Back at the shop, which fronted a lane off the main road through the village, Joben saw his neighbors bent under their loads, driving their carts, leaving their homes and farms and heading anywhere away from the dark blot that grew from the low hill behind their fields.

But he had built this life over many years. His own father had taught him the trade, and he had come to Mourmenir from the next village to start his own business without encroaching on his father's. At first he had gone from house to house, carrying his kit on his back, even his wooden shoe stand. He saved his coin and built his shop, and married the daughter of the farmer who sold him the plot by the lane. She had been such a good wife to have, his Anaba. When it seemed clear they would not have children, she had taken in those unwanted by others, and had raised up five little boys and girls to adulthood. But none had stayed, they had ventured out to Dastenn or married into other families, coming at whiles to visit. But less so since Anaba had passed.

It was many days that he passed from room to room, from shop to kitchen to bedroom to parlor, the little house that had been so bright with laughter growing darker by the day. His dark hair became unkempt, his beard untrimmed.

Finally on a morning, Joben hunted out all the gold and small treasures he knew were there. The gold coins went into his strongest tooled wallet. The treasures he lined up— Anaba's ring, a gold bracelet he had given her, a pair of pearl earrings, and a ribbon festooned with tiny pictures of her and the children. These went into his wallet as well. The rest, beads and such, he left on the table. He rolled up the best woolen blanket and packed some clothes into a saddlebag. The other carried the essential tools he needed. He hunted out his old portable shoe stand, made from hornbeam, which his father had given him. Finally, he packed some food.

A passing neighbor had sold him a spare horse some days before. He had a stall at the side of the shop for fitting saddles and harness, and there the sorrel mare stood swaying back and forth, bored. Now he fitted her out with everything, including what rolls of leather he had left. She kept nuzzling him, and finally he went back into the pantry and put the last of the apples into a sack. He halved one and offered it to her. Then he slipped the bit into her mouth and led her from the stall.

The sun did not strike him as he came out from under the lean-to, it was obscured by the mass that lowered with stone splinters that smoked the air and blackened the land. It was just a stone's throw away now. The front door of his shop was open. He left it so and led the mare away. The cat showed up, meowing, and he lifted her to the horse's back, where she rode clinging, hissing at what lay behind.

***

As he moved through the village, there was a dark and desperate tone. It was as if everyone's throat were dry as they called "Peace" to one another and hurried on. He had numerous offers to buy the mare, and he held tighter to his reins, finally mounting her and nudging her to a trot, Smoke, the cat, on his lap.

It was a bit less so in the third village, but there were creases in many foreheads, and a hushed and hurried air as people moved about. The children only sat and huddled together; not running or playing. He stopped at the house of an adopted daughter and supped with her family. He told her what had happened. It was a sad supper, although the children were happy and excited by the child-sized leather shoulder bags he had made for each of them in the idle hours before he departed his shop. He left early in the morning after embracing her and her husband, and kissing her children. It was a long way to where he wanted to be that evening—across the Deep River.

Late in the afternoon he approached Sheaf, the next town, and saw the bridge crowded with travelers, most on foot. The last group he had passed, they had begged him to sell the mare, to let them or their tired children to ride. Joben was tired himself. A group of desperate looking travelers had muttered among themselves as he passed, gesturing towards the mare. He knew there was another way through to a less-used route to Dastenn, and inquired about it. He was directed along a street that went west.

But even as he set out that way, the stragglers seemed to cast an envious eye on his mare, his kit, and the stupendous effrontery of the cat riding queenly on the front of the saddle. Evening was falling. He decided to camp far off the road. He turned the mare off through sheep fields, after letting her through the gate from the lane, and led her along a low stone wall toward the wood. Finding a stream a short way in, he followed that, and made camp in the shelter of a rocky outcropping.

For his supper, he had purchased a good-sized fish from a boy who had several on a string near the river. He filled a feedbag for the mare. He shared the fish with the cat, who then laid contentedly on top of him when he rolled into his blanket.

It had been long since he had slept out—since before he had the shop—and as tired as he was, he lay awake while Smoke dreamed of mice, twitching, and the mare drowsed, standing. The red moon peeped wanly over the shadow to the south. Even the night creatures seemed more furtive and anxious than usual. He didn't know when he fell asleep, but suddenly it was dawn, and the cat was stretching and yawning on his chest.

In the morning light, he boiled water in a small pot and poured half the water in a cup to make tea, and with the other half he made oats porridge. The cat wandered off and came back with a wood mouse, which she hunkered down to devour. He went to the stream to wash himself.

When Joben stood up, he saw through the trees that he was not far off from a group of standing stones. It made him shudder, although there was no feeling of dark or cold coming from them. He determined to avoid the stones and go back to the lane the way he came.

After eating and washing his small pot and cup, he broke camp and led the mare back to the pasture.

He walked to stretch his legs, leading the mare. The cat followed, hounded by the shadow.

\*\*\*

An hour down the lane, he saw a house to his right, with a small barn. He would have paid it little heed, but there was a handful of men gathered near the door. The way one glanced over, he felt he recognized one of the ragged roadsters he had tried to avoid the day before. He paid more attention. One of the men had a pry bar, and was working at the front door of the house.

Joben calmly tied the mare to a tree on the other side of the lane. From his cobbler's kit he drew a long-handled hammer for his right hand, and an awl for his left. Then he calmly walked toward the group around the front door.

They were aware of his approach and spread themselves out. The one with the pry bar came forward first. "State your business," said the one who seemed the group's leader. He smiled through teeth that were half gold. He wore a stained and ratty velvet coat that clearly wasn't made for him. His body was lean and tense.

"My business is making sure you don't break into that house," Joben stated.

"You gonna take us all on? It's all or nothing, brother." He smiled viciously and attacked suddenly.

Joben's hammer was long, and his arms thick. Still, he wasn't a fighting man. He dodged the pry bar and swung the hammer. He felt a kick from behind, and suddenly he was on the ground. Kicks came from all directions, but he put the awl to work, and it was sharp. The hammer met a kneecap and the shriek caused the group to jump back, startled.

Joben took the opening to jump to his feet, and wasted not a moment moving in on young Gold Teeth. He blocked a blow with the hammer and stabbed with the awl. The awl missed and he swung away, swinging the hammer towards the heads of the others. He felt more than heard Gold Teeth stepping up behind him and ducked as he swung the hammer at the young man's ankles. Then Gold Teeth was rolling on the ground, growling with pain. Joben turned to the others. There were only two left, and they were afraid now. He stepped towards them and they backed off.

The pry bar broke his ribs with a sickening sound as he turned back, and his turn became him collapsing on himself. "Got you now, daddy, don't I? Don't I?" The gold-toothed man lifted the bar to bring it down on Joben's head. Joben tried to scramble out of his reach, but then the pry bar was falling from useless hands. An arrow protruded from Gold Teeth's neck. Shocked, he tried to speak. Blood streamed down the filthy velvet. He grasped the feathered end of the arrow and pulled. Joben heard the arrow snap as it broke, and then blood was coming in spurts. These slowed as the young man crumpled to the ground.

"Gasper! Gasper!" One of the other men cried, but *pop* silenced him and he too fell to the ground, an arrow protruding from his mouth. The other man fell to his knees, crying for mercy. A third arrow answered his cries.

Joben turned to the house. The door was open, now, and an old woman stood, nocking another arrow. He stood silent, slowly raising his hands into the air.

Finally she spoke. "Are you the 'brother' he was referring to?"

"Yes, mother. P-peace to you." The tip of the arrow had swung towards him as he spoke, but she didn't draw.

"Who are you and why are you in my yard, fighting with thieves?"

"I was a-passing by. I saw men, prying at the door. I thought I ought to intervene."

"Who are you, and where from?"

"I'm a cobbler, mother. Joben Falat, from Mourmenir. Just traveling by."

The arrow pointed at his feet, now. There was something odd about her gaze, like she was looking past him. The mare snorted in the silence, trying to reach the grass at the foot of the tree where she was tied.

"Are you hurt, Joben Falat?"

"Only when I breathe, mother." He lifted his shirt. The day had been warm, and he wore just one. "One got me in the ribs with an iron."

"You're traveling alone?"

"Aye, just the mare and myself. And the cat." He wondered where the cat had got to, when it came meowing up the walk, and wound around his legs.

"A cat?" The old woman smiled and dropped the arrow she was holding back in the quiver on her shoulder. She hung the bow and quiver from a peg on the house and came off the doorstone. As she approached him, he now clearly saw the milky irises searching the bright day. To his surprise, she came near, grabbed his shoulders, and put her ear to his chest. She listened, then stood.

"Seeing as you took your life in hands for my sake, bring the horse. And the cat. I'll see what I can do to tend to those ribs. Sounds like your lungs are okay, but you never know." She turned toward the house and went inside.

Joben fetched the mare and led her up the walk. Every breath was a red-hot poker in his chest, below his right arm. The old woman reappeared with a basket over one arm and a bowl of goat milk in the other, which she put down for the cat. She waved toward the barn. "Let's put the mare in the paddock for now. There's a lean-to left of the barn. Lay down in the straw and let's see to you."

Joben did so, creaking and groaning. He rolled to his back, lifting the shirt, exposing the redness and swelling. "Put my hand where you're hurt."

He took her hand and laid it on his side. She probed gently, causing him to suppress his whimpers. Unmoved, she pressed on a spot. He could hear a slight crunching sound and gasped, biting back a curse. She just nodded. From the basket at her side, she drew a stoneware pot with a softwood cork for a lid. She opened it and took a couple of fingers' worth of a balm from within. He smelled lavender, clove, and something bitter. She smoothed it liberally on and around the bruised and swelling area. She took a folded cloth and laid it over the injury.

"Just rest there for the night. We don't want a broken rib gouging you up inside. I'll get your things. The mare, what's her name?"

"Uh… Shar. Shar's her name."

She put the basket inside the house and called the mare to her. Shar wouldn't come, so she went to the side of the barn and pulled some grass that grew there. Now, the mare came, and the woman tied her to the fence. She proceeded by feel to unpack his heavy, clunking kit, rolls of leather, blanket, and saddlebags, and laid them nearby in the lean-to. Then she removed the saddle and put it on the railing that composed the lean-to's outer wall. Finally, she came back with the bridle and laid it over the saddle.

"The boy will see to the mare when he brings our own horse back. I'm going to get you some tea."

She bustled back into the house and returned sometime later with a cup of bitter tea, some honey to mask the bitterness. Joben recognized the willow bark flavor and drank it gratefully. Then he laid back. He heard her dragging the bodies of the men behind the barn and when he attempted to rise to help her, whimpered loudly enough that she yelled at him to stay put. He was impressed, even a little intimidated, by the old powerhouse and gladly passed out in the warm, westering sun.

***

Joben awoke when a chill stole across his body and started trying to figure out how he was going to get up to empty his bladder, and where he should do that. It was dusk. The last thing he needed was to trip over something in the dark and fall, so he'd better get at it now.

Coming back from the other side of the barn, he decided he needed to stretch his legs for a few minutes. He walked around the yard a few times. There was light in the house now and smoke from the chimney, and voices other than the old woman's.

Presently the door banged open, and two children tumbled out. "Peace to you!" They called to him and he returned the greeting. The boy hobbled to the paddock, which Joben's mare now shared with a grey gelding. He led them both the barn, chattering happily with them. The girl was gathering firewood from the stack near the door.

The door opened again, and a middle-aged woman emerged. Her eyes found him. "I'm glad you're up. Come inside for supper when you're ready."

"Thank you kindly. Where can I wash my hands?"

She gestured towards the well. He moved towards it, dreading pulling the bucket up, but thankfully, it was full and sat to the side. There was a wood bowl to scoop with, and a sliver of soap. He washed his hands, and then his face and neck. Then he drank two full dippers of the sweet well water.

The boy appeared, and did pretty much everything Joben had just done, if not so thoroughly. Then the girl, whose ablutions seemed far more attentive. The boy turned to him, swiping his sleeves across his dripping face. "Gama says you fought with some men who tried to break into the house! We were in the woods! We have so many things to tell Gama! What's your name, sir?"

"Joben. What is yours?"

"Finder. Are you coming in the house for supper? I'm starving! I mean, not like I used to be, but a fellow does get used to eating regular after a while."

\*\*\*

As was the custom, Joben paused at the woodpile to collect a few pieces to bring into the house, helping to warm it. He managed to keep the few pieces away from the injury. He paused at the doorway to hullo the house and was invited in and offered a chair at the table. For a few minutes the women and the boy bustled around, and then they sat to the meal.

The old woman spoke. "Brother of light, bless us."

"And those that have none," they responded.

The boy began to prattle straight away, but the older woman silenced him with a look. "Eat well first. You need it and so does our guest."

"Joben Falat, cobbler, from Mourmenir."

"Lylaba Davey. This is Gama Davey, Onna, and Finder."

"And Ba!" cried out Finder, pointing to the dog who sat near the table, looking hopeful.

"If we're going to include the animals, there's Shar, my horse, and Smoke, the cat. Although I'm not sure where she's got to. But Mistress Davey gave her milk, so she'll be back for more, I'm sure."

There was quiet for a few minutes while they ate the hot stew and bread. Joben could cook for himself, but since his wife's death usually had a neighborhood cookhouse send a plate over for his supper. He hadn't realized how much he missed a hot, home-cooked meal. His eyes watered, and in the blur he could almost imagine Anaba and their adopted children around the table. *Stop it,* he told himself. He took the cloth napkin, and dabbing his mouth quickly wiped his eyes as well. He ran his hand over his brown beard and cleared his throat.

He wanted to ask what had become of the bodies of the thieves but decided against it. The children's faces were shining with excitement and he already knew the boy was bursting to talk on some event of the day. He didn't want to dampen their joy. Finder ate quickly, then sat staring obliquely at Lylaba, who added a slice of bread to his plate. He tore into it as he had the first. Joben observed that Finder was likely not Lylaba's son, but the girl was surely her daughter. The boy lacked the freckles and light hair the women shared; his skin was more olive, like Joben's own. Suddenly he realized that he had seen the boy before.

"Are you from Turla?"

The boy looked at him from under heavy brows. "Yes, sir."

Onna piped up. "He can't remember what his parents called him, because they died and he lived in the barn with the people in Turla. They just called him Boy. But we started calling him Finder." She smiled as if that was all as it should be, but Finder wasn't eating the bread anymore, just shredding it onto the plate. Suddenly his face brightened.

"You fixed my shoes for free! And gave me a belt for my trousers!" Joben nodded. The "shoes" could hardly even be called that, being the legacy of someone far larger and who had had all the good out of them years before. Joben had carved the sole shorter and sewn the flapping upper down, slathering the whole thing heavily in grease to keep out the snow, and given him a strip of hide to tie the rags he wore about his lower bits up so they weren't continually falling. He had also given him his old jacket and slipped a handful of almonds in the pocket. But he didn't mention that. It had been winter and he was at the house to buy pelts. From the condition of the boy's hands, it was clear who had been set the task of scraping and washing them with lye soap. He had offered to buy the boy, in fact, but was refused. Anaba would have fought harder for him.

He found he couldn't speak, and the conversation lulled for a moment. But then Lylaba rose to carry her plate to the sideboard, deftly lifting his own from his place. The children carried theirs and Gama's to the sideboard. Lylaba was pouring water from the kettle into a basin. She soaped a rag and quickly washed the wood bowls and plates, then the iron spoons and knives, and rinsed and set them to dry on a cloth on the sideboard. Meanwhile Onna wiped the table clean and set out a wooden cup for each of them. She filled the pitcher from the urn, and put it on the table.

Then everyone was seated again, and Gama said to Finder, "Now you can tell me."

\*\*\*

They had breakfasted and cleaned up, had stacked wood by the fireplace for Gama's use, and filled the urn, and Finder was just bursting to go. Lylaba had looked at him limping around and told him to bring out Feef. "Why do we need the horse?" he asked.

"Don't you think horses like adventures too?" He smiled and hopped to the barn, returning with the horse, saddled with the worn-out old thing the seller of the horse had given her for free as the tree was cracked and she had had to mend it. She cinched it tighter and put some dried berries and fresh bread in a saddlebag. Then she told Finder to climb on and helped shove him up to the saddle. He and Onna had been riding Feef a little each day, as he was a cart horse and not much used to being ridden, although he did not object. He actually did seem to be happy to be out on an adventure. *Me too, pal,* thought Lylaba. She hadn't had many of those in recent years.

Onna happily led the way, although Lylaba was reasonably sure of finding it on her own. The stones stood on a small rise in the woods. Although the story said it had been a prairie once, and the Plainwood was flat for miles around, perhaps the hill had grown over time. Or maybe they were just stories.

It was less than an hour before they reached the knoll crowned with a ring of stones several times taller than a grown woman. Onna and Finder ran around and through the stones, weaving in and out. Lylaba stood and surveyed. The gaps between them were uneven. Some were almost joined by the growth of vines and mosses; while to the south, two stood many yards apart. From one side of the circle to the other, it was perhaps thirty paces. A few trees grew inside the circle, their yellow leaves quivering in the breeze, squirrels and birds making their homes there. Under one such tree, Lylaba found owl pellets. She called the children over, crumbling one so they could see the tiny bones and teeth of little creatures, birds and mice. Onna picked them over with fascination, arranging the tiny bones and guessing what they were.

"Is it their poop?" Finder had asked. Lylaba laughed.

Onna replied, "No, silly, the owls cough them up. From their mouths."

"You mean their *beaks*, silly."

Then they were off, chasing each other again and calling each other silly this and silly that and so on. Meanwhile, Lylaba walked slowly around each stone. They were no different than she remembered. Each was three to four times human height, a beautiful dark brown, almost black. That is, where they weren't covered with bright mosses and tiny mushrooms and pale lichens, with vines and stonecrops and even salamanders. She put her hand to one, and it was as she recalled — while it looked like rock, it wasn't rock-hard, somehow.

The last time she had been here, she realized, Onna hadn't even been born. She had come out here with Gama. She hadn't yet killed her husband.

By the time she had made a circuit of the stones, the children came running, begging for the berries and bread.

They sat down to eat, smearing the bread with fresh goat cheese and studding it with the dried berries. She had filled their water bottle at the stream, and they drank that off. Then the children laid back and talked quietly. The afternoon sun was warm, and they all drifted off to sleep, even Lylaba.

But her nap was troubled by a feeling of being watched. Her eyes opened suddenly and she sat up. She looked around, and then upwards. Near the top of the stone nearest, there was a glint. She stood and drew nearer. Yes, in a brow-like recess, there were deep, dark orbs, like obsidian nodules a trader had once shown her.

Unblinking.

Patient.

Wise.

Lylaba could only stare back.

What had she expected? Was she going to ask questions? Get them to help? The stone loomed over her.

"Brother of Brightness, protect us," she whispered.

There was silence for a long, long moment.

Then the stone began to vibrate. The vibration became a rumble. Yet it was deep, not threatening, like the rumbling of the river cows she had seen as a girl. It even made her want to reach out, as she had reached into the water and touched the river calf, whose friendly face had bobbed above the surface and met her gaze with deep, dark eyes. The moss on the standing stone shivered and the head of it seemed to bow down slightly.

A mouth opened and an exhalation stirred her hair. The breath was that of cold stones and green mosses and cut wood, a fragrance she knew well. "Bright Brother," she whispered.

The breath became a deep yet sibilant voice.

"Ssssseeeek thhhe ssssiiiissssssterrrrrr...."

The eyes gleamed at her as the dark head slowly became erect once more. The quivering ceased, and there was again silence.

"Mama?"

Lylaba turned to find Onna and Finder both awake, both faces filled with wonderment.

"It's looking at us, see?" Finder jumped up and ran to the stone, bobbing up and down and pointing. Onna came and stood beside Lylaba and took her hand. They gazed upon the dark eyes, which were becoming darker. It was soon almost difficult to think of them as seeing.

Had it really happened? Had the stone *spoken* to her?

The children ran off and played around the stones for another hour or so. Lylaba peered at them, one by one. But there was no response, and the eyes were dark and closed.

***

"The stones looked at you?" said Joben. He looked to Lylaba for confirmation, but she was lost in her own thoughts. There was quiet for a moment. The fire collapsed in the fireplace, sending a spray of sparks up the chimney. Finder suppressed a yawn, worn out from excitement.

Gama nodded. "Finder, you told the story well. There's a story about why the stones are open toward the south. But that's a tale for another night, children. Time for sleeping."

Lylaba snapped out of her revery and looked at Joben. "How are your ribs?"

"I'll do, thank you." He rose, gingerly, and stepped away from the table. He could feel stiffness settling in and wondered when he'd be able to swing a hammer again. He moved toward the door. Lylaba said, "I'll be out in a minute. I want a word."

He nodded and made his way to the lean-to. Suddenly she was there, with an old mattress tick over her arms. She kicked the straw about in the lean-to and laid the tick on it.

She had also brought an extra blanket. "Nights are cool, now. The warmer you are the less stiff you'll be."

"I thank you kindly, Lylaba."

She was frowning. "There's a bit more to the story of today. While the children were asleep, the stone said something to me." She hesitated, he frowned. "'Seek the sister.'"

"It spoke that to you?"

"Aye, it did. As I'm standing here."

"'Seek the sister'."

"I suppose I had just said, 'Bright Brother'."

"And the 'sister'..."

"Well, that's it, isn't it. A 'sister' of Brightness?"

"Or something else entirely."

They stood in silence. A few crickets whirred sleepily, and the horses shifted in their stall. An owl screeched. Lylaba shook her head. "Rest well tonight. Brother of Brightness heal you." She turned toward the house.

"Brother of Brightness, bless you."

The westering white moon cast her shadow behind her and shone translucent through the hem of her tunic. He noted the outline of her body, the shoulder-length honey-colored hair, and then felt surprised at himself. He hadn't looked at a woman as a woman for a long time. Her shoulders were strong, but her waist and hips womanly. He turned toward the lean-to, worked himself down on the tick, and wrapped the blankets around him.

He would have chuckled then, if it wouldn't have pained him so badly, that he hadn't given a thought to a shoe, or a hobnail, or the quality of rawhide, for most of a day. Why had he lingered so long in the shop, when the shadow glowered over him and there wasn't even custom to busy him? He had passed the point of grieving for Anaba many seasons ago. It was good to have a new chapter in his book, even if a short one, while he healed before moving on.

He relaxed and found a position even more comfortable, with room to breathe without too much pain. Speaking a word of gratitude into the night for that and for the warmth stealing over his limbs, he found himself wondering about what the stone had supposedly spoken to Lylaba. Could she have imagined it? She said they had all dozed off. But the idea of her being carried away by imagination seemed very much in opposition to her personality, which seemed as imaginative as a block of wood from her shop.

That caught him by surprise, and he did chuckle, and then moan in agony. But the pain was worth it. He lay with his shoulders shaking, and a tear slipped down his temple into the brown hair above his ear. As much as it hurt his ribs, he hadn't laughed like that for an age, and it felt good. He slept as well as might be expected after that.

Chapter 3

When I came out of the house the following morning, Joben was greasing the old saddle and mending a stitch here and there. I was impressed he had hauled it out of the barn by himself, in his condition. It hung over the railing. I was painfully conscious of the stitches I had used when I had repaired the saddle tree. Sewing was never my strong suit. Making conversation, I asked what kind of grease he used, and he told me he boiled his own from kine foot bones, and clary sage. I asked what the clary sage was for.

"My wife told me it was to make the leather bitter, so the rats'd leave off. But I think she wanted something to make it smell better. I added the lavender as a sort of joke, but then she liked to so well, I kept it up." He didn't need to add the "after she died" part. "If I have to use it, I wind up wearing it. I might as well like it." Later when I passed his leather apron laid over the railing, I noticed the herbal scents there.

Some days passed like this. Joben had become part of the rhythm of our lives. I was thinking of the colder nights and of partitioning him off a room somewhere, but I didn't know if he would stick around long enough. There was room behind the chimney piece, large enough for a narrow bed and a chest. He could work his cobblery in my shop... I wondered at myself, thinking like this, and dismissed it out of hand.

And there was that damn shadow, lurking in the south, growing day by day. Occasionally the bracing odor of falling leaves and harvested fields was tainted with a foul exhalation and a chill in the air like that of a crypt.

The king, I had heard, had sent more delegations. Wizards, mages, priests. All had hung about and plied their trades for some days and gone back to Dastenn again. The runners and outgrowths were low to the ground now—for I had ridden Shar to look upon them myself one day—but no less foul. They rose higher here and there, but not as high as the knoll where the original stone had stood, now a no-man's-land almost a mile off. That now rose yet higher, thrusting its murk up against the innocent sky. Abandoned houses stood here and there, but the trees and all kinds of plants were bare and blasted. There was speculation about what might happen when the blight reached the river. As I crossed the river on the way home, I gazed down and imagined the blackness and what it would likely do to the fishes and the shimmering eels and the river cows. To the deer and livestock who drank from it. To the children of Sheaf. Even some in Sheaf were leaving, some stopping at the house to say goodbye.

When we went to the house of the Brightness on the next worship day, it was half empty. The small circular temple, whitewashed within, with its soaring conical roof of bleached thatch, amplified the voices of the seekers, and if I closed my eyes I could almost imagine it full of white-clad men, women, and children. When we sang the Parting Hymn, there wasn't a dry eye.

> One Brightness shines within us,
> Filled we are, and full we be
> Of grace the Brother brought us
> Brightness in you, and Brightness in me.
> Come together, seekers all,
> We have heard the Bright One's call.
> Now to part but for a time,
> Let us go forth now to shine.

Sadly we stood about outside after the rite. Furtive glances flicked toward the lurking dark south. The villages that way had emptied, and half of Sheaf. I caught conversations all around.

"Dastenn? But everyone is going there. Surely..."

"It's likely there's not a chicken coop left empty to sleep in."

"Nor work to be had."

"The price of oats..."

"It could reach the river by Spring. And then what?"

"The salmon run…"

"My uncle Campo…"

That caught my ear, and I moved in the direction of the voice. "… he sent a message back, he found my cousins in Till. He says it's a small house, but they're willing to let us stay until we find our own place." The young man talking was not from Sheaf, by his slight twang. "I thought Sheaf would be safe, but the blight doesn't stop for anything. It's coming…"

I was glad to hear that the old man had found a place to land, and having nothing to add, I drifted away, found the kids and Joben and Gama, and we walked home.

***

Back at home, I realized for the first time, looking around, that the likelihood of my little family living out our days here, seeing Onna grow to maturity, and even Finder, and… well, I was getting used to having Joben around but I had no claim on him. If people were leaving Sheaf, who would buy my woodworking services? Where would we get food?

I know that at dinner I was distracted. It was Gama who brought it up. "How long are we going to put off deciding what to do?"

Silence.

I looked at the kids. They rose, and took our plates to the sideboard, and went about washing them. "Let's get some fresh air," I said, looking meaningfully first at Gama, then Joben. Gama, Joben, and I rose and went out into the yard.

The last dusk was fading from the west. It lingered long because of the ocean that lay just over the horizon in that direction. I had been there once, as a child. I still had a shell they called a whelk, on the sill of the window of the marriage bedroom. Its rosy inside seemed harder and stronger than the delicate spokes of the rim. Somehow I had protected it from my husband, who had a way of breaking fragile things. But I hadn't been one of them.

But right now, I did feel breakable. This was my home, the only one I had ever known. There was little question that it would become a blasted waste, hard and lifeless, just as Joben's had. I felt a rush of compassion for the man, who had not complained although he had lost his family, his home, and even temporarily, his trade... although his strength returned day by day, Gama would not yet allow him to use his hammer. But that day would soon come. Even that tenuous connection felt like breakage, thinking of him going off on Shar one morning.

"I've been remembering," said Gama. She cleared her throat. "I wanted to be sure I remembered it aright. There's a story that would bear telling."

Joben and I waited.

***

Sintramalala and Mehanaba had stood long in the circle, swaying among the trees their long, steady motion while the seasons passed over in waves, green and brown and white and green again. There were others, and some say they were called Maral, Ounaba, Jobenoben, Tenjeh, and Faniraba. Jobenoben and Maral were a pair, and had parented many of the younger Stone Folk, but the rest were unpaired.

Tenjeh and Ounaba had walked within sight of one another for a thousand years, but even then, the way of the Stone Folk loving each other and having families was fading to memory. When they came to the circle, they stood beside Mehanaba, for he and Ounaba were siblings. Across the circle was Sintramalala, Jobenoben, Maral, and Faniraba. And Faniraba was lovely to look upon.

Ounaba wanted the others to look upon what she and Tenjeh shared and admire it. She stood closer to Tenjeh than the rest to each other. As they stood long, swaying their slow dance, Tenjeh's eyes met Faniraba's. Long they looked upon one another, through drought and storm, golden autumns and sweet springs. It was long before Ounaba looked and knew that she had lost Tenjeh's heart. He and she would not walk together more, for he was drawn to Faniraba.

By the time she knew what she would do, the dance had all but ceased. Sintramalala and the others were almost lost under the growth of moss and lichen, garments they did not shrug off. Faniraba was steady within the circle of peace; there was no desire in her. But Tenjeh no longer gazed upon Ounaba as he once had. Ounaba began to turn away from the circle, then to move away.

Slowly, slowly she made her way south, so that she could gaze upon the sun and not feel so alone, although to her it swooped through the sky dragging the stars and the red moon and the white in its wake until it returned to outshine them all. Ounaba knew Faniraba outshone her, had dragged the splendor of Tenjeh's soul in her wake. She kept moving, over hills and streams, until at last she slowed, and at a promontory, she turned to see if any in the circle had marked her departure. But the trees had grown so high, she could no longer see them. And so, alone she stood for a long, long time. When others joined her in a circle, she hardly knew it. She barely marked their presence, having thought only for Tenjeh and what she had lost, and gazing north, away from the circle she was now part of. Over the years, she bowed, and that was how she was known to our kind, as the Bowed Stone.

\*\*\*

"Bowed Stone?" said Joben. Gama nodded. "Mourmenir."

I said, "Mourmenir? I thought that meant 'broken stone'".

"My wife's father told me how in the old way of speaking, 'broken' and 'bowed' were the same word. Or rather, they sounded so close, only one who spoke that tongue would hear the difference. His grandfather was one of the last who purely spoke it. The village was named for the stone circle that was on the hill about a mile behind my shop. My wife… that is, I owned a field that ran right to its foot. Mourmenir was where the shadow began."

After a moment, the pieces fit together in my mind and I said, "Sister."

The door banged open then, Onna and Finder and the dog tumbling out, laughing as always since Finder had come along. They were about pulling water from the well and closing up the barn for the night. I shivered as the cold night air came down. It looked like rain; while we had talked, a veil had moved across the countless stars. I told Joben to bring the tick and blankets into the house, and we would find room for him. He looked so grateful I had to turn my eyes away after a moment.

Gama nodded, then said, "We haven't decided anything."

"Not everything, Gama. But some things." Her gaze followed mine toward Joben, who was collecting some of his things. I turned towards the house to arrange a space for him in the nook behind the chimney piece where we stored the winter things. The cat had already made it her own, which was good on account of mice.

***

I forgot to mention that it wasn't only people that made up the exodus. Herds of deer, forest hares, foxes, even ferrets and badgers, snakes and bobcats could be seen picking their frightened way through the surrounding trees. Even the water deer left the river and crept along the creek. We hunted and ate plenty of meat and dried it for the winter. I was surprised at how guilty I felt at our opportunity. The barn was tacked with pelts drying in the sun, and Finder helped Joben brain and scrape them, and afterward I saw Joben rubbing his and Finder's hands with balm. Flocks of birds darkened the sun at times, and butterflies beat their gentle paths through the woods. All headed north, although it was autumn. It was all wrong.

There was but a trickle of folk passing by at this point, hushed and hurried. None wanted to speak of the state of things in the south.

Winter set in rather suddenly. One day it was crisp autumn, and the next morning the ground was white. Sleet made the outdoors distinctly unappealing. We all found something to do indoors. Joben was showing Finder how to sew himself a cap with the fur inside. He sewed us each rabbit fur socks and mitts. Gama had finally approved that he use a hammer, but there wasn't much work to be done on our shoes, and only a few people had heard that a cobbler was staying with us, although I let it be known at the House of Brightness. We settled in, having heard that the blight had ceased to spread with the sudden freeze.

The snows were deep for many weeks. The sad parade of refugees all but ceased. Finder was ill with a fever, and we almost lost him. When his fever broke, I sat by his bed and told him he was our Finder now, and I was his Mama, and he need not ever trouble his mind on that account. He started crying and I lay down next to him and held him close for a long time, until he slept. It was a bitter cold night and I begrudgingly left the narrow cot that was his—it was uncomfortably small for two—and bid Ba lay down on the foot of the bed. When I looked in on him later, the dog had insinuated himself alongside Finder, whose arm was draped over him.

On the way across the house, after stoking the fire, I looked to the nook that was Joben's sleeping place. He happened to be peeking out. I stopped and we looked at one another for a long moment.

"How's Finder?"

"He'll do," I said. "He'll be okay." I smiled because I was genuinely happy that I had thought to tell Finder what I had. Joben smiled and nodded.

"Thank the Bright One," he murmured with feeling.

Then we had nothing more that needed saying, but we both stood there, our smiles changing into something else. I wasn't really surprised at what I felt inside, but I also knew the time was not yet ripe. Joben must also have known, for he said "Brother of Brightness give you rest," and turned away, still smiling a little.

***

The shortest day of the year, there was an almost holy quiet over the world. We went to the temple deep in the Longest Night, long before dawn, having stayed up eating our best dishes, giving each other gifts, and telling stories and singing songs. We were each bearing lanterns and carrying many candles which we lit once we arrived. The white walls reflected the light and the House became warm from all of the flames and bodies. Most of the children were asleep on blankets along the wall. It didn't seem half-empty that night as we sang songs about knowing that the light would return to us and grow brighter from that night forward, and warm the earth and wake it, and cause the green and growing things to smile from the land, and the forests would be filled with singing and the barks of deer again. For what was more reliable than the cycles of the heavens? No matter what fire or flood or plague or war might do to us here below, the sun and the moons, the slow red moon and the swift white moon, would continue their transits. The Brightness is faithful, the Brightness is true.

Dawn came late that winter morning. We emerged from the temple when the timekeepers said the moment was approaching, when the sun—the Messenger of the Brightness—would soon show face, bearing witness to our hopes. We came forth into the frozen morning, expecting at least the first blush of dawn. But it was long we waited in the dark before the sun climbed suddenly above the shadow. For it had grown.

Some days later a thaw came. Though the sun rose late, it was hot and bright, and the snows revealed patches of ground on the exposed places. It was then we realized that it was too late.

Chapter 4

Joben was first out on the third morning of the thaw. His ribs had mended well, and he wanted to split plenty of wood. As he moved around the yard, he quickly removed his scarf and fur cap. As the sun brightened the sky, he took a break from splitting and stacking to let the horses out of the barn.

There was a place Shar and Feef would like to stand because the sun shone strong there. But as the two of them trotted about, nervously snorting, Joben noticed that they avoided that end of the paddock. He moved over closer to see what was spooking them.

His heart skipped a beat.

The ground was black, and stinking. It seemed to smolder, and there was a hissing sound. He had seen that before.

He almost ran back to the barn, and when he called the horses, they came willingly to go back inside. He stood outside in the wintry quiet. Now that he had heard the griping sound that had emanated from the blighted spot in the paddock, he recognized that it was coming from other places. From far off, a voice screamed, and others shouted. A child wailed. Dogs barked.

He strode to the house and through the door. Gama looked, and seeing Joben's stricken face, stopped where she was, a stack of wooden bowls in her arms.

"Bright Brother," she gasped. "Has it..."

He swallowed, but it felt like swallowing sand. "It's here. In the paddock. Who knows where else, under the snow? Lylaba!"

She emerged from the sleeping rooms. Joben almost shouted, "No one should leave the house. There is blight outside. We've been here all winter and it's been growing all the while and we didn't see it."

"The snow. And the trees would be bare anyway."

They heard voices all morning as people from Sheaf hurried by — many of them. There was a knock on the door. It was Marna, a woman Lylaba had been friendly with for many years. Lylaba invited her in.

"I cannot linger, Lylaba, but I wanted to be sure you know..."

"Joben here just found it outside."

"The river's still frozen over, but the blight has crossed it. We met in the wee hours in town and decided we all needed to leave, but that we can't use the road that follows the river. This road goes more directly west. What will you do?"

"We haven't figured it out yet."

Marna put a mittened hand to Lylaba's shoulder. "I need to go, they're waiting." She hugged Lylaba tight. "Peace to you, Lylaba."

"Brother of Brightness, protect you," Lylaba said hollowly, and let her friend out the door, watching her go down the walk to where her family awaited. She returned their wave as they turned to leave.

They all stood in silence for a few moments, even the children, who had emerged from the sleeping rooms.

"We won't make good plans on empty stomachs," declared Gama, moving to place the wooden bowls on the table. "That blight isn't going to swallow us in the house, is it."

They ate porridge with stewed dried apples and the last of last year's maple sugar, and slices of hard cheese, and no one seemed to know what to do next.

Joben's brow was furrowed. He suddenly put his hand on his forehead, his eyes closed. Lylaba started to ask if he was well, but he held a finger up, as if stalling for time. Then he said, "The blight won't swallow us in the house, will it."

Gama stared at Joben, but Lylaba's breath caught. "When I rode out to see it, I saw houses still standing. Nothing living, but the houses weren't changed."

Joben looked at Lylaba. "Wooden shoes. Have you ever made them?"

"Aye, for a few stone workers, farmers, and the like. Some of them like the protection."

"The blight burned my leather shoes. But it doesn't seem to affect wood."

"They're time consuming to carve out and get a good fit."

"We could help," said Onna.

"Yes, your small hands would do well carving the insides out. I've got the tools. We'd need green wood as it's too hard to carve dry."

"What if only the sole were wood, and the top part was leather?" said Finder. They all looked at him.

"Clever Finder! Why not? I could make those much faster. But maybe have a bit of a wood cover in front. Or all around. But having it be open for carving out would make it a quicker process."

Gama was bringing a sheet of parchment and a charcoal pencil. They sketched out how the clog-soled boots would be constructed. Lylaba and Onna went to the barn to hunt up the tools. There were three alder trees she had skidded from the woods during the freeze. She sawed a round, and split it into chunks. The first was in her bench vice and chips were flying from her chisel before the noon meal. In the afternoon, Onna was carving the inner surface of a pair to fit Joben's feet. By supper, he had cut the rawhide to fit. He wanted to nail the uppers on right away, but Lylaba said they needed to dry for a fortnight, and not by the fire, which could split them. They argued about it. Finally they agreed that since they didn't know what would happen, and this was a trial pair, he would go ahead and finish them and try them out in the morning, so they would know if it worked or not.

Finder was pale and upset at dinner. Onna asked him what the matter was. He just shook his head. Finally he blurted, "Lylaba and Joben were fighting! It scared me and is Joben going to go away now?" He burst into tears.

Onna put her arms around him.

Joben looked at Lylaba. "I'm sorry we quarreled."

"As am I."

Joben looked at Finder, whose face was constricted and wet with tears. "I am sorry we frightened you, Finder. We are all scared. We are trying to figure out what to do. As long as it's okay with Lylaba, I don't want to leave." He looked at her.

Lylaba's heart squeezed into her throat. She also looked at Finder. "I don't want Joben to leave." She looked suddenly at Joben. "Please don't leave." Her eyes blurred with tears.

He sat up straight. "Never." His hand found hers, and she found she couldn't breathe for a moment. She sniffed, and nodded.

"Nobody's leaving, unless we all leave together."

\*\*\*

Joben was up for hours after, finishing the half-wood, half-leather boots. Then he slipped rabbit fur socks on his feet and the boots, trying them on. He was satisfied, and greased them all over before going to rest on the tick behind the chimney piece.

In the morning, he pulled them on to go to the privy. They kept the wet from the thawing snow out, and although the hard wood sole was hard to get used to, Joben thought they worked. Before going back to the house, he entered the paddock, and walked through the slush to the black patch at the end. He stopped and looked at it with trepidation. Then he tenuously stepped one foot on the fouled earth.

Nothing happened.

He stepped on with both feet, and stood. His feet felt warm, and there was no burning odor as there had been when he had kicked a knurl of the blight so many months ago. Satisfied, he returned to the house. After the morning meal, he laid out leather for more uppers, while Lylaba worked on a pair of soles for herself.

\*\*\*

They were granted a reprieve when two feet of snow fell and covered everything. The temperature dropped and the snow looked like staying for a while.

The experimental pair did not crack, but the damp of the wood crept in and made Joben's feet cold, so they let the rest of the soles dry before finishing the work. After a fortnight, Joben began forming the uppers to the lowers. He added a layer of cow skin to cover the wood, not sewn in, but removable to dry if needed. They all began wearing them about the place to break them in and become accustomed to the clunky, solid feel of them. One day Lylaba looked at the remaining goat that was foraging about. Then at Shar and Feef. Could she make wooden horseshoes? By evening she had made a set of ironwood horseshoes and partially sized them to Feef's hooves.

But in the morning she wondered if she had wasted her energy. Maybe iron would resist the blight just as much as wood. What was worrying, though, was either material left the frog, the soft portion of the hoof exposed. If she made the shoes solid, that might solve that problem, but it would be difficult to clean the area out. She went out to her shop after breakfast, and ended up throwing chunks of wood here and there, sketching abortive designs on wood with charcoal, consumed with the problem. The horses were lowing in the stalls because they were being kept in, for fear they would come into contact with the blight, and it preyed upon her anxieties. In the end, Lylaba split ash palings and pounded them through the snow and into the ground halfway across the paddock, and wattled them to make a fence. Then she let the horses into the reduced paddock. By then it was time for the noon meal. Joben came looking for her.

He saw the workshop a wreck, which was unlike her. She saw him glancing about, and began sorting and tidying almost frantically. But the big man was there, in the doorway, when she turned to leave the workshop. His arms closed about her and she collided woodenly with him, and then collapsed, her arms going around him in return.

"We'll figure this out."

Her hands became fists, gently thumping his shoulders for a moment, before relaxing again.

"We will." She sighed. Then they straightened and turned for the house.

\*\*\*

Winter had settled in, but despite the covering of snow, every time they left the safety of the house it was to walk with trepidation upon the treacherous ground. Joben accompanied Lylaba to cut hickory, more for something familiar to do than from hope that spring would bring orders for new plow beams or cattle yokes. But when the tree fell, it was black within and much of it simply shattered when it fell. The snows were deep, but she feared for Feef and quickly she and Joben returned her to the barn, leaving the ruined tree where it lay.

That evening Joben took blanks of ironwood and scribed Feef's hoof shapes on them. Lylaba and he argued again over the idea, but in the end she cut the shapes and that evening he fashioned boots for the horse. In the morning he put them on Feef, who stomped and nibbled at the leather, but Onna distracted him with carrots and in the end, he allowed himself to be led out of the barn for a few turns around the paddock, being talked to continually. Back in the barn, he acceded to having the boots taken off. Joben didn't like that snow fell into the tops of them, and Lylaba hunted up the gaiters her father used to tie around the old horse's lower legs when the snow was crusty and logs needed dragging from the woods. They were dried out and too large for Feef, but Joben managed to use them as a model to make gaiters that would work for the gelding. Over the next few days he repeated the process for Shar. Finder found the horses wearing boots an endless source for giggling.

When that was done, then Joben and Lylaba and Gama began to talk intently about the journey that seemed inevitable at this point. The road they must take was not suited to carts—especially in the winter, because it would be impossible to see what was under the snow and the trail was said to have subsided in many places. From the rafters, Lylaba pulled down two ash splint baskets designed to be worn on the back. Joben mended and oiled the straps. She showed Finder and Onna how to hammer ash wood to create splints, and she and Gama wove additional baskets—larger for Joben, and smaller for the children.

They sorted clothing, and packed food into parcels. They were eating their way through the few chickens until they were gone. That left just the goat. No one wanted to kill her, though, so it looked like she was going to come along.

"What about Ba? And Smoke?" Onna asked one morning, when we spoke of departing the follow day.

"I wouldn't worry about the dog and cat. I've seen Smoke hiss and spit at the black patch in the meadow, and back in Mourmenir, most animals steered well clear."

They were planning on having Feef pull a narrow travois for times when Gama or Finder needed rest, and to start their journey with plenty of extra food, and a carpet of pelts for sleeping on. Gama chose a few cooking implements and pots and dishes. They made bedrolls.

Joben made fur collars from the best of the fox pelts, even for Finder, who rubbed his face in the dusky fur over and over. He threw his arms around Joben, as did Onna.

"Why did you make us these wonderful collars, Joben? Is it because you love us?" We all laughed so hard, Finder hid his face in the fur again before laughing along with us. Joben squeezed his shoulder.

"Aye lad. I guess I do love you. All of you."

Finder slept that night with the fox collar bunched against his smiling face.

***

Joben rode to the village not far from Sheaf where two of his adopted children had lived, but both houses were still and empty. On the eldest's' house the door had been marked with charcoal: *Gone north.* He came home somber.

Finally, on a morning, they were ready to go. The horses were saddled and Feef rigged with the travois. The goat was tied to Shar's saddle. The house was closed and cold, the cat was closed in a basket on the travois, and everyone had their clog boots on—even the horses. They set off upon the road when the sun was just peeking above the shadow.

Chapter 5

They had gone but a few miles when they passed what appeared to be a fresh grave. The road was a wide trail, the passage of many feet and hooves having beat the snow and packed it down, and even the fresh snows had not effaced it. Some had passed even since that, two days since. There were shallow streams to be crossed, and fallen trees; although most of these had been moved, or the trail diverted around them. There was another grave, dirt and snow packed in a hasty mound, before they stopped for a bite of lunch. The sky became overcast. The days were still somewhat short, but it didn't seem they had come far at all before twilight fell and they made camp.

First, a fire. Thankfully there was a previous traveler's fire ring, and for the past hour they had collected sticks. Finder was fascinated by how much snow had to go in the pot to become enough boiling water to stew a few potatoes and onions and half-shriveled carrots, dried venison, and a handful of dried herbs. There was bread that had been hot that morning.

They laid down furs and blankets and covered themselves with the same. All were too tired for stories.

They woke to a fresh dusting of snow, and the horses shaking the snow off of their heads. All had removed their boots but kept them under the furs, but Finder had somehow kicked one of his out from underneath and he complained bitterly that it was cold. When they had drank tea and journey bread, they set out and within an hour he reported that his foot was warm again.

Lylaba walked in front, leading Feef, with Gama walking or riding as she was able. Finder walked with Onna, who led Shar. Joben took up the rear, the hatchet and a flaying knife in his belt.

By the end of the fourth day, it was clear that the journey was taking a toll on them all, especially on Gama and Finder. Both of them were riding more than walking. It was early afternoon when they came upon a well-worn trail leading up the right-hand bank, and they stopped while Joben went to inspect it. He came back saying this was a good place to spend the night.

It was a large, dry cavern. There was even some wood left from the last group that had stayed here. Joben and Lylaba spent a good hour hunting up as much wood as they could and they had soon had a fire roaring. Their boots were lined up near it, even the horses', and when they were dry, Joben set Finder to work oiling them, leather and wood. Ba curled up near him and Onna at the other side, watching the pot while Gama rested.

Suddenly Gama was on her feet, drawing her bow. Ba jumped to her feet and barked. The horses nickered and a small group of figures entered the cavern. Joben swore to himself that he ought to have been watching; he had not forgotten the young man with gold teeth and an iron bar. But Lylaba was greeting the newcomers, and clasping shoulders among them. He recognized Lylaba's friend, Marna. They came to the fire and sat down, thanking the Brightness that they had found rest and a fire already burning. Gama leaned the bow within reach against the cavern's wall and sat back down cross-legged.

Joben settled himself closer to the cave entrance. After the greetings and introductions took place, the new arrivals told their story.

They had left Sheaf a few days after the thaw that sent many of them on their way. They had made good time and had even seen afar off the bay into which the Deep River emptied. They knew Dastenn was only days away.

But the trail was mired in many places. They could see and smell the blackening blight coming through, although until then they ground had seemed as normal. It took longer and longer to work their way around such places and stay on snow. After a time, it became impossible.

They had arrived at a large, open field where the sun had melted all of the snow away from wet and mired ground. This ground was littered with dead of all kinds. Birds, people, beasts tame and wild. From this they had turned back. And they had just kept on going for lack of knowing what to do, where to go. Their food was running out. They had managed to stone a squirrel or two along the way. Lylaba added water and dried meat to the pot, but Joben saw that she was counting the pieces with her eyes, and looking at what they had left.

Joben spoke, finally. "There was another road that went toward the sea, a day's travel back. If I remember aright, that road goes down to the coast, to a road that runs north and south from Dastenn to the cities of the South."

Lylaba looked at him. "If that road does go down that way, we would have options after that. Dastenn, or south." Neither of them could confess to how hopeless either way seemed to them.

The next day, everyone rested again in the cavern. The trees were dripping, and around the entrance to the cavern as well. Marna's eldest son managed to bring down a small deer, so they ate well that evening, their fears of starvation staved off.

They all looked forward to leaving the next day, and dreaded it, but looking forward was better than giving up.

\*\*\*

One good thing that had come from the mass exodus was that in the places where the old road had washed out, people had industriously laid logs across, or dug away the landslides. The group moved together. Marna's family displayed no envy of the horses, although it was clear they anxiously wished for wood-soled boots once Lylaba had explained why they were wearing them. But they did not envy riding the travois as Gama often must now. Even horseback was too hard on her old hips, she said. The hammock-like seat was the most comfortable thing in the world, she insisted, and she was warm as toast on the sheepskin rug covering it.

They made a sad camp under a drizzling rain. No one slept well, although they were fairly well sheltered under an oilskin tarpaulin Marna's husband strung up. The rain did not soak them, but it worried them. By morning, many dark patches of exposed earth showed along the trail. Lylaba's group went first, and kept careful watch for the blight.

They arrived at the branching of the road before nooning and were surprised to meet a small party of persons there. The groups approached one another cautiously, but then Lylaba called out, "Campo?"

"Peace to you, Lyla is it?" She did not correct him. She swung down from Shar's back and clasped his arm.

"Peace to you, Campo. I heard you found your way to Till and found your people."

"Aye, I had word that more were coming, but they never arrived. I was hoping if I started along the road, we'd meet up. These are my grandchildren, Benbo, Shaw, and Faran." Three fine-looking young men nodded and greeted her. They were all armed with bows and long knives. Lylaba introduced her family, Joben, and Marna's family.

Lylaba told Campo how she had overheard some relative of his at the House of Brightness on the New Morning. "I didn't know him, but he spoke your name and it caught my ear."

"Aye, they arrived, but they said more were on their way. I don't suppose you saw a group of three, two women and one man?"

"We saw no one on our way from Sheaf, until we met with Marna coming back along the road." She and Marna related how the last couple of days had gone.

Joben had gone to check the horses' boots and returned to the group. The young man called Benbo asked about the boots and Joben started explaining them. While he did, he saw a faraway look come over Lylaba. He knew her well enough by now to recognize that she was thinking, hard.

One in Marna's group had a fire pot and decided to boil water for tea since they were stopped. The group collected around the small fire, although no one sat because of the snow. Joben looked at Lylaba, caught her attention, and cocked his head meaningfully. She stepped away from the circle and he went with her. "What are you thinking about?"

She stared down the road, the direction of Sheaf. Her mouth worked, her head shook slightly. Joben waited.

"I am thinking I need to go back."

"Have a word with the Stone Folk."

She looked at him. "Aye, that."

Then she looked at Gama, Onna, and Finder. Her face became more worried. Her grey eyes rested on his face. "What about them? I can't take them back, I can't just leave them here. Will you go with them, down to the sea?"

"And leave you? I should go. You go with your family. Somewhere safe. Let me go back to the Stone Folk."

"It was me they spoke to."

"I'm not letting you go back alone."

"You're not letting me?" She hissed. Her eyes were filled with fury.

Joben closed his eyes. "I'm sorry. It's not for me to let you or not let you. But I will go with you. Or without you. But I am going back. I have no idea what I'm in for, but we can't keep running away from this thing. I have a suspicion, Lylaba, that it's going to keep spreading to wherever we run until we're surrounded and there's nowhere to go. So if those stones can tell us anything at all that might stop it, we need to go and have a word with them."

She looked sadly at her family, who was now looking back at them, understanding that a decision was being made. Gama told the children to stay put, and she came over to them. They told her what they were talking about.

"We can go with Marna, follow Campo to wherever some place safe is to stay. We'll leave word wherever we go. You go and do what you must. Onna and Finder will be as safe with me as they will be anywhere." Despite her brave words, her eyes filled with tears. The children came by her, one on one side and one on the other.

Onna put on a brave face. "We'll take care of Gama, Mama. And Ba, and Smoke too." Finder was weeping.

"You said I was your own Finder, Mama." Lylaba pulled them all into an embrace.

She kissed Onna's two cheeks and held her face in her hands. "My beautiful girl, I know you will take good care of Onna and Finder for me, and we will find you again soon. Finder, you will always be my Finder, and Gama's, and Onna's Finder. Gama..." She ran out of words then, and just held her grandmother, feeling her strength and frailty beneath the woolens and fur.

Marna attempted to dissuade Lylaba. She couldn't understand what Lylaba was going to do, and when Lylaba tried to explain she stopped herself and told her, "Marna, I've always trusted you. Trust me. I *must* do this." Marna stared at her, unhappy, but nodded. "Brother of Brightness, protect you."

"Brother of Brightness protect us all."

The horses and the dog would go with Gama and the children. The cat was confined to her basket. While Lylaba packed a packbasket with a little food—they would stop at her house to resupply—Joben went to Campo and his grandsons.

He told them that even though Lylaba's family weren't his family, they could be sure he would come looking and move heaven and earth until he saw their faces. But if he found them well, they would be welcome to the mare, Shar, and all that was in his power to repay them. Campo looked him in the eye and said that none of that was necessary. He was only repaying the kindness Lylaba had shown him and that he would be sure to be listening for word. Marna assured him that they would not be far away either, if they could help it, especially keeping her eye on Onna as a pretty young girl among men.

Lylaba was telling Gama that Onna was welcome to use those few tools she had brought, in order to establish a new life wherever they went, and that Finder must continue his letters and be treated as Onna's brother, no matter what. She stopped herself. "As if you wouldn't know." She held the woman who had raised her up, and told her she loved her, and hefted the pack on her back. Campo handed her a belt with a sheaf that held his long knife. She hesitated, but then thanked him with a hand on his shoulder. With many more such goodbyes, it was midafternoon by the time she and Joben set off back east, while the horses and her family followed Campo down the road toward the sea, where they would go north to Till, not far south of Dastenn. Lylaba looked back to watch her daughter, and Finder, and grandmother disappear into the woods, and tried to swallow the sharp stone that had lodged itself in her throat.

Chapter 6

It was raining still when they made camp under a fir tree where the snow had not washed away, and a piece of oilcloth with sheepskins made it a tolerable bed. They huddled under the fir boughs and coaxed a smokey little fire to life. Joben stared at it, combing his beard with his fingers. By staring at it he afforded Lylaba a bit of privacy for her tears. They drank fir needle tea and chewed dried venison and a few dried plums. They curled up on the sheepskins. At some point in the night, the rain became snow before the skies cleared and a wind blew up cold. Joben woke shivering, tucking his hands into his stomach and contracting himself smaller. He could feel Lylaba moving uncomfortably. He peeked out at the red moon and decided it was near dawn anyway.

"Let's not bother with a fire," said Lylaba groggily. "Let's just get moving."

"There's nothing to drink, and too cold for sucking snow." Thankfully a few embers had survived, and it was a matter of blowing them up under the last sticks they had and warming snow so they had a drink to start with, and could fill their bottles. There was plenty of the red moon's light to see as they packed their things. As they started down the road, which now showed a brown strip down the middle where the rain had washed away the accumulated snow, Lylaba handed Joben a piece of journey bread and they ate and walked hurriedly in silence while the dawn came up.

Not a bird peeped. The trees should have been budding out red at the tips by now, and some were, but in significant patches, there were no signs of life. There was the sound of water gurgling under the snow, and the crossings were flush with ice water which they avoided. The day was warming with the sun.

The sun came up, crossed the sky, and sank in the west. They had barely stopped all day. They camped, slept a few hours, rose, and went back to the road. When the sun came up, it was a dreary revelation. Many black and foul areas seeped poison. Dead trees had fallen with the wind the night before. The farther they went, the more bare and blackened ground there was. Only patches of dirty snow remained here and there among the grey and silent trees.

As evening fell, Joben said, "There's no stopping anymore. There's nowhere we could lay down."

"Aye. We'll be to the house about dawn."

But they hadn't factored in the circling around fallen trees they had to do. Some of the blackened areas were pushing up from the ground, creating stumbling stones in the dark. They had to pick their way slowly. In the end, they clasped a hand and an arm in order to support each other. When the red moon sank, they almost came to a standstill. They leaned on a tree to rest.

Thank the Brightness, the white moon came up an hour later and helped them make the next push forward. But her crossing of the sky was swift, and soon they were picking their way down the black road, and it was hard to tell the road from anything else.

Just when Lylaba was sure they were lost, she heard the murmur of a stream. She prayed it was the one that ran not far from her house. The pre-dawn chill came down. Then the sky began to blush in the east, except for near the horizon. Because Lylaba was afraid of falling into the ravine that the stream ran in, she suggested they rest. There was a fallen tree they sat down on. They waited, and Lylaba was passing out from exhaustion. After she had nodded several times, Joben pulled her head down to his shoulder. How long she dozed, she wasn't sure, but she was awoken by Joben's voice.

"Brother of Brightness preserve us" he gasped.

The sun was risen suddenly over what looked like a vast mountain of black. All trace of snow was gone. The land was a blasted waste, the house barely visible some distance away amid a snarl of tree falls. There was an odor of carrion and something even more acrid. It was under their feet, smoldering and crackling. Lylaba stood swiftly, then almost lost her balance forgetting the pack basket, although the weight was not much. She began to walk quickly toward the house. It took some doing because of the snarls of limbs everywhere. But when she got close enough to see the house she breathed thanks that no trees had fallen on the house itself. It was as they had walked away from it several days ago. Only now it sat in a lifeless desert, a wreck of trees around it.

The snowmelt that ran over the ground was dark and not a hint of green blade nor moss showed, even where the earth was still soft.

They made it to the front door and Lylaba fished the brass key from the small bag of treasures that hung from her neck inside her tunic. She opened the door and they went in, dropping their burdens on the ground.

Wordlessly, Lylaba went to her sleeping room, pulled off her boots, and laid on the bed, an arm across her face. Joben found the tick where he had left it, unrolled it, and also slept.

\*\*\*

In the late afternoon, Lylaba woke to the sounds of Joben moving around in the next room. She crept from the room, to see him shirtless and drying himself with a cloth. He had started a fire and found the rain barrel to draw water from. He was heating the kettle, but had clearly already bathed himself as well as he could, and she longed suddenly to do the same. He noticed her and reached for a clean tunic he had hung over a chair and drew it over his head. He ran his fingers through his damp hair.

Lylaba filled a pitcher with hot water and found a cloth, and went back to her bedroom to clean herself up. It felt wonderful, the almost scalding water leaving her skin reddened and fresh. She scrubbed at her face and neck, and everywhere else, finally plunging her head in the basin to do what she could about her rough, dusty hair. The water was black, and she wrapped in a sheet and went to see if there was more. It wasn't warm but she didn't care. A rinse did wonders for the way it felt.

She dressed in clean long tunic, small clothes, and wide trousers, and wadded up the clothes she had traveled in. She would have liked to toss them in the fire, but they were her most practical and warm, so instead she filled the dish basin and tossed them in. The cobbler was bent over their boots, oiling and rubbing them. "Joben, give me your clothes, please. If we hang them up by the fire they should be dry by morning." He brought out his own wad of woolen clothes, black about the bottoms. Lylaba wondered if it would wash out. She added a large handful of soap flakes to the water and stirred them about with a paddle. After a meal was eaten, she would scrub them.

Suddenly she swore. "What is it, Lylaba?"

"The root cellar. There was a good bit left in there."

"And it's likely all gone to rot."

She swore again, and strode to the pantry. She was reassured by what was there, although it wasn't a lot. She brought out a small bowl of barley, and one of lentils. There was a few handfuls of Gama's dried vegetable mix of onions, carrots, leek, celery, and some thyme and other herbs. These all went into the pot with what was left in the pail of rainwater.

She slipped on an old pair of shoes to refill the pail. The rainbarrel stood at the edge of the doorstone, so she would not have to step on the ground.

Outside was an eery quiet. She stood in it for a moment. The sun was getting low and it sank into a tangle of half-fallen trees. She looked west and wondered if her children and grandmother had reached Dastenn yet. If it was safe. If she would ever see Onna and Gama and Finder again.

No sense in dwelling on what must be. She bent over the rainbarrel and caught her reflection for a moment. She had combed the rats from her fair hair as best she could, but the tiredness and worry marked her face. Ah, well. She was nearly two score summers. What must be, must be. She filled the pail with the clear, cold rainwater and lugged it back inside.

When the food was ready, they both slurped it unapologetically. Their scant rations had run out the day before their night-long trek, and the hot meal warmed and filled their bellies. They each filled their bowls again and ate more slowly this time. They drank tea afterward, staring past each other.

Finally, Joben put his cup down. "Lylaba."

She looked at him.

"I guess we're going up to the standing stones in the morning." She nodded slowly. "I can't believe we're going to ask Stone Folk for help. Beings come alive from old stories. But there are a lot of things that I never would have believed. Things coming alive I thought long dead." He reached across the table.

She pulled her hands away and put them under the table, suddenly uncomfortable.

"Joben. You never asked about Onna's father."

"I figured you would tell me when you were ready."

She gazed at her cup, unseeing. "Well, I'll likely never be ready, but here goes. I killed him. Right behind me, by the fireplace. With that very sword you see hanging there."

He looked horrified, but held himself still.

"Might I know why?" he rasped.

"He struck Gama. Knocked her right down." He could see the old rage building in her eyes, a righteous wrath. She looked at him, defiant. "He was getting ready go after her more, kick her. As he'd done to me more times than I could count on both hands."

"One time is too many. Lylaba, you did the right thing. He might have killed her. He might have killed you, too. Or Onna."

"Onna wasn't born yet. I wasn't even sure I was with child." Her hands covered her face. He let her have a few moments, and then reached for one of the hands and held it.

"I'm sorry you had to do that. But you did right, as far as I can tell. You surely did what you had to. I know you're not looking for my judgment. But I think no less of you knowing it, if anything I think more. You are an amazing woman, Lylaba. Brother of Brightness, bless you."

She allowed her hand to rest in his for a time. She didn't know how to say what was in her mind, so she cupped the back of his hand with her other one. His second hand joined the knot on the table.

\*\*\*

In the morning they were up early, washed even cleaner, dressed in more layers. They had agreed to find the stone circle on the knoll, and then come back to the house — whatever came of that. Lylaba filled a water bottle and they set out. It was even warmer than yesterday. The ground was thawed in most places and water was trickling everywhere, much of it vile and toxic. They again held hands to prevent either one from stumbling. Both wore stout leather gloves, just in case.

They had the same difficulty with so many fallen trees. The sun was almost overhead by the time they reached the rise.

The stones were not there.

"This can't be the right hill. We must have gone the wrong way," said Joben.

"The Plainwood is mostly flat. This is the only knoll this high for miles around," said Lylaba doubtfully.

They gazed in every direction. Lylaba mounted a tree that had fallen against another, and climbed until she was well over Joben's head. She looked about and then called Joben up the fallen tree. He climbed carefully until he was just below her. She pointed toward the east—where the shadow loomed, massive and dark. "You see what I see?"

Joben frowned. The noon sun seemed to shine upon something that stood out against the dark and blasted distance. A few somethings. They were perhaps three miles distant, maybe more—it was hard to gauge. Between the figures and the knoll they were on, a wide path was cleared in a straight line through the ruined woods and fields.

"Those are the Stone Folk. They're moving towards the east."

"Towards the shadow." She began to move that direction and Joben said, "Lylaba, listen. The Stone Folk move slowly because they derive their strength from the earth. You and I need food and water—especially water. We should go back to the house and prepare ourselves. We don't even have our coats." She stopped, but her eyes never left the backs of the slow, dark giants to the east. The land stretched out before them, a wilderness of ruin and smoke, the Folks' road leading straight to them.

Her eyes turned to his. "Please, Joben. We must hurry. I don't know why, but I feel so urgent about this. Let's just go."

"I could go back to the house and get—"

"Don't leave me." Her fingers clutched his sleeve. "I don't know what I'm doing, but I am terrified to do it. Please stay with me."

He nodded, unable to speak. He wrapped his hand over hers, and they turned to follow the Stone Folk, along the way that had been plowed for them, almost smooth. They knew if once they fell, they were likely done for.

So they walked for about two hours. The sun fell into the west. The red moon rose lurid over the fume to the east, which gained in height incrementally. So also did the Stone Folk. But despite the slowness of the progress of the Folk, they were still far off when dusk fell.

Not far off the trail was a farmhouse with two chimneys. Lylaba recognized it by those as one where she had done several jobs. Those people had left months ago, and the house stood forlorn. It was a prosperous house and boasted several blown glass windows. They made their way to the house after some discussion, knowing they would need rest and fearing some pitfall along the way that might prove fatal. Lylaba brought out the long knife Campo had given her and tried to pry a frame open. She cursed her good workmanship, which seemed oddly humorous and lightened their weariness for a moment. She turned the knife handle first and broke one of the panes, reached in and unlocked it. Joben boosted her inside and she opened the door for him.

The house, of course, was dark and cold. They had not brought fire implements with them, but thankfully there was a flint, steel, and box of charcloth by the hearth. The former occupants had left kindling and a few logs behind. Some time later, they sat before a good fire.

Joben found and lit a candle and looked about, locating the pantry that had not much in it, but there were a few wrinkled apples and some walnuts in the shell, and a few pickled eggs in a crock. They blessed and ate these hungrily before the fire. There were some inches of water in the urn, stale but drinkable. They refilled their bottles and drank their fill. Joben dragged a couple of mattress ticks near the fire, and blankets.

There was no longer anything like awkwardness between them. They rolled their tired bodies into blankets and laid down near each other and slept until the light came up.

***

In the morning they made tea from the water in the urn, drank as much water as they could hold, filled the bottle and another bottle Joben found that fit in his tunic pocket, and with the last bit cleaned their faces and hands as best they could. They ate the last of the pickled eggs and filled their pockets with other odds and ends they found. Then they returned to the Stone Folks' road.

The dark mountain that rose before them swallowed, it seemed, more than half the sky. But it was toward this that they moved. The sun warmed a landscape of sable, charcoal, steel grey, obsidian. It became hot as they marched along. As fast as they moved, the Stone Folk seemed no closer. But the mount of shadow only grew before them.

Hours later, Lylaba stumbled over her own feet. It was only Joben yanking her arm that kept her from hitting the ground. They clung to each other, gasping with fear. Joben took the bottle from his pocket, pulled the cork, and held it to her cracked lips. She gulped it, but stopped herself. He took a modest swig and replaced the cork, dropping it back into his pocket. He looked around, and seeing a fallen tree not far away, he pulled her over toward it. She sat, staring dumbly at the black road into more black that lay before them. It seemed forever they had trudged down this road, but by the sun it was early afternoon.

Here, the blight was like roots of an old tree, snaking in and out of the dead ground. Some of the houses and barns had been pushed against and distorted, walls caving in, roofs buckling. Off the road they were on, it looked almost impossible to navigate. Broken trees were heaved this way and that. Boulders had been uprooted. Broken buildings were heaped upon each other, farther down the way east.

"We're closer to the Folk than we were. But if they're going to Mourmenir, we should soon have to cross the river."

She pulled a small and wizened apple from her pocket and took a bite and offered the apple to him. He took a bite. They chewed very slowly. "Bright Brother," she whispered.

"Lylaba, do you ever wonder why we talk of the Brother, and not the Brightness Himself?"

"I confess I do. Gama says it's that the light is too much for us. We need the Brother between us and the Brightness. Just as we can't gaze upon the sun — it'd blind a person."

"That's what the old folks said to us when I was young, as well. Can I tell you a story I once heard?"

She chewed the last of the apple, which she had eaten core and all, and nodded.

"Let's walk while we tell stories."
***

Two Stone Folk grew a beautiful house for themselves in a circle of mountains. All the walls were living wood — madrone, like living stone, coaxed and shaped into walls and arches and a leafy roof. Madrone trees were long-lived, and could be renewed by the speech and will of the Stone Folk.

Now, the Stone Folk did not call themselves that. That name was given them by those who came much later, whose lives were hurried and seemed at first not to signify. To themselves, they were simply the Folk, or in their tongue, *Elledun*.

These Elledun in this story grew many young ones, for they loved each other long and well. But the time for children passed, and one spring, stray twigs were growing from the walls of their home, and they looked at them and said, "Why not let the tree grow as it will, and not as we will?"

They sat long and watched their home become something else, of its own shaping. As they watched it strive toward the sun, they understood that it was shaped by the light that fell on it from above. Every leaf sought to drink the sunlight. Each branch sought to lift itself higher. The madrone tree was already old beyond its time, however, and so it began to die out.

The Elledun thought long on this. They might add their strength and will back to the tree and make it to live again longer, but perhaps that was not the point. Perhaps they should be reaching for the light, not hiding themselves in the shelter of those beings who did so on their behalf.

So the Elledun stood long in the sun, reaching for the light. They gazed upon the sun, dizzying in its swift course across the sky. They drank in the light of moons and stars.

One of the Folk closed its tired eyes one day. Then it looked upon its partner, standing as they now had for so long that the madrone tree had melted into the earth, and new trees had taken its place and grown over their heads.

"I miss you," said the one to the other.

Surprised, the husband turned to his wife. His arms were still spread. He gazed at her. Then he gasped.

"There is light in you, my wife."

"And also in you."

Their arms spread round one another, and there they stayed long.

\*\*\*

While Joben had been speaking, they noticed, they approached the last in line of the Stone Folk much more quickly than before. They quickened their step but avoided any water — where it splashed on their clothes, it ate holes in them. The grease on their boots was the only thing keeping the leather intact, as the liquid ran off faster than it could erode the rawhide. The dead trees and heaved stones piled higher by the sides of the road. At one point, Joben looked behind them. In the distance the road was closing in, the blight effacing the road the Folk had made. He said nothing, but a short time later Lylaba looked back, and gasped. Their eyes met with understanding. They kept moving. The sun was going down.

"This last one—it's stopped. It's just standing there," Lylaba observed. Some time later, they approached it. Their steps faltered and they stood gazing up.

Two dark eyes met their gazes. Slowly it nodded at them. Then it inhaled, a rush of breath which expanded it slightly, made it seem to stand even taller than the heights of three or four men it already stood. It was still covered with mosses and mushrooms.

Again Lylaba felt the exhalation upon her face, a scent of moss and rock and green wood—although there seemed a tinge of decay and acridity. The eyes seemed sad.

"Seekers... with us." It breathed more than spoke the words, long and subterranean. It nodded once again.

Then it stood silent, looking down.

Finally Lylaba said, "Yes, Ancient One. We are afraid of the shadow, but we are drawn to it. We... want the light to return. But we don't know what to do."

"Yesssss..... the sister remains hidden from us, as well. We go to find her. You also will come, and see if she awaits us?"

"We will," said Joben. "But we are weak, and this land may poison us. We will go with you as far as we may."

"I am Lylaba, Lylaba Davey, and this is Joben Falat."

"Joben Falat. A good name. It reminds me..." She trailed off.

"May we know what you are called, Ancient One?"

"Maralalam, you may call me, although my true name is long for you, and has not been spoken by any of your kind in a long time as such. The last I heard it, it was from the heart of Jobenoben, the father of my children."

"We speak of Jobenoben in the old stories. And of Maral."

"Ah, yes. Your lives come and go so quickly. No time to spare on long-winded names. Come, let us walk, although I am tired. It is many, many circles of the white moon and the red, and even the black moon, since I moved so. And the earth here cannot sustain me long, for it is sick. Sick with the sorrow of the sister. Let us seek her together."

"The black moon..." murmured Joben. "My grandfather told me it passed over slowly, had been sinking since he was a lad, and it went down the year my mother was born. He wasn't sure when it would rise again."

"I have heard of it, too. In the stories, and some have written of it. They claim to know the date of its rising again, since men and women of old once gazed upon it, measured its passage with instruments, and wrote it in the books."

Maralalam spoke. "Joben Falat, I heard the story you were telling, and I knew I must await you and Lylaba Davey. For this shadow lies heavy upon me as well as you, and I fear going into it. But then, this fear signifies not. For into it I must go."

"Why did the shadow grow? Your folk have stood unmoving as long as any of us can recall, as long as we have been writing in books. Somehow we have old stories of your kind, but nothing of this darkness consuming the land as it is doing."

"I cannot answer this. Your stories bring back memories long buried. It brings me back to the times when we built our great homes of living wood, and crossed oceans and mountains in search of knowledge and beauty. The truth we had already. We longed to see how it expressed itself in many forms, but in the end, there was just the truth of who we were."

"Do you wish to speak of those times, or is silence more to your liking now?"

Maralalam was quiet for what seemed to the small humans accompanying her a long time in which the sun went down, and the red moon after it. The white moon spun by almost a smear across the panoply of stars.

Finally, she spoke. "It was as in your story. We came to a standstill because we thought we were home. But home is not a place. No." She was again quiet for a time. "Home is us."

By now most of the sky was blotted out, and only the fading of the stars showed that the next day's dawn was upon them. The poison was working its way through Maralalam's root-like feet and causing her thinking to slow even more. So it was that she did not notice the small people by her side when they stumbled from weariness. The one called Joben Falat fell onto one hand, but his other arm swung behind him, catching the other one before she hit the dead ground. But she soon heard, as they strove to keep up with her, his labored breathing as he suppressed his pain. She knew that the flesh was being poisoned just as the trees had been. There was nothing she could do to save him from the burning pain, but she stopped and lifted the both of them in her arms. They clung to one another, praying to the Brother to heal him and protect them.

\*\*\*

I might have been asleep on my feet when we fell together, but Joben was awake enough to plant his right hand and forearm while his left arm swung up in front of me so that I fell atop him into the vile muck. I scrambled back to my feet and helped pull him up. He pulled off the leather glove he wore; it had burned through to his palm. He held it up, but it was too dark to see anything by only the light of the red moon, and that halfway obscured by the shadow. I poured water from my bottle on his hand and pulled the hem of my tunic up to wipe it off as best I could. I tore that off and threw it away, and tore another strip to bind his hand, although I wondered if it would do any good.

Maral kept moving and by the time we caught up to her, Joben's breath was tight with pain. He was clutching his arm. She lifted and carried us in her embrace. Her arms were rough, but gave like redwood bark, and they cradled us as gently as she might do. I held Joben as he shivered. As the sky paled, I saw his fingers were grey. I prayed, but it was more just *Brother of Brightness Brother of Brightness Brother of Brightness* because I didn't know what to say. I had lost my children and my grandmother. I had lost my home, my community. I had lost the landscape in which I had lived my life; the beautiful trees and the song of birds and the skip of deer in the woods, the laughter of children and greetings of friends... all ruined and dead around me. Would I ever have any of these back? I walked with alien creatures from another time, and my only companion, a man whose soul was knitted to mine by all we had been through, was doomed to wither and die before me. With his well arm, he held me to his breast and I wet it with anxious tears. The dawn was coming up but I did not look to see the dying world around me. We passed through the river which stunk with dead creatures and that acrid poison. Maral kept us above the cold, dead waters, but part of me wanted to end all the pain and sink into that blackness.

But a thought came to me of Onna, my silver song; and of my dark, lovely Finder; and of Gama. Where were they now? What if they could see my thoughts? Did they still hope that the world might again go green and brown and white and green again? How could I not hope to see their faces again? My tears stopped, and I rested my head on Joben's shoulder. Finally I lifted my head, and looked at his face.

"Joben." I smiled. "Thank you."

"For what?"

"For being here with me. For being a friend. For showing us the light in you. For your kindness to me, and to Onna, and Finder, and Gama. I don't know what is going to happen, but I am thankful that you have been with me through... all of this."

"Lylaba..." he whispered. His fingers were in my hair. "Thank you for... no, I'll just say it. I love you. How I would have wanted for us to have a life together." I kissed him on the mouth. Our lips were dry and cracked, but that kiss was sweet, and sealed something between us. I brought out my water bottle and we drank the last of it, and then laid down in Maral's arms and we slept.

## Chapter 7

We woke and walked on our own legs for a time while there was light. The sun was but a dull coin until past noon, when it finally gave its full strength. Our trouser legs were in tatters, but our boots were holding up well for now. The sun had dried much of the dead rubble that surrounded us and black dust blew on the wind. We each tore a sleeve from our tunics and tied them round our faces. Our water was gone and no hope of finding more. We dropped the bottles and followed Maral, Joben's good hand in mine. Our dinner was a last, small apple that we nibbled and savored. There was nothing in the world like that half-shriveled apple. The wine of summer seemed distilled into it. It was like tasting a world gone by where sun shone and rain fell and the land gave its good things. That world seemed a hundred years gone.

As Maral walked her straight line into the dark, there was not just stones and broken trees. There were fragments of the life that was gone. A cup here, a child's toy there. A trowel, a nail, a lantern, a pail. As the sun made a brief showing from the west as it fell that day, Joben stopped and bent over, gingerly plucking something from the dust of the ground and examining it briefly. I didn't see what it was, and he straightened and kept on. I wanted to ask, but my throat seemed full of sand. When the sun set, we climbed back into Maral's arms. Sleep did not come except in short visits.

By dawn, we felt Maral slowing. A wan light showed that the Stone Folk had spread, some to the left and some to the right. We knew not to ask Maral to explain. We could feel that her strength was almost gone. We climbed down from her arms and followed. The mosses that furred her shoulders and head were brown.

Finally, she came to a stop. Slowly, she turned to face the deepest part of the shadow. And broke her silence.

"My children, now is when we ask of you to help us. It is you who must find the heart of light within this dark mountain.

"Our sister, Ounaba Tahembalai, has done this. Or so we believe. For we do not know what lies at the center of the darkness, where she once stood. We believe it is her, and therefore we trust that there is also light to be found. And perhaps an answer to this spreading death. Will you go?"

I looked at Joben. His eyes were closed from pain and exhaustion. I said to her, "I will go. He must stay here, with you."

Joben's eyes opened. He weaved as he stood. I saw in his eyes his anguish, and his death. I knew this was goodbye. Another goodbye. I wrapped my arms around him, tucking my face under his chin, into the warmth of his beard, where I could still detect a suggestion of clary sage and beeswax. He kissed my forehead. Then I let him go. The sun was barely breaking the dusky shadows where we stood, and I was glad he could not see the tears streaking my face. I turned to Maral.

"How shall I go?"

"We are very close now. Stay in the light of the sun. Find your way among the roots. I do not know what you will find. Brother of Brightness, bless you, as you people say. Amongst ourselves, we would say, There is light in you."

I found that these words resounded in my soul. I don't know how to explain it. In the House of Brightness, we sang of light in each being. It was understood that there was also darkness, the kind of darkness that caused my husband to mistreat Gama and me, and for me to respond in kind. For that, we trusted that the Bright Brother would purposely bring light to those dark places in us. Just the thought of him brought light, and as one candle could dispel the dark of a whole room, one thought of him could bring grace to our souls.

I knew I needed that grace right now, if the darkness around me was not to swallow me whole.

***

Lylaba turned to face the darkness. The afternoon sun was behind her head. Tall roots like gnarled knees, sharp as knives in some places, rose to either side of her. She began to step forward, finding her way between.

The way opened before her. She walked into the darkness, but the light of the sun followed her. It did not penetrate near her feet, so she had to step cautiously, but she was not in any hurry. For what seemed like hours, she moved into the deepening dark. But the sun stayed with her, as if it were standing still. It was a crown above her head and she knew that as long as she walked, it would not desert her.

The walls of black stone were narrowing. They hissed and suppurated. The strange vine-like and moss-like growths, with their vile fruits, brushed against her. But they could not harm her as long as the sun was her diadem, lighting the way forward, its warmth pushing her on through the murk.

Was it hours, or days, or years that Lylaba moved towards the darkness? Her feet were numb, her legs were heavy, but it did not matter. She would never stop so long as the way opened, and the sun rode her. The sun was growing, she knew, although she couldn't see it behind her. It was larger than the red moon. It shone brighter and warmer until it glowed through her. She became translucent as an alabaster stone, vibrating with a bell-like intensity.

Suddenly she stood before an opening. That is, the way was closed and blank before her. But gathering her will, knowing she carried the light not only of herself but of those she loved and who loved her, and of the Bright Brother, and of the Brightness itself which now burned in her own breast; she moved into the blankness and it opened to her, like moving through the night air.

Then she reached the heart of the shadow.

An arched chamber glowed dimly before her, yet she could see every detail. The walls were bas-relief that glowed warmly from within and told stories of travels and adventures and family and companionship. They were beautiful, and the arched alcoves and pillars and chambers that seemed to spread in every direction were apparently full of these wonderful works. For a time, Lylaba gazed around her.

She was suddenly aware that she was alone — for the sun no longer blazed within her. And yet, she was not alone, for a figure knelt bowed in the center of the largest chamber. She moved toward this figure.

She stopped a few yards away. She knew that it was one of the Stone Folk. Bowed — the broken stone from which Mourmenir had taken its name. Lylaba blew a breath from pursed lips. Then she addressed it.

"Ancient One, whom they call Ounaba," she said. Her voice echoed in the chamber, but there was no response.

"Ancient One, I have come to find you and speak with you. For this house of yours is beautiful within. But outside there is death and poison, and we would plead with you to know what we can do, for it has taken our homes and lives from us, and we cannot live in your shadow."

She thought that she was not heard, but when she considered speaking again, the bowed figure shuddered. Over several minutes, it straightened, and then stood. Lylaba herself shuddered, for the surface of the Stone Folk roiled with strange exudations, ridges and striations forming and receding.

Finally Ounaba stood tall over Lylaba. She saw the dark, deep eyes looking down upon her.

Lylaba felt, more than heard, the subterranean, slow speech. "Who are you, child, to intrude upon my holy home?"

Lylaba swallowed, although her mouth was dry as paper. She closed her eyes for a moment, remembering how the sun had been her very crown. She breathed a few moments, and said, "I am a child of Brightness. My name is Lylaba Davey. And I have lost everything because of the greatness of your mountain of shadow. So I have come to see if there is light in you yet.

"Your sisters and brothers stand around you. They believe there is light. They have come, and they have sent me, because I am small, and I have nothing left to lose."

"Do you not know, Lylaba Davey, what I have lost? I lost the heart of the one I loved. And in that, I lost my chance to be loved, to have family, to make a home and have a companion. All you see around me are memories. Memories that are very old, even to me. But they are all I have left to me. I would rather have my memories and shut out the world that hurts to live in, and I care not for what losses you tiny beings with your frantic and brief little lives may imagine you suffer for a few moments."

"Ounaba, I have also lost the one I love. He is outside with your sister, Maral. He is dying because of the poison waters that flow from this thing you have created. I have had to leave my children and my mother far, far away. Though our lives are brief, compared with your length of days, we too know love and loss. In this we are perhaps more like you than you realized. Ounaba, while we live, we carry our pain with us, and we must work and strive and carry on while we carry that pain. You may stand in one place, nourished by the earth, and nothing more is asked of you. While we must go on, for the sake of others we love. We cannot afford to give up hope.

"And you do not have to. There are still those of your kind who await you outside. They have come because they understand that you need them. They want the world to be beautiful again, and they want you in it, too. They could have come, breaking and battering you down" — she didn't understand how, but Lylaba knew this suddenly to be true — "but they await you with love.

"They believe there is light in you still."

The expression in the eyes was unreadable.

Lylaba looked around her. "Your memories are beautiful, wondrous. You still hold on to things you found lovely in the world, and the persons you loved. That tells me that there *is* light within you still."

"If there is, it is but a dying ember."

"An ember can be fanned to flame."

Ounaba gathered a long, long breath, and stood higher, seeming to fill the chamber, causing Lylaba to retreat a few steps.

Then she thundered an unintelligible roar of rage, passion, grief, blame, and pain. But instead of terrifying Lylaba, she gathered herself, remembering the sun blazing within her. Soundlessly, she raised her arms toward Ounaba, feeling more than seeing the light burning out of her. She moved toward the giantess with her arms open. It did not occur to Lylaba that she was small, or weak, or mortal. Somehow as she approached Ounaba her heart swelled with compassion, and she wrapped her arms—how was it possible?—around Ounaba, holding her close. The light consumed the poison weeping off Ounaba's body, and it did not burn her. Her arms seemed to grow around Ounaba, whose scream continued louder and longer, echoing in the chamber until it began to shatter around them. The massive pillars crumbled, and the walls exploded in every direction. Lylaba was ablaze, holding Ounaba within the circle of her arms, until the scream was exhausted and Ounaba seemed to implode on herself.

Lylaba was holding a collapsing monolith of stone shards, sharp blades that should have cut her arms and hands and face as they collapsed into a heap, but Lylaba still blazed with light. The air was full of dust, and stones rained down upon her. But something was changing. The taint of the air was being diluted, as if someone had opened the door on a smoky house.

The ground rumbled as they approached, the Stone Folk. They came close, rolling slowly over the heaped ruins of Ounaba's chambers. Lylaba slowly untangled her arms from the heap that had been Ounaba. She saw Maral approaching, Joben curled like a child in her arms. She ran to him, and Maral laid him on a clear place on the ground.

What light was left in her she wrapped around Joben's cold form. She pushed it all into him, praying, "Brother of Brightness, heal him. Brother of Brightness, heal him. Brother of Brightness..."

Somehow, the sun was in the east. The shadow was settling as black dust. It no longer stung, but drifted softly down. A soft wind was blowing it westward.

Joben stirred in her arms. His eyes opened in his dust-covered face, and he rolled to his back, looking up at Lylaba, a look of alarm on his face. But she simply smiled and embraced him, giving thanks. When she pulled away, finally, the sun was no longer blazing from within her. She was just Lylaba, and Joben looked relieved. Joben sat up.

They heard a sound like glass clinking and looked over to see the Stone Folk collecting the shards that had been Ounaba and forming a cairn with them. Maral moved over to them.

She stood over them, nodding slowly. Her dark eyes shone from within her deeply-furrowed face.

"You have done well, Lylaba Davey. We were right to call you to us."

They weren't sure what to make of that, but before they could ask questions, they heard a childlike voice. Lylaba knew it must be the one called Tenjeh who lifted the reborn Ounaba into his arms. The dark stone child curled into his body and seemed to sleep. The Stone Folk began to move off as a group.

Maral turned to them once more. "We have much to do, many reparations to make. The land must be healed. And we must find those of us who have drifted apart. We see now we are not meant to live alone forever.

"Brother of Brightness, bless you."

"Brother of Brightness, protect you!" they called back.

They stood to their feet and watched the Folk moving off into the sunrise.

"Shall we go home," Lylaba asked, "Wherever that is?"

Joben brushed dust from her face. "Home is us."

## Chapter 8

By the time they found a house amid the confused landscape that was intact, rain had rolled in, and it was sweet. Joben and Lylaba opened their mouths to it, and let it run over their faces. The rain barrel was intact and they drank deeply. They found what little there was to eat in the house after breaking in, and ate and slept long and hard. In the morning, there was enough water that they were able to bathe in turns, and change into clothing abandoned by the former occupants. Joben found a pair of boots that fit him. It was odd to feel the flex of them after so many days walking on wood. Joben gave Lylaba what he had found in the ashes as they followed the Stone Folk—a beautiful ring with a sapphire stone in a gold setting, like a piece of the summer sky.

It was several days of finding their way over blackened fields, at times having to climb through tangled deadwood stories high, before they were able to find Lylaba's house by the road. Each day they slept in a strange house and ate what food had been left behind.

As they moved through the wasteland, they discovered that not everything living had been destroyed. A few trees were budding out in patches, here and there some tender grass, a few coltsfoot blossoms. These were a shocking joy amid the devastation, the stench of decay only growing stronger in the warming weather. A few birds passed overhead. They found a turtle.

\*\*\*

It took them longer than they had hoped to find their family. It was *their* family, after finding the first House of Brightness with people in it, and having their wrists tied with scarlet thread before the community. The children and grandmother had been in Till with the others for some time but left there with everyone else when the river turned black.

Lylaba and Joben traveled down the coast, where rumors led, asking at every House of Brightness along the way. Finally, someone remembered the group from Sheaf passing through, but did not know where they were headed.

It was high summer before Joben caught sight of Finder, walking with a hitch in the marketplace in a coastal town called Ygeddanis, trading balls of twine for food items. Finder jumped into his arms and celebrated volubly. After they picked up the balls of twine he had sent rolling every direction, he took him to where he and Onna were living over a wood shop owned by distant relations of Marna, where Onna was carving boxes and selling them. Onna fell into her mother's arms and wept loud and long. Gama had passed suddenly along the road, as they slept in a guest house. They found among her things a handful of gold teeth which had paid for her burial, and then some, but the teeth mystified them. Joben promised he would explain the teeth later, when less important stories were being told.

They crowded into the low rooms above the wood shop. On the Longest Day, they went to the House of Brightness. Joben lifted Finder, causing laughter, and spoke his name.

"Finder, Finder," the people murmured.

Furious rainstorms set in that flooded the rivers and washed the tangled corpses of animals and trees in great rafts into the sea, where they moved off to the horizon, harried by gulls from above and fishes from below. By the time the storms ended, it was early autumn and there was no profit in traveling back to what was left of Sheaf. The family spent the winter in the tiny apartment, with Ba, and Smoke.

In Spring, they ventured back to the house at the edge of Sheaf. There were only a very few pilgrims returning to their homes, and a few looking to loot, or even to squat in abandoned farms. Thankfully, surrounded as it was by dead trees, no one had desired Lylaba's house. They stayed for some days and explored, but they agreed the land needed more time to heal, and it was lonely there. They were tradespeople, not pioneers. They weren't ready to live in an outpost in the wilderness. Soldiers arrived to clear out squatters and looters, and to spread the decree that the land should heal for one year before residents returned.

But before they left, Joben and Lylaba rode out to a hill past the bridge—which bore deep cracks, having endured a massive jam of downed trees that spring, but just barely. They rode the horses up Turla Mount and looked over the land. There, they could see the group of Stone Folk moving almost imperceptibly across the plain, clearing pathways for the deer to return, freeing streambeds of blockages, dragging down the worst of the massed snarls of dead trees, burying the dead of all kinds together in great mass graves and setting saplings to grow over them. At least, that was what the couple imagined they were doing.

Then they rode west, the Stone Folk behind them. As they descended the far side of the bridge, they both turned to look until the Folk were out of sight.

Acknowledgements

Thank you so much to Luke Wildman, who was my beta reader. His input was invaluable. My daughter, Sarah, has always encouraged me to keep writing, and I need that! My husband, Bob, is always encouraging me to be who I am and do my best at what I believe in — that is indispensable. And all who read my previous efforts — thank you!

Author Note

I hope you enjoyed *The Stone Folk & other stories*. Please rate and write an honest review, and check out my other books, *Blackbirch Woods, Ardinéa,* and *Follow Jesus Through the Gospels, a One-Year Devotional*.

Meredith Anne DeVoe is an elementary school principal in Jos, Nigeria, where she and her husband have served as global workers for the Gospel since 2006. They have two grown children, one daughter-in-love, one grandchild, and a one-eyed parrot named George.